JITTERBUG

Loren D. Estleman

jitterbug

a novel of Detroit

A TOM DOHERTY ASSOCIATES BOOK   new york

This is a work of fiction. All the characters and events portrayed in this
novel are either fictitious or are used fictitiously.

JITTERBUG

Copyright © 1998 by Loren D. Estleman

This book is printed on acid-free paper.

A Forge Book
Published by Tom Doherty Associates, Inc.
175 Fifth Avenue
New York, NY 10010

Forge® is a registered trademark of Tom Doherty Associates, Inc.

Design by Sara Stemen

LIBRARY OF CONGRESS CATALOGING-IN-PUBLICATION DATA

Estleman, Loren D.
    Jitterbug : a novel of Detroit / Loren D. Estleman. — 1st ed.
        p.   cm.
    "A Tom Doherty Associates book."
    ISBN 0-312-86360-8
    1. World War, 1939–1945—Michigan—Detroit—Fiction.   I. Title.
PS3555.S84J58   1998
813'.54—dc21   98-21185
                                                                         CIP

First Edition: October 1998

Printed in the United States of America

0 9 8 7 6 5 4 3 2 1

For my mother,

Louise A. Estleman,

who dances still

War, my lord,
Is of eternal use to human kind,
For ever and anon when you have pass'd
A few dull years in peace and propagation,
The world is overstock'd with fools, and
    wants
A pestilence at least if not a hero.

—Lord Jeffrey

Part One

Kilroy Was Here

Whe stood outside himself—as he did most of the time, being an authentic objective—he compared himself to a house cat: ordinary, invisible, the most efficient hunter in civilization.

Others, uninformed, saw him differently. A girl he had taken to the movies told him he looked like Robert Taylor. That had pleased him, because he had liked Taylor ever since he'd seen *Billy the Kid* at the Capitol and had bought a wallet at Hudson's with a picture of the actor in it and torn it out and stuck one corner inside the frame of the mirror on his bureau. He consulted it from time to time as he combed his hair, straight back with a wave up front. Only his hair was light brown, not black, so he darkened it with old-fashioned pomade from a jar he'd bought in a barbershop. He was working on a pencil moustache like the one Taylor wore in *Waterloo Bridge*, but it was coming in red and he was thinking of shaving it off. Taylor was clean-shaven for *Bataan*, a war picture he couldn't wait to see, having read about it in *Parade*. He went to see nothing but war films since Pearl.

WJR predicted showers, but WWJ and WXYZ were sticking to partly cloudy. He despised indecision. Didn't they get their reports from the same U.S. Weather Bureau? He wondered if he should snap on a hat protector. The rest of the uniform was wool and absorbed water without spotting, but he was worried about the visor.

He took pride in the uniform. It was Army Air Corps, chocolate tunic with amber corporal's stripes on the sleeves, khaki trousers. It had been left in the closet of his last furnished room by the former tenant, who had been invalided out after Guadalcanal—shell shock, he supposed, or the man would never have forgotten it. The corporal was an inch taller and heavier through the chest and shoulders, but he had taken it to Schmansky Brothers' and had it tailored to his fit, selected a khaki shirt and matching necktie at Richman's, and gone to three shoe stores with his stamps until he found the right kind of brown oxfords in his size at Cancellation on Broadway. He applied Kiwi polish, spitting into the lid of the can, and buffed them with a horsehair brush until they gleamed like furniture on his feet. When he put it all on and looked at himself in the mirror, it was he who had been forced to leave combat after a fifty-caliber round had shattered his left tibia, whereupon a grateful War Department had assigned him stateside to sell bonds. When people asked him where his medals were he said he kept them in a safety deposit box at Standard Savings & Loan because he felt uncomfortable wearing them while better men were lying dead on beaches without a single decoration.

It helped that he was young and attractive, with a shadow of recent pain fluttering behind his clear brown eyes; but mostly he was convincing because he believed himself when he spoke. On those rare occasions when he did not stand outside himself, he could hear the thump of the mortars and chomping of the heavy machine guns behind their sandbags on the hills. The army psychiatrist who had interviewed him in the Light Guard Armory had diagnosed him as a paranoid schizophrenic with persecutory patterns and delusions of grandeur, and stamped his file 4-F. Face burning with anger and mortification, he had gone home and written letters to FDR, MacArthur, Governor

Kelly, and Mayor Jeffries denouncing the psychiatrist, whose name was German, as a fifth columnist. None of them had replied, but he was certain they were just being careful of the mails and had opened a file on the Kraut doctor.

The *Free Press* said partly cloudy, with scattered showers after two P.M. He expected to be back by then. He left the cellophane protector in the drawer and brushed the closet lint off the flat-crowned cap that made him think of a postman; he wished the army had come up with something more arresting, like the Afrika Korps. Hitler knew a thing or two about style.

As he turned to leave, his gaze went to the *National Geographic* map of the European Theater on the wall. He checked the paper again, the front page this time, and added another pin to the map. The navy and marines were pounding hell out of Pantelleria, an island the size of a decimal point sixty miles off the coast of Sicily, and the Italians were expected to surrender any time. The pin had a tiny paper American flag attached. He'd bought two packages of them at Woolworth's and intended to use them all.

The fat woman's name, he had found out, was Anna Levinski. She lived in the 2600 block of Dequindre in Hamtramck, one of those same-looking houses the Polacks had flung up five minutes after they stepped off the train. It had a peaked roof and a four-paned window directly above a plain front door, like a house in a picture drawn by a child. The first time he'd checked out the address he swore he saw squiggly brown crayon-smoke coming out of the chimney.

He'd gotten the number from the butcher at the Holbrook Market at Eight Mile and Dequindre, where she'd bought a six-pound pork loin, two pounds of sliced bacon, and a whole boiled ham, all in one visit. Total red points: 102. Elsewhere in the store she bought butter and eggs, paid for the whole she-bang in cash with more ration stamps than he'd seen at one time since his last trip to the OPA, and drove off in a big green gas-guzzler of a Pontiac Torpedo four-door sedan—with an "A" card on the windshield, to boot.

Watching the house, he'd learned she was married to a fore-man at Dodge Main, a hulk with small ears and a dented black lunch pail who inspected engine blocks for the M-4 tank. The couple had no children, but they liked to throw a party once a month, hoarding stamps so they could serve delicacies to other line workers and their wives and listen to the Tigers on the radio. The husband was probably a saboteur, passing on blocks with fissures that split open on the first steep hill, stranding the crews out in the open for the first German 88 to get them in its sights while the wife made sure their bunkmates went hun-gry and couldn't fight.

When he stepped outside himself he didn't really believe that. Then he knew that they were what they seemed, a pair of hoarders who lived on rodent fodder and shank's mare for weeks at a time so they could show off for their friends one night. Such practices caused shortages at the front, where a can of K rations and a bit of powdered egg were as important to victory as gasoline and ammunition. They might as well be saboteurs. Just thinking about them made him walk faster, as if by getting there five minutes sooner he might save the life of some dogface who would never know he existed.

He made himself slow down. Sole leather was blood in time of war, and anyway some 4-F shirking cop seeing a man run-ning down the street in the uniform of his country might shoot him for a deserter. Irony of ironies.

Walking up the narrow strip of concrete in Hamtramck, rough and porous as bread, he unbuckled the straps that secured the flap of his briefcase. It was plain tan leather, double-stitched, with cardboard-reinforced dividers, a close match to the dispatch cases carried by army couriers, $12.98 at Saks. He knocked.

He heard feet shuffling from the back of the house, the tiny squeak of the hinged lid being lifted away from the small glass peephole. He was all house cat now, beneath the surface; all his senses were on end. He gave the fat woman on the other side of the door a full second to take in the uniform, then snap open the lock. She didn't disappoint him.

"Yes?" Strong accent. She might have been in this country thirty years, but she wouldn't have much need to practice her English in that neighborhood.

Standing close to her for the first time, he was surprised that her head barely came to his epaulets. She'd seemed so imposing giving her order at the butcher counter. Her graying hair was tied back in a bun, tightly enough to smooth the creases in her face. It was a pretty face despite the fat, or perhaps because of it. Younger-looking than the gravity of her carriage suggested.

"Good morning, ma'am." He touched his visor, smiling his Robert Taylor smile. "Corporal Adam Kolicek, United States Army Air Corps." Her face smoothed out further at the sound of the name. "I wonder if I might interest you in a subscription to *Boys' Life* or the *Saturday Evening Post*. I'm selling them for the war effort."

"No boys in this house," she said.

"The *Post*, then. I have some samples." He took out November 29, 1941, and April 11, 1942, both Rockwell covers. Older women loved Willie Gillis.

"Mr. Levinski likes *Argosy*." She raised herself a little, trying to peer down into the briefcase.

He tilted it toward him. "No, ma'am, just the *Post* and *Boys'*

Life. Fifty percent of the subscription price goes to feed and clothe our men fighting overseas."

"How much is it?"

"Just two dollars. That's sixty cents less than the price at the newsstand."

She mopped her hands on her apron. He was confident of her decision. Hoarders always felt guilty.

"Come in."

He stood in a tiny dark living room crowded with over-stuffed furniture. The usual portraits in glazed oval frames hung on the papered wall above the heating stove, opposite a large wooden and ceramic crucifix looking down on the sofa. A floor-model Zenith gleamed in a corner under an embroi-dered shawl. Uncovering, he tucked his cap under his arm.

She asked him to wait and shuffled down a narrow hallway lined with more pictures, an ornate wedding certificate in a plaster frame with cupids. He watched to see which doorway she went through. It would be the bedroom, where the valu-ables were kept.

The place smelled of old meals, heavily seasoned. He thought of all the meat that had been consumed there while American flyers were starving in Nazi POW camps. He laid his cap on the radio and twisted the knob. The tubes warmed. "Trickle, trickle, trickle, trickle, nickel, nickel, nickel, nickel." The Pepsi jingle.

She came back clutching two crumpled bills in her fist. She frowned at the radio.

He smiled, embarrassed. "Hope you don't mind, ma'am. My wife works at Ford Willow Run. She expects me to keep her up on *One Man's Family.*"

"You are married?" She smiled for the first time. It made her almost beautiful.

"Next week's our anniversary. I shipped out the day after the ceremony." He reached inside his case and took out an order form, grasping the stainless-steel handle inside as he did so and bringing it out behind the sheet.

"You were wounded?"

"Yes, ma'am, in the leg."

"Such a terrible war."

"Yes, ma'am." He leaned down and propped the briefcase against the base of a pedestal table, shifting the handle to his other hand at the same time. Holding it behind his leg, he gave her the form, unbuttoned the flap of his left breast pocket, and uncapped his fountain pen one-handed.

She held the form close to her face, moving her lips as she read. Then she took the pen, spread the sheet on the table under a lamp with a fringed shade, and filled in the blanks, bracing herself with her left hand on the table, the bills pinned beneath the palm. She drew a horizontal line through her sevens.

While she was signing her name he stepped behind her, curled his left forearm across her throat, and pulled her back into an arch, all in one movement, like a cat springing onto a high shelf. He crossed the hand holding the bayonet to the left side of her abdomen and slit her diagonally from pelvis to clavicle.

She filled her lungs, but her mouth flooded with blood and the cry came out in a pink bubble. Her body shuddered and began to sag.

He lowered her gently, backpedaling to lay her on her back so she wouldn't bleed onto the floor where he might walk.

"Trickle, trickle, trickle."

He switched off the radio, used the end of the shawl to wipe the knob, then cleaned the ten-inch steel blade with the order form and wrapped the form around it, clean side out. He put bayonet and paper back in the briefcase and found the pen and capped it and returned it to his pocket, buttoning the flap. Then he went down the hall to rifle the bedroom for the hoard of ration stamps while Anna Levinski finished dying.

chapter two

I t's psychology."

"What's psychology?"

"It's the study of the mind."

Canal rolled his eyes, so eminently made for rolling. Zagreb was convinced he never wore dark glasses because his eyeballs bugged out so far they'd touch the lenses. "I know what psychology is," Canal said. "I'm asking how it applies to the present situation."

They were standing near the third-floor landing in the California, a residential hotel on Hastings in Niggertown. A grubby plaque on the ground floor announced that Theodore Roosevelt had stopped there in 1907. It didn't say he'd stayed. Zagreb was pretty sure the old Rough Rider had taken one look at the lobby and charged straight from there to the Pontchartrain. He didn't believe any establishment could deteriorate this much in just thirty-six years. It had been at least that long since anyone had replaced the dead flies in the bowl fixtures.

"This pimp used to work for Big Nabob." He tipped his head toward the door at the other end of the hall. "You can't grill him in his own dump. That'd be like interrogating Dick Wakefield at Briggs Stadium."

"Wakefield's One-A, I heard."

"Who gives a shit except Wakefield? You can see my point."

"Sure. That's why we take the pimp downtown."

"That's no good either. It's like his second home. If you looked in the basement you'd find his handprints in the cement. You've got to see it from his point of view: Four big white guys bust down his door, cuff him hard and pull him out. He thinks he's headed downtown, only when it's time to turn right we go straight and then turn left. Drag him up to a little room in some stinking hole he's never been in."

"We don't know that. Maybe he brings some quail here, bangs her every Saturday night in that same room."

Zagreb lifted and settled his hat; letting the exasperation out. "The *point* is we aren't playing by the rules. Not even the unwritten ones. So what *else* aren't we doing? Up to now the worst he expects is we haul him down to the furnace room at Thirteen Hundred and strip him and bounce him around the coal bin. Could be we're going to shove him out a window instead."

"He won't like that. Spooks are scared of heights."

"You don't want Eleanor Roosevelt to hear you talking like that."

"Fuck her and fuck FDR. I'm voting for Dewey."

"I thought all you Polacks registered Democrat."

"I ain't a Polack. I'm Ukrainian."

"No kidding. My mother was born in Bulgaria."

"Who gives a shit except your mother?" Canal grinned, rare event. "I get where you're going, but it don't make sense. If you want to grill a jig outside his backyard you don't use a hotel room in jigtown. Why not take him up to Grosse Pointe?"

"Rent's two hundred a month in Grosse Pointe. You want to feed that kitty?"

"I don't know why we're feeding this one. The department should pay."

"The department doesn't know about the California. If they found out they'd make us get rid of the room. Our conviction record takes a nosedive, the papers stop writing about us, the commissioner breaks up the squad like he's been wanting to do ever since he got in, and the next thing you know you and I and McReary and Burke are freezing our peckers off walking Griswold in January."

"That happens I join up. At least I'd get combat pay."

"Not to mention a Kraut potato-masher in your shorts."

They were two men in black suits and gray snap-brims standing in a stairwell stinking of stuffed cabbage and urine. Sergeant Starvo Canal—it had probably been *Kanal* until his father hit Ellis Island—took up most of the space. Zagreb, slighter and not as tall, had selected him for his size, and had been delighted to learn he had a cool head as well, not normally to be found in big men of his background. Canal had chronic blue chin, a squidgy little nose that looked ridiculous in the middle of his fleshy face, and those eyes. He could lift a good-size man six inches off the floor by the throat one-handed and turn an experienced defense attorney into a sputtering maniac during cross-examination. Canal and Zagreb took the same size hat, which when the lieutenant removed it to show his bulging forehead explained why some of the men at 1300 Beaubien, Detroit Police Headquarters, called him Donovan, after a radio show called *Donovan's Brain*. His Christian name was Maximilian, but he refused to answer to Max. Canal, Burke, and McReary called him Zag. No one called him Lieutenant, except of course the people he was in the habit of placing under arrest. When he put his hat on he became invisible. Together he and Canal made up half the Detroit Racket Squad.

After a few more minutes Zagreb looked at his Wittnauer and said it was time to see how the other half was coming along. They went back and gave the knock.

McReary opened. He had freckles on his young bald head and an expressive mouth that sent all the wrong signals—like last week, when he'd smiled while reporting the death of Edsel

21

Ford, a man he admired, as if it were Mussolini who'd died. Ford had once tipped him a hundred dollars for helping to arrange security at a party in Grosse Pointe.

"Anything?" the lieutenant asked.

The bald officer grinned and nodded. "Not a damn thing. We thought we'd wait for you before we got impolite."

"Who's Jekyll?"

"That'd be me."

Zagreb and Canal went in. It was a narrow room with faded sunflowers on the paper above scarred wainscoting and a window looking out on the yellow brick wall of the secondhand clothing store next door. The squad had picked it for the view. There was a painted iron bedstead with the mattress rolled up against the headboard, exposing the springs, a table by the door where Burke and McReary had laid their service pieces, and two upright wooden chairs, both occupied. Burke, several years older than Sergeant Canal but still just an officer, sat astraddle with his beefy furred forearms folded across the back of his chair, facing a Negro in his fifties, sitting with his wrists cuffed behind him. The Negro was naked. His ribs showed and his chest was hollow, but he had a huge penis even when flaccid—one of the rare examples Zagreb had seen of that racial tall tale in practice. The wooden seat of the chair between the man's spread thighs was soaked, not entirely with sweat. The rank ammonia stench had been detectable from the hall.

The newcomers squeaked their revolvers from their underarm holsters and placed them on the table before approaching the seated pair. The precaution was the lieutenant's, inspired by the death of an officer in Ecorse in 1931 when a small-time bootlegger got hold of his piece during interrogation and shot him in the head.

"What's the holdup?" Zagreb asked Burke.

The officer in the chair didn't stir or take his eyes off the Negro. "Ask Mac. I wanted to toss the shine out the window but he said no."

"There's a war on. Rationing, you know? Before you go anywhere you have to ask yourself: Is this trip necessary?" McReary looked mournful over his little joke.

Canal swiveled his eyes, registering his opinion of McReary as Jekyll to Burke's Hyde. Burke was large and soft and moon-faced and smiled when he was amused and scowled when he was upset. He cried when Kate Smith sang "God Bless America." Burke inspired trust.

The naked man sat with his chin on his chest, staring at the floor. He'd vomited in his own lap; bits of green vegetable and what looked like bean sprouts had dried in his pubic hair. Chinese? Zagreb stood over him with his hands in his pockets.

"You're a lucky man, Richard, bet you didn't know that. You sold Sergeant Canal a brand-new set of Uniroyals, complete with spare. You're not a licensed tire dealer, you're not registered with the OPA. You didn't ask for stamps. We could've turned you over to the feds. They hang black marketeers. Michigan hasn't hanged anybody since eighteen thirty."

"I'm a lucky man," mumbled the Negro into his chest.

"Lucky as Andy Hardy. It just so happens the sergeant's got a mad on for J. Edgar Hoover. Isn't that right, Sergeant?"

"Fuck J. Edgar," said Canal.

"The sergeant wanted to be a G-man. It's all he ever wanted since he read in *Liberty* about how the feds got Dillinger. His application with his picture got all the way up to Hoover's office. Hoover tossed it in the ashcan. What was it he said, Sergeant?"

"He said I looked like Eddie Cantor."

"That's what I meant when I said you were lucky, Richard. Turns out the sergeant's a Jolson man. Sing 'Swanee,' Sergeant."

"I left my pitch pipe in the apartment."

"Too bad. You ought to hear him. Close your eyes, you swear it's the radio. Now, McReary's all for Cantor. He'd just as soon the feds put your neck in a rope. Burke's tone-deaf, but he doesn't like paperwork. That's two for, one against."

Now Richard lifted his head. One eye was swollen shut. His nose had bled and the blood had dried into a black crust on his lip, but he still didn't look much like Hitler. "How about you?"

"I like Crosby."

The naked man seemed to find that amusing. He snorted. His nose started bleeding again.

"Der Bingle for me," Zagreb said. "So you can see I'm undecided. I know what I don't want, though. I don't want to see the feds hang you out at Fort Wayne and spoil our perfect record. Well, perfect since eighteen thirty. Where'd you get the tires?"

"Found 'em on Outer Drive. Somebody dumped 'em."

"Why would anyone dump a brand-new set of tires when the governor's driving on recaps?"

"Maybe he didn't have no stamps neither."

"Was it the Conductor?"

"I don't know no conductors. My daddy was a porter on the B-and-O."

Burke leaned back, hooked an ankle under the rung of Richard's chair, and lifted the front legs off the floor. The Negro's bare feet dangled.

"You're not a stupid nigger, Richard," Zagreb said. "You ran numbers for Big Nabob until he got capped. You still run whores for Frankie Orr. Doesn't he let you call him the Conductor? You know why they call him that?"

Richard shook his head. Zagreb nodded at Burke, who straightened his leg with a snap. Richard's chair went back and down with a bang. The glass shivered in the window frame. Somebody in the room below thumped at his ceiling with a broom handle.

The lieutenant stepped forward and stood astraddle the Negro where he had rolled off the chair onto the floor. Zagreb's hands were out of his pockets and clenched at his sides. Instinctively Richard coiled himself into a fetal ball. The skin of his buttocks was loose and wrinkled.

"They call Frankie Orr the Conductor because he garroted another guinea to death in front of a carload of passengers on the Seventh Avenue El, just before Sal Borneo brought him out here from New York. But you knew that, Richard. Big Nabob knew it when Frankie shot him and took over his racket and you with it. Now he's taken over the black market, and that's where you got the tires you sold Sergeant Canal."

"I don't know no Frankies."

Zagreb snatched up the fallen chair by one leg and swung it up over his head. The back struck the bare lightbulb dangling from the ceiling. The bulb exploded with a hollow plop. Richard coiled himself tighter, burying his head between his knees. The lieutenant hovered, then swung the chair back down and let it drop. It glanced off the naked man's bent back. Richard took in his breath but made no other noise.

The thumping started up again from below.

Zagreb was exhausted suddenly. "Where do you live, Richard?"

"Sojourner Truth."

"Jesus." McReary grinned.

"Give him his clothes and take him home," Zagreb said.

Canal goggled. "Money changed hands!"

Burke said, "What about Frankie?"

"You heard him. They never met."

"He's a lying nigger."

"Any nigger who'd lie for two hours in room 309 of the California would lie his way onto the slab. I've been with the department since I got out of knickers. I haven't killed anybody yet. I'm not going to do it over a fucking set of tires."

Canal said, "We'll put him in a cab. He ain't stinking up the Olds."

"Put him in a Zero if you want. Just get him the hell out." The lieutenant fished in a pocket and came out with two zinc pennies and a streetcar token. "Who's got a nickel?"

McReary had one. Canal followed Zagreb to the pay telephone at the end of the hall. The lieutenant called downtown, said "yeah" three times, wrote an address on a bare patch of wall, and hung up. "Hamtramck cops need a hand with a homicide on Dequindre."

"That's Brandon's detail."

"Killer walked off with the deceased's ration stamps. Could be black market."

"Four-F shirking bastards."

"Half of Hamtramck's stationed in England. We're all in this together, right?" He tapped a Chesterfield out of his pack.

"So they say." Canal watched him light up. "That was some Hyde in there."

Zagreb snapped shut the Zippo. "I used to be Jekyll."

chapter three

The department had issued them a 1941 Oldsmobile sedan, black, with a two-way radio and blackout headlights. Burke, the snazziest dresser inside a detective's budget, with a charge account at Hudson's and eight payments to go on his walnut console Philco radio-phonograph, thought the car looked like a carpet beetle. He'd refused to ride in it at first, but cabs were getting scarce and he'd relented finally, although not without making an acid comment every time he put a foot on the running board. When the squad was created in 1939 they had been promised a new unit every year. Then Pearl Harbor came along, GM, Dodge, Ford, Chrysler, De-Soto, and the others switched to tanks and bombers, and Baldy McReary added regular tours of all the junkyards in south-eastern Michigan and Greater Toledo to his job description. So far he had managed to scrounge a transmission, steering column, AM radio, and the entire rear end of a 1940 model, all of which he stashed in a barn in Oakland County, dividing the storage fee with the others, against the inevitable breakdown. The farmer who owned the barn had threatened once to donate the contents to the government scrap drive if they failed to pay up the first of every month, but after a visit from Canal he had reconsidered and granted them a two-week grace period.

The cop on the scene in Hamtramck was a skinny albino named Walters. He wore a seersucker suit that hung on him like a sail and a half-inch coat of Noxzema on his white face to protect him from the June sun. Pinkwater eyes swam behind eyeglass lenses as thick as ashtrays. His obvious Adam's apple went up and down like a piston when he read Zagreb's ID.

"The Four Horsemen! I was beginning to think you guys were invented by George Stark."

Stark was a columnist with the *Detroit News.*

"Not hardly."

"I hear you keep those Four-F assholes in line down at the beer gardens. Bust their heads and throw 'em out in the alley with the swizzle sticks."

Canal said, "Jesus H. Christ," and turned his back to enjoy the view of the identical house across the street.

"We're not supposed to bust them," Zagreb said. "Just lump them up so they remember us every time they put on a hat."

"Long as I don't have to take part. They pulled me off Records for this detail. The regular guy's in the Pacific. I'm a librarian."

"No kidding. You want to check out the stacks for a stiff? They told us you had one here."

Walters pulled the chain on his vacant smile and stepped aside from the doorway. Zagreb and Canal entered, followed by Burke and McReary, who with a hat covering his bald head looked like a kid from the reserve.

The living room was gray, not much wider than a hallway, and lit only by a single lamp and stuttering flashes from the Speed Graphic in the hands of a Detroit police photographer. Zagreb knew him slightly, a pudgy youngster with a cold cigar stub screwed permanently into the middle of his face and always the same baggy suit belted just under his sternum. He started basic training at the end of the month. Henry Brandon, inspector with Detroit Homicide, moved with him, shuttling backward and from side to side in a crouch like a fight referee, pointing out new angles. He ran toward lightweight gray double-breasteds, a white Panama hat between Memorial Day and Labor Day, and gold-rimmed spectacles. His temples were prematurely white.

The rest of the room belonged to a middle-aged woman with a face straight out of a newsreel from the Warsaw Ghetto, round, puffy, and dough-colored. Someone had cut her open like a deer and stretched her out on her back on the rug, a fern-leaf pattern with fringes. The eighteen-inch slash had begun to draw flies.

Brandon spotted Zagreb and stepped over the body to join him.

"Thought you'd be called up by now," he said by way of greeting. "All of Stationary Traffic shipped out last week. Uniform's up to its ass in ugly meter maids."

"Essential duty," Zagreb said. Brandon was too close to Commissioner Witherspoon for him to like. "I hear there are stamps missing."

"The husband says whoever did it took every ration book in the house. He won't say how many. Hoarders. Nothing else was stolen, he says. They had forty-six bucks in cash in a cigar box in the bedroom dresser, right where they kept the stamps. They still have. So whoever did it's looking for a black market sale. Thought you might want a look."

"Where's the husband?"

"In the bedroom, bawling his head off. Polack, works at Dodge Main. I don't think he did it. It's a deep wound. There's a carving knife in the kitchen, but it's clean."

"Forced entry?"

Brandon shook his head. "Way it looks, he grabbed her from behind and cut her backhanded. She trusted him enough to turn her back on him."

"But it wasn't the husband."

"He's got fists like sides of beef. He wouldn't have to cut her. Anyway, she's been dead a couple of hours. He called us as soon as he got home from work. You can go back and talk to him if you like."

"Take a look first. Okay?"

"Be my guest."

He didn't bother looking at the wound. There were no slashes on her palms, just a purple stain at the base of the third and fourth fingers on the right one. He sniffed at it. "Ink," he said. "Find a pen?"

"No. But we haven't moved the body yet. Coroner's late." Brandon fitted a Lucky into a black onyx holder and lit it off a gold-and-enamel lighter. He didn't look the least bit like Roosevelt.

Zagreb finished with the body. His gaze alighted on a pedestal table. He lifted the fringed shade off the lamp that stood on it and tilted the lamp. The glare of the bulb showed a pattern of indentations on the table's varnished top. "She used this to write on. Can you get it?" He looked at the photographer.

The photographer squinted. He had the best eye downtown. The army would probably make him a cook. "Sure." He snapped off a dozen shots from every angle, catching the spent bulbs and replacing them on the fly. Zagreb turned the lamp this way and that on the young man's command. When he stopped to crank in a fresh roll of film, the lieutenant set the lamp on the floor and fished out one of the folded sheets of newsprint he used to take notes.

"Anybody got a pencil? No, a pencil."

Brandon, who had produced a fountain pen, returned it to his double-breasted, patted his pockets, and shook his head. He looked at Walters. The Hamtramck cop took inventory and came up with a gnawed yellow stump, sharpened with a penknife. Zagreb took it. He smoothed out the sheet on the table and scrubbed the side of the lead back and forth across the page.

"Look at Charlie Chan," said Brandon.

Zagreb held it up and squinted, then handed it to McReary, who had the best eyesight on the squad. The bald officer squatted on his haunches to look at it in the light of the lamp on the floor.

"Looks like she signed something," he said. "A signature, anyway. Did some printing too. Numbers. What's the address here?"

"Twenty-six ten Dequindre," said Walters.

"Yeah. There's an H and an A and maybe M."

"Hamtramck."

Everyone turned to stare at Burke, who looked away and didn't contribute anything more.

"And O-S-T," McReary said.

"OST?" Zagreb looked at Walters, who touched the Noxzema on his cheek.

"Well, there's Botsford Street. But that's a mile north."

"That's OTS. See anything else?"

"Not that I can read." McReary stood.

"How soon can we have those shots?" Zagreb asked the photographer.

"Tomorrow night. I'm still processing the stuff from the Brzezicki shooting."

"Tomorrow morning's fine."

Brandon said, "Hold on. We've been working the Brzezicki twenty-four hours."

"Wartime priority," Zagreb said. "You made the call. You can have this one if you want."

The inspector said nothing.

Zagreb said, "Let's get a look at the husband."

The bedroom was a coffin, two-thirds the size of the living room and dominated by an antique bed with a six-foot walnut headboard. Joseph Levinski was sitting on the edge of the mattress with his big feet on the floor in their steel-toed brogans and his big shaggy head sunk between his shoulders as if to deflect blows. His face was red and gullied where tears had furrowed through the grime. He was still holding his black lunch pail on his lap. Zagreb guessed: liverwurst, an apple, maybe a Baby Ruth for after, milk in the Thermos. In November it would be chicken noodle soup. A pair of officers in the uniform of the Hamtramck Police Department, Polacks both from the look of them—ox-eyed, slate-jawed, arms bent at the elbows even in repose, the tendons shortened by generations of heavy lifting—took up the space not occupied by the bed and a new-looking chest of drawers in contrasting colors of wood. They looked relieved by the fresh company.

Levinski didn't look up. He breathed noisily, snuffling up snot and exhaling through his mouth. The lieutenant stood in front of him with his hands in his pockets. "He found her?"

Brandon nodded. He was the only one who had gone in with Zagreb. There wasn't room for another occupant. "Walters says the sergeant who took the call spent five minutes getting him calm enough to give the address. Half of it was in Polish. Which in this town is no big problem."

Zagreb went to the chest of drawers. The top drawer hung open. "Print boys been in?"

"On the way. Everything takes longer now."

He peeled back a stack of sleeveless undershirts and looked at an R.G. Dunn box in the corner of the drawer. He was still holding the pencil Walters had given him. He used the eraser end to tip up the pasteboard lid. Inside was a pile of wrinkled bills and a scattering of change. "This where they kept the ration books?"

"According to Levinski."

The lieutenant looked again at the man on the bed, inventorying him along with the rest of the room. "Any domestic calls, complaints?"

"Walters says no."

"I won't get anything out of him the locals haven't."

Brandon sucked hard on the onyx holder, coaxing all the good out of his cigarette. A recent memo from Commissioner Witherspoon had urged all upper-level department brass to cut down on smoking by way of setting an example, freeing up cartons for America's fighting men. Zagreb hadn't seen a butt longer than a quarter of an inch in an ashtray downtown since before the memo.

"There's a reader on my desk from the cops in Flatrock," the inspector said. "They pulled a fifty-eight-year-old man out of the river three days ago, cut up just like the Levinski woman. Local character, carried a fat wallet stuffed tight with stamps and no one ever saw him spend one. The wallet wasn't on the corpse."

Zagreb felt his face getting haggard. "Shit. One of those."

"I'll send over the paperwork."

"How come you're so good to me?"

"Save it for show-up, Lieutenant. I got no shortage of homicides. There's no need to ration those. Most of my best men are in England. It isn't as if we aren't all in the same boat."

Zagreb lit up a Chesterfield by way of reply. The memo didn't cover lieutenants.

Back in the living room, Walters was looking out the window into the window of the house next door. Except for the corpse at his feet there wasn't a compelling difference between the room he was standing in and the one he was staring at. He turned around when Zagreb asked him about the neighbors.

"I've got uniforms out knocking on doors. Don't get your

hopes up. All the housewives are catching rivets over at Rouge."

Zagreb gave him a card. "Ring me up if you turn anything."

"I sure will. The Four Horsemen." He was looking at the card as if that was what was printed there.

Out on the sidewalk, Zagreb told the others about Flatrock.

"Jesus H. Christ," Canal said. "One of those."

"That's what I said."

Burke, standing at the end of the walk, motioned to the rest of the squad. They joined him just as the coroner's wagon, a green Chrysler panel truck, pulled into the driveway. Burke pointed at a smeary chalk drawing on the yellowed concrete between his wing tips: a crude cartoon showing a pair of goggle eyes and a long nose and two sets of sausage-shaped fingers overlapping a horizontal line, like someone peering over the edge of a fence. Underneath someone had printed KILROY WAS HERE.

"Anything?" Burke asked.

"What if it is? They're all over town." The lieutenant dropped his cigarette and crushed it out on Kilroy's face.

And now the killer had a name.

chapter four

Sid Yegerov had owned and operated Empire Cleaners on Twelfth Street for thirty-seven years. Before that he had apprenticed to his Uncle Yuri for six. Yuri, one-eyed and bent over—family legend said the eye had been put out by Cossacks and his spine damaged when imperial cavalry trampled him during a Marxist demonstration in St. Petersburg—was Sid's godfather. He had traveled by train to meet his nephew in Battery Park after the doctors at Ellis Island had pronounced the young man fit enough to set foot on U.S. shores. Sid remembered the occasion as the first and last time Yuri had addressed him by name. After that the old man had developed an elaborate vocabulary of grunts whose tone and timbre indicated whether his apprentice was in disfavor or merely that his assistance was needed at the counter.

In 1906 the old man died, leaving the business to Sid, then twenty-three. The new owner knocked a hole in the front wall, installed a plate-glass window to let light into what had been a gloomy cave stinking of mildew and candle wax, replaced the Hebrew sign with the store's name lettered in English on the glass, and bought a new steam presser, retiring the one that had been in use since 1889. At that time he also acquired a wife, Chanah, whose photographic portrait, smoky at the edges and tinted with oils according to the custom of the age, still stood on his bedside table at home with black lace around the frame, although she had been dead eighteen years. She had been standing near the window, examining a customer's cotton blouse by natural light to determine whether it had been damaged by bleach, when the glass exploded. The police determined that the bomb had been made by filling a smudge pot stolen from a street construction project with paraffin and inserting a flaming rag. The entire front of the store was gutted by fire and Chanah was hospitalized with third-degree burns over eighty percent of her body. She died that night—fortunately, they said, without regaining consciousness.

That was the beginning of the Cleaners and Dyers War, from which the Purple Gang took its name. Sid Yegerov, who paid no attention to territorial disputes and did not keep company with others of his profession, had known nothing of the business until he returned from the bank to find black smoke pouring out of the front of the shop and a hook and ladder clanging up the block.

Sid wasn't impressed with the police investigation, even when it produced an arrest at the end of just three days. The suspect, a nineteen-year-old neighborhood youth whom the dry cleaner knew by sight, had turned himself in at the local precinct house and confessed, saying he had intended only to destroy the shop as an example to those establishments whose owners refused to align themselves with the Cleaners and Dyers Protective Association, of which he was the local representative. Guilt over the death of Mrs. Yegerov had proven too much for him to bear in silence. Hearst's *Detroit Times* ran a picture of the suspect on its police page, face buried in his manacled hands on a bench outside Recorders Court before his arraignment on a charge of felony murder.

The widower was unmoved. It was clear the youth had been put up to take the blame, probably in place of some more valuable gang member, and that he had been promised good representation and a sum of money to compensate him for the inconvenience—in this case, seven to ten years of his life for the lesser crime of involuntary manslaughter, to which he pleaded guilty. He was out in three.

Sid didn't bother to attend the sentencing, or to keep track of what happened to the boy, although he heard a rumor that something had happened during his confinement in the Southern Michigan Penitentiary at Jackson and that it was bad enough to prevent him from returning to the neighborhood, where the story was known. That meant he was in Toledo. The Purple Gang owned that port on Lake Erie down to the manhole covers and the storage buildings where the Department of Public Works kept the piles of salt it spread on the streets in February, as well as several hundred cases of Old Log Cabin sourmash whiskey, a favorite in Capone's Chicago. By now he was probably a street commissioner.

What Sid did, instead of interest himself in the fortunes of the young man who the law was satisfied had taken Chanah's life, was buy a gun.

It was a seven-millimeter Luger that Krekor Messarian, the Armenian tailor in the next block, had acquired from a German in the trenches in France during the 1917 Christmas truce. The trade had cost him six cartons of Fatimas. The cleaner gave him fifteen dollars. The pistol, an ugly brown length of pipe with checked wooden grips and a firing mechanism that worked on the same basic principle as a cigarette lighter, shared a White Owl cigar box on a shelf below the counter with an extra magazine loaded with brass cartridges. At night he took it home, box and all, and carried it under his arm to work each morning. Everyone in the neighborhood knew about the pistol in Mr. Yegerov's White Owl box. Boys who came to pick up their parents' cleaning sometimes worked up courage enough to ask to see it. He always refused. He knew the gun would save his life one day.

When the little copper bell mounted on a spring clip above the door jangled and a young man came in with an army tunic folded over one arm, Sid didn't examine him any more closely than he did any other customer, although he didn't get much business from strangers. The uniform didn't surprise him. He saw them often on streetcars, and had wondered if the young men who wore them used civilian cleaners or whether the service was provided by Uncle Sam. The tunic itself, closely woven wool dyed a rich brown, promised a welcome change from Herman Schwemmer's out-of-date mustard suit he wore to synagogue and invariably befouled afterward, in summer with dripping ice-cream cones at Sealtest and in fall and winter with matzoh at Berman's, and Mrs. Tolwasser's cotton print dress, which attracted mud and grease like lint every time she stepped off the running board of the Edison electric she had been driving ever since Mr. Tolwasser had his brains kicked out by his milk horse on Woodward in 1913. Sid knew every detail of every item of nonwashable apparel in the neighborhood as well as he knew his own.

The young man himself was pleasant-looking in that bland, characterless way of unworn youth—dark sandy hair brushed back from a prominent widow's peak and features well enough balanced for Hollywood, or so Sid concluded from the pictures he saw in *Parade*. (He himself hadn't been to see a movie since Chanah, had never watched one whose dialogue wasn't restricted to preprinted cards.) The fellow had on a military-style trenchcoat too heavy for a warm June day over a khaki shirt and trousers with a necktie to match. He was carrying a briefcase.

He brushed aside Sid's greeting with a question. "How are you with ink?"

The cleaner turned his attention from the eyes beneath the liquid black visor of the young man's cap—clear, brown eyes, anxious about his uniform—to the tunic, which he took and turned inside out without asking questions. The blue-black stain was where he expected to find it, at the base of the inside breast pocket.

"I never carry a fountain pen myself," he said. "The only thing you can count on them to do is leak."

"Can you get it out?"

"Is it fresh?"

"It happened yesterday."

"I can do something if it hasn't set." He hung the coat on the rack by the register and slid over the receipt pad. "Name?"

"Taylor."

He wrote it down, tore off the original, and held it out. "I can have it for you tomorrow night."

"I need it sooner."

"Lots of people ahead of you. Nice weather. Barbecues. They pour on plenty of sauce so they don't notice there's not much meat."

Corporal Taylor laid a five-dollar bill on the counter.

Sid couldn't believe this war. Only five years ago, five dollars was a hundred. He smiled at the eager young soldier. "Inspection?"

The corporal grinned shyly. He was just a boy. "Yes, sir. The captain's a good man, but he seems to think the war will be won by the side with the sharpest creases."

Sid grunted. "You can pick the coat up at eight A.M. The chemicals will need to dry tonight or they'll run and bleach the lining. It will be a dollar twenty." He pushed the bill back across the counter.

The corporal thanked him and put the money in a trench-coat pocket.

"Where are you stationed?"

"Fort Wayne."

"What outfit?" Sid took the tunic off the rack and folded it.

"Hundred and Seventy-seventh."

"Really? My nephew's in the Air Corps. This looks like their insignia."

"That's right."

"I thought the Hundred and Seventy-seventh was Field Artillery."

Corporal Taylor hesitated. The cleaner felt embarrassed for him. "I guess you can't expect the army to tell us what it's up to. All we're doing is paying for this war."

"I just go where I'm assigned."

No more words passed between them. The young man left the shop.

Sid was troubled by the exchange, and returned to it from time to time throughout the day, not thinking about it only when he was forced to respond to a customer's comments on the war, Roosevelt, rationing, and the mysterious ability of chocolate and cream sauce to migrate to one's lapels unobserved, or when he made change, which after thirty-seven years still required all his concentration. Particularly when he was daubing at the indigo stain on the rayon lining of Corporal Taylor's tunic with a sponge dipped in a mixture of mineral spirits and naphtha—his own blend—he wondered about the bizarre lapse. There was no Army Air Corps installation near Detroit. Both the 182nd and the 177th Field Artillery regiments had shipped out months ago, leaving only the Quartermaster Corps at Fort Wayne to receive and store military vehicles produced at the automobile plants. Perhaps the young man had served overseas and been wounded, either physically or mentally, and was confused about details. Certainly there was an air about him that suggested something vital was missing.

Rotten war. They were all rotten. It didn't matter if they were endorsed by governments or cheap punk crooks. They were thieves of life and youth. They left ugly stains that all the mineral spirits and naphtha in the world could not eradicate.

He left the tunic to hang overnight, inside out to dry completely and dispel the fumes, locked up, and struck off to board the streetcar home, carrying the White Owl cigar box with the Luger inside. He had become another of those old Jewish shopkeepers plodding along the sidewalk with their shapeless hats pulled low and all their ambitions reduced to the next square of concrete. Lately he had ceased even to think about that, had begun to become what he had beheld. His kind blended into the gray city background like lichens on a stump.

He would never get used to the quietness of the street at that early hour of the evening. The day shift at the plants had let out an hour and a half ago, the night shift was well along. Gas and tire rationing had erased the weekday shopping and entertainment traffic from his neighborhood as effectively as alcohol erased tomato sauce from cotton. If he closed his ears to the bleating of the odd horn over on Woodward, the hollow whistles of the trains shuttling iron pellets and coils of copper wire and donated scrap back and forth across the grounds of the sprawling Rouge plant, he could imagine he was back in St. Petersburg, delivering bread and paper collars to customers of the shops in the narrow twisted streets that had known nothing but horses, carts, and sore feet since before Tamerlane. There, as here, the sudden scrape of a strange heel on pavement echoed off the brick walls as if it were immediately behind him, making the hair on the back of his neck prickle. His fingers tightened on the cigar box. It calmed him with its tactile reality, the reassuring weight of the German automatic resting inside.

He heard the steps for a long time, not increasing in pace but faster than his so that they must overtake him unless he ran, and this he would not do, not at his age and station in life, not while he had a weapon. He assumed they belonged to someone who, like him, was on his way home from work. The man was in a hurry. A young man, then, with a wife awaiting him whom he loved. Probably his route was long and he was walking to save fuel and rubber and wear and tear on his automobile. Sid, who was not so pressed—why hasten home to empty rooms?—slowed his own pace and moved in close to the wall to give the fellow room to pass.

When the footsteps behind him slowed as well, he turned to look over his shoulder. He felt relief when he saw the man was in uniform. It was only a G.I. hurrying to catch the streetcar and be back in barracks before taps. Then he recognized Corporal Taylor, and for some reason he felt a twinge of apprehension. He stopped and turned to confront it—and him.

"Your uniform will be ready in the morning," he said. "It must dry overnight, and then I need to press it. There is no use your hurrying what takes time to correct."

The young soldier had stopped in front of him. His briefcase was open and he had one hand under the flap. When it came out, something came out with it, a long strip of reflected light from the streetlamp on the corner. And then the briefcase was falling and the other arm was curling up and around to encircle Sid's neck.

He fumbled at the lid of the cigar box, but it slipped from his grip. The box struck the sidewalk, tipping open and dumping out the Luger and the extra magazine. By then he was being spun on his heel, spun and pulled back against the long hard length of the young man's body. Something tugged at the front of his waistcoat; something that encountered no resistance from the wool or the cotton shirt beneath or the undershirt beneath that and pulled a string of fire from his pelvis to his collarbone. A warm wetness spilled down his leg like urine. Then something broke, a string inside him, and he felt himself folding to the sidewalk like a coat sliding off a hanger in his shop. He never felt the sidewalk.

chapter five

Canal said, "Which one tonight?"

"I don't know," Zagreb said. "You pick."

"I picked last time."

"So you're in practice."

McReary said, "I'll pick."

Canal laughed. "Forget it. You'll pick the Ladybug because you got a hard-on for that tall barmaid."

"What's wrong with that?"

Burke said, "Give it up, Tim. Dames like that wipe their asses with guys like you."

McReary tried on a leer. It made him look like Mortimer Snerd. "Sounds pretty good."

"Jesus H. Christ." Canal relit his cigar, a lost cause once the glowing ash reached that part of the wrapping saturated with saliva. "Let's hit Rumrunner's."

Rumrunner's occupied a former Michigan Stove Company warehouse at the end of one of the narrow streets that led to the Detroit River. It had been a blind pig during Prohibition. Boats loaded with Canadian whiskey had delivered their cargoes through a door located under the dock, bricked up long since. The front entrance retained its ornamental iron grillwork, designed to slow down raiders while personnel inside hid incriminating liquor paraphernalia. Double-tiered tables had allowed patrons to keep their drinks out of sight from the windows, and now proved convenient to provide a dry surface on top for euchre. Then as now, such features were cosmetic, intended merely to pique the customers' love of the forbidden;

in fact, most of the overhead had gone to the Prohibition Squad to discourage interruptions. Since Repeal, the establishment had become one of the many beer gardens along Jefferson, dispensing Altes and Fox DeLuxe beer, nickel bags of potato chips and pretzels, and steaming plates of bratwurst and sauerkraut to the city's largely German population. Here, polka was king, swing merely the prime minister, and few denounced the Nazis for their nationality, rather for their friendship with Hirohito.

Patriotism was in evidence, however. Various colorful posters, inspirational (PRODUCTION IS AMERICA'S ANSWER, SAVE FREEDOM OF SPEECH—BUY WAR BONDS), recruitment (I WANT YOU FOR THE U.S. ARMY, IT'S A WOMAN'S WAR TOO—JOIN THE WAVES), and admonitory (LOOSE LIPS SINK SHIPS, SOMEONE TALKED!) decorated the brick walls just below the canopy of tobacco smoke, and snapshots of various area soldiers, sailors, and airmen in uniform shingled a bulletin board near the blackboard menu. But most of the adornment was nostalgic: framed front pages from defunct tabloids shrieking of gangland massacres, blowup photos of men in cloth caps and fedoras unloading crates of whiskey from the trunks of touring cars, snapshots of rum-running boats, sleek and speedy. Twelve years of Depression followed by six months of rationing had restored the romance to the excesses of the Roaring Twenties.

The place was filling up, but not with the kind of crowd that had come there in the dry time to drink to lawlessness and the rebellious American way, or in the hard times that came after, to float away their unpaid bills on a stream of alcohol. There were women, plenty of them now that they had their own money from working in the plants and no place to go but empty houses and apartments with most of the male population in foreign stations. They were there to drink with their friends and cast hungry glances at the men in the place; some in uniform, others wearing discharge pins, still more with double hernias and flat feet: 4-Fers, and a troublesome lot when they got a couple of drinks under their belts and uncorked their opinions about how MacArthur should have handled the Philippines. There was heavy chatter, people trying hard to have a good time despite the combination of bad news and no news at all from the war theaters, and a little music from the jukebox, a red-and-green Rock-Ola trimmed in ivory Bakelite, overstocked, as usual, with Glenn Miller. While McReary was watching through the glass porthole in the front door, a reedy youth of twenty—no Detroit bartender had asked to see ID since Repeal—in peg tops and saddle shoes slid a nickel into the slot and selected "St. James Infirmary." McReary strolled back down the street to where the black Oldsmobile was parked and planted a wing tip on the running board.

"Getting ripe," he announced. "Give me ten minutes."

"Somebody mouthing off?" Zagreb lit a Chesterfield off the dashboard lighter.

"Not yet, but a kid just got gutbucket going on the juke."

"No shit. Shine? No shit." Burke leaned forward from the backseat and folded his hairy forearms across the top of Canal's seat.

"Not in there. You kidding? You know these kids and their nigger jazz. Those hillbilly production workers won't sit still for much of that."

"Any servicemen?" Zagreb asked.

"No, the army and the navy both posted this place O.L. after the last fracas."

"Good. I hate working with those fucking M.P.s." Canal pushed his cigar to the other corner of his mouth. It had gone out for good.

Zagreb checked his Wittnauer. "We'll give you fifteen. It's early."

"What are you going to use?" Canal asked.

McReary looked glum; he was enjoying himself. "Old Reliable."

Burke grinned for him, a wolfish snarl against his chronic five o'clock shadow. "Better make it five, Zag."

Zagreb said nothing, ending that line of argument. When McReary left to enter Rumrunner's, the lieutenant looked at Canal. "Got your call key?"

The big sergeant patted his pockets and looked sheepish.

"For Pete's sake. You keep losing them we're going to have every hophead in town calling his connection from a police box. Open the glove compartment."

There was a collection of identical hollow-shafted keys inside. Canal put one in his vest pocket. "I don't know why we just don't use the radio."

"Because every beer garden this side of the river has one," Zagreb said.

Burke sat back. "If we keep giving Baldy more time, he's going to walk out of one of these places with his head turned backwards. Those Four-effers fight dirty."

"So does Baldy." Zagreb flicked his Chesterfield out the window and lit another.

There were two empty stools at the bar, but McReary didn't like either location. He hung inside the door, pretending to be waiting for the caller in the telephone booth to finish, while a slope-shouldered Pole in a threadbare denim jacket with a block-plant tan at the base of his neck settled his bill and slid off his stool to use the men's room; then he moved in to claim the vacancy. The drinker to his right was a skinny towhead in a leather vest, work pants, and scuffed cowboy boots, with a Confederate flag tattooed on the back of his left hand. His other neighbor was less obvious, but McReary had heard a twang when he'd ordered another round.

The bartender was a squat Corktown Irishman, built along the lines of a fire hydrant, with humorous blue eyes in a face that was otherwise as friendly as a skillet. When he asked McReary what he'd have, the officer glanced down the row of shot glasses and beer mugs lined up along the bartop and ordered a grasshopper.

"Saint James Infirmary" growled to a finish. While the bartender, without taking his eyes off his customer, assembled the primarily green ingredients, McReary left the stool, punched a nickel into the Rock-Ola, and scowled in delight when he found Bessie Smith's "Gimme a Pigfoot (and a Bottle of Beer)." He wanted to meet the man who had that juke route. As he made his way back to the bar through Bessie's wailing opening, he heard a voice in the crowd say, "Holy shit!"

He paid for the neon-colored cocktail, counting out an inordinate number of pennies and no tip; that guaranteed no interference from behind the bar when he started getting his head kicked in. He could feel the stare the redneck on his right was giving him out the corner of his left eye as he raised his glass. The lumpy-looking number on his left was glaring down at his beer with both broken-nailed hands wrapped around the mug.

"Here's to Eleanor Roosevelt!" said McReary, and drank.

Zagreb watched the sweep hand on the face of his Wittnauer pass the twelve. He turned to nod at Canal just as the first glass broke inside Rumrunner's.

Canal didn't wait for the nod. He chunked down the door handle, sprinted when he hit the sidewalk, unlocked the police call box on the corner, and called for the wagon. The others meanwhile were moving toward the door of the beer garden.

By now more glass had broken inside and the music had stopped—whether because the plug was jerked or because of a direct assault on the front of the machine had yet to be determined.

The fighting inside was not general, after the manner of a Hollywood Western saloon brawl, with customers slinging punches at whoever wandered into their path and stunt doubles jackknifing off balconies. A crowd had gathered near the end of the bar, where McReary and a narrow-gauged party in a leather vest and cowboy boots run-down at the heels were on their feet, circling each other in a cleared section of floor.

Baldy's dour expression told Zagreb he was enjoying himself. The shitkicker had his back arched and his fists up, neither guarding his face. McReary, in a crouch, face concealed behind his hands, kept his weight on the balls of his feet and pivoted quickly whenever his back was turned to the bulky fellow seated on a stool with his elbows behind him on the bar, minimizing the latter's opportunity to attack from ambush. There was a dark spot on McReary's right temple, a sickly green puddle on the bar and pieces of broken glass winking on the floor in front of the rail. He had taken the first blow.

Just as Zagreb and Burke moved in, McReary ducked a shoulder, feinted with his left, and when the redneck stepped back to avoid it, resting his weight on his heels, the officer stepped forward and connected with his right, a short jab straight from the shoulder that struck the point of the other's chin with a sound like ice cracking. The skinny towhead took two steps backward and shook his head. Then his jaw dropped, his eyes went out of focus, and he teetered forward, falling in a long clean uninterrupted arc onto his face on the hardwood floor. Zagreb felt the impact through the soles of his shoes. Then the pile of bulk seated at the bar came down off his stool and slung a ham fist into the side of McReary's neck from behind.

The punch lacked momentum. Burke, who had had his eye on the fellow from the start, had stepped in just as the skinny man fell and drove his left forearm into the bulky man's throat as he hit McReary. His windpipe collapsed. He wheezed to force air into his lungs, his face bug-eyed and terrified; by then Burke's other hand was coming out of his own coat pocket. Brass gleamed as he pistoned his fist into the man's mouth. Blood geysered.

McReary, dazed by the blow to his neck, grasped at the bar for support. Zagreb turned his back to the officer and spread his feet, blocking him from the others in the room as in a smooth ambidextrous movement he produced both his gold badge and his short-barreled Colt .38. "Police! Stay where you are!"

The crowd's hesitation was brief. Then it split in two directions, some patrons heading for the door, others surging toward the three men standing by the bar. Canal, who was now standing in the doorway, pointed his starter's pistol at the ceiling and fired. The blank glass cartridge made a noise like a heavy crate hitting a sidewalk. The echo of the report rang through the silence that followed.

Then the wagon was there, accompanied by four black-and-whites and eighteen Detroit police officers in uniform, who formed a flying wedge as they entered the building, fanning out inside and surrounding and disarming and herding the patrons across the sidewalk and into the wagon, the two men who had attacked McReary in the lead. They stopped loading when there was no more room inside. When the bar was closed, Zagreb, Burke, and Canal helped McReary out the door and into the black Oldsmobile.

Canal got the flat pint of Old Grand-Dad out of the glove

compartment and passed it over the back of the seat to Burke, who unscrewed the cap and held it out for McReary. The officer declined assistance, seizing the bottle and tipping it up. It gurgled twice. The smell of fermented grain filled the car.

"All square?" Zagreb was watching him in the rearview mirror.

Baldy wiped his mouth with the back of his hand and tested the sore spot on his neck with two fingers. "Either those hillbillies are hitting harder or I'm getting old. This what it's like?"

"How would we know, you little pissant?" Burke was grinning. "Maybe you need to come up with a toast that won't rile them up so much."

"Yeah. Try calling Robert E. Lee a faggot." Canal confiscated the bottle and swigged.

"I don't see why we need one at all," McReary said. "Why don't we just wait for a fight to start and come in then?"

Zagreb said, "You can wait all night for that. This way we make an example early on. Word gets down the street, the bartenders in the other joints put the screws on, and we're all home in time for Charlie McCarthy."

"Yeah, but is it legal?"

"What's it matter? Everybody's looking for U-boats in the river." The lieutenant leaned over and spun up the volume on the two-way.

"One-ten, one-ten." The dispatcher didn't sound as if he had any hope of a response.

Zagreb unhooked the microphone and thumbed up the switch. "One-ten."

"One-ten, see Inspector Brandon at the Wayne County Morgue."

"Holy shit." Canal screwed the cap back on the bottle and returned it to the glove compartment. "I hope they want us to identify him."

chapter six

Zagreb hated coroners' hands.

This one's were like all the rest, pink and puffy, with round antiseptic nails and no hair growing on the backs. They got that way from immersion in alcohol and formaldehyde. The fingers resembled bunches of scrubbed sausages and made the lieutenant think of mannequins and the newly washed hands of corpses lying in state. He didn't mind the specialists' coarse jokes, intended to weed out the squeamish, and the sight and even the smell of flayed human flesh had ceased to bother him, but when introductions were made he always found something to be doing with his own hands to give him an excuse to avoid grasping those naked pink fingers.

The rest of the fellow was ordinary enough, although Zagreb would never get used to the extremes of age made necessary in the workforce by wartime personnel shortages. Dr. Edouard (he'd taken pains to spell it for the lieutenant) was seventy if he was a day, with a ribbon of hair combed across the top of his bald head, satin white against pink scalp, and glass blue eyes under thistly brows that had needed plucking five years ago and now required mowing. He wore his white coat over a tweed vest that made Zagreb itch on sight, with a row of stubby yellow pencils poking out of one of the pockets and a red bow tie, the kind you tied, with yellow polka dots.

"County pulled Edouard out of retirement," said Inspector Brandon, in his trademark Panama hat and gray double-breasted. "He owns a mortuary, which his son runs. He worked in the old morgue when it moved into the basement of the County Building in 1905."

"Busy first week. Omnibus ran into a horse trolley." The old man laughed without making a sound. His chest bellowsed and he opened his mouth to display a horseshoe of gold molars.

Zagreb made a noise that seemed appropriate and the three went into one of the three autopsy rooms, bypassing both the viewing room with its comforting furnishings, chosen to lessen survivors' shock, and the long, low-ceilinged cold storage room where unclaimed corpses awaited identification behind refrigerator doors. The medium-size room where they ended up gleamed with white porcelain and ceramic tile and contained a fixture that was more sink than table, white enamel with a dull zinc lining, a faucet at one end, and a drainpipe running into the floor. The metal shade of a hydraulically operated lamp hung suspended above the naked male carcass stretched out inside. The dead man was about sixty and balding, the gray skin of his face shiny where the bones seemed to be wearing through. His eyes were half-open and sunken into their sockets. His fingers and toes were long and bony, barnacled with callus, and his circumcised penis lay to one side of his deflated scrotum. His torso from collarbone to pelvis was an open, empty cavity in which Zagreb could see the inside of his ribs. A pile of entrails lay atop a rolling steel cart parked next to the table. It was a sight that never failed to remind the lieutenant of his annual hunting trip north to Grayling and the process of dressing out a slain deer. The fishy smell of stale blood and butchered meat, washed down with carbolic, was a presence in the room, very nearly alive.

Edouard's bright eyes were on Zagreb as they entered the room. The lieutenant's reaction to the corpse, or rather his lack of it, seemed to disappoint the specialist, who promptly lost interest. He hung back at the door, hauled out a thick pocket watch with a nicked steel case, and held it in the pink palm of his hand throughout the visit as if he were timing it.

"Simeon Yegerov." Brandon read from a spiral pad he took from an inside pocket. "We're still waiting for a positive, but that was the name on the papers in his wallet. He owned Empire Cleaners on Twelfth. We found him six blocks away, dead maybe ten minutes. Probably on his way home."

"Any cash in the wallet?" Zagreb lit a Chesterfield. His throat was raw from smoking but he wanted to take the edge off the carnal stench.

The inspector turned a page. "Thirty-three dollars. It wasn't robbery."

"Ration stamps?"

"Third of a book, in the upper right-hand inside pocket of his coat. Butter and eggs mostly."

"So why am I here?"

Brandon turned to Edouard, whose glass blue eyes brightened. "Single laceration, proceeding upward from first penetration at a thirty-degree oblique for sixty-six centimeters, right to left, beginning at the ilium and ending at the clavicle. Complete severance of the external iliac, inferior epigastric, sternal, musculophrenic, and superior epigastric arteries. Death by desanguination in less than two minutes. First time I ever conducted an autopsy without touching a postmortem knife." He made his noiseless laugh.

"Shit." Zagreb blew out smoke with the expletive.

"There's more," the inspector said. "Owners of businesses carry keys. No keys were found on the body. First uniform on the scene went to the dry-cleaning shop and found the door unlocked, the key still in the hole with the ring hanging from it. No sign the place was tossed, but maybe the killer knew where to look."

"Maybe Yegerov left his keys."

"Not on the outside of the door, on his way out. Forensics is dusting."

"Stamps?"

"Haven't found any. If our man knew where to look we won't."

"Doesn't make sense. If he went to all that trouble he wouldn't have left the ones on the body. He must've been after something else."

"Something like what?"

The lieutenant took a haul, dropped the cigarette, and crushed it out on the tile. He was burning more these days and smoking less. "If this was Prohibition I'd say he was after cleaning fluid. Maybe he left his shirts."

"He was probably in a hurry when he tossed the body. Maybe he overlooked the ration book."

"It'd be the first one he's overlooked. Any scribbles by the body or near the shop? Walls, sidewalk? 'Kilroy Was Here,' anything like that?"

"No, and I wouldn't let that out if I were you. The newshounds will sniff this one out soon enough without a hook like that."

"How long are you suspending the uniform for?"

Brandon measured out his diplomat's smile. With the white temples he looked more like an ambassador than the son of a German brewer. "Reprimand. Can't spare the manpower. There's a war on, you know? He expected me to boot him up to the squad. I said he must've been home sick the day they told his class at the academy it isn't a uniform's job to go through a victim's pockets."

"You should've booted him up. He's got a better head on his shoulders than all of Homicide."

"We'd've got to the store eventually."

"After some Four-F burglar found the door open and tossed the place."

The inspector stopped smiling. "The M.O.'s Kilroy's. Right-handed sweep from behind. You want it or not? Wartime priority," he added, showing his teeth.

"I'll tinker with it." Zagreb looked at Edouard. "Weapon?"

"Long blade, razor-sharp, no give. At a guess, high-tempered steel, probably double-edged. A fighting weapon."

"Bowie?"

"Too clumsy. This was more like a long incision."

"You mentioned a postmortem knife."

"Possibly. Probably not. I wouldn't want to attack a living body with a hiltless knife. The idea is to spill the victim's blood, not yours."

"That eliminates Jack the Ripper." Brandon put away his notebook. "Have fun with it. I've got a nigger killing on Second I ought to poke my nose into. Probably just some hillbilly, but Jack Witherspoon wants brass on the scene. He had his picture taken with Eleanor Roosevelt once."

"Once'd do it for me," Edouard said. "She's got a face like a Chihuahua's ass."

Zagreb wondered if all the Democrats were in Europe.

He remained behind to ask the coroner's man a few questions. Edouard's answers were brief and desultory; his interest in the lieutenant had vanished when the cut-open corpse had failed to draw the proper reaction. When he was finished Zagreb went back out to the general offices, where he found the rest of the racket squad taking up space in the reception room.

He was irked by their inactivity. Canal, who had a talent for buttonholing supernumeraries and sending them out on errands, was finishing a bottle of Coke. Two empties were already lined up on the edge of a battleship gray steel desk with a covered typewriter atop it; he averaged two minutes per 6.5-ounce bottle. Baldy McReary stood with his hands in his pockets, studying a chart of the female anatomy on a bulletin board next to the door, all its secrets exposed like the tunnels and chambers of an ant farm pressed between panes of glass. Burke had claimed a chair with square steel legs, sitting with his knees at right angles and his hands, surprisingly small and fragile-looking at the ends of his big wrists, gripping his thighs. He looked like someone determined to hold the position against a couple of regiments of Japanese. In reality he was probably struggling to maintain the flow of oxygen to his brain. The carbolic smell that dominated the autopsy rooms had penetrated to every room of the building, and Burke, who had shot and killed two men when he was with the uniform division and been suspended for strangling a third nearly to death in interrogation, hated corpses to the point of phobia. Recently he had refused to serve as pallbearer for the aunt who had raised him.

A portable radio encased in tough fabric with a Bakelite grille was going on about Pantelleria, but nobody appeared to be listening. No one in the room had ever heard of the island before the marines hit it. The announcer sounded as excited as if they'd taken Rome.

"Ladies, I guess I'm the stiff-watcher for this outfit," said Zagreb, being sure to make the comment general. Burke was inclined to sulk.

"One gob of guts looks pretty much like all the rest." McReary blew a kiss to the anatomy chart and turned away. "Is it our boy?"

"Brandon thinks it is."

Canal clunked down his empty bottle and belched dramatically. "That means he don't think he can tie it up. They ought to issue us brooms. All we do is sweep up everybody else's crap."

"We'd better get to sweeping quick. Three's the limit before the papers catch wind." The lieutenant gave them the details on Simeon Yegerov.

"It don't figure," Canal said. "Boys like Kilroy don't light out till they get what they're after. He'd frisk the stiff in the middle of the Hudson's parade."

Zagreb said, "We'll park that for now. Twice he's taken ration stamps. A lot of ration stamps. Either he likes big breakfasts and ball-busting auto trips or he's laying them off somewhere. And there's only one place to sell them in this town."

Burke came out of his trance. "The Conductor."

"Frankie Fucking Orr." Canal tasted it, liking it more with each syllable.

McReary touched the tender spot on the side of his neck, as if it alone had prevented him from coming up with the answer first.

Zagreb's Wittnauer had stopped. He shook it, wound the stem. The sweep hand started moving. His Timex self-winder had given up the ghost just before Dunkirk. All the other self-winders had gone to war and he hadn't gotten into the habit of winding regularly. "What time is it?"

McReary checked the Curvex strapped to the underside of his wrist. "A little after eleven. Roma's stopped serving an hour ago."

"Roma's stops serving when Frankie goes home," the lieutenant said. "We've been turning over Kilroy's dry turds long enough. Let's just this once get out in front of the cocksucker."

chapter seven

That was the best movie," the girl said.
"It was great. I like Robert Taylor."

He thought it was the finest movie ever made. He'd been eager to see *Bataan* ever since it went into production. He had read about it in *Parade*, seen a picture of Taylor, in combat fatigues and smoking a cigarette, going over the script with the director, and had been checking off the days on the calendar before the release date as conscientiously as he kept track of allied engagements with flag pins on the war map in his living room. The final shot of Taylor, the last American on the island, chopping away with a water-cooled machine gun at swarms of victorious Japs like a twentieth-century General Custer, thrilled him, filling him with nationalistic pride and validating his conviction that the U.S. could never be beaten, even if it lost every battle but the last. He knew he would go back to see it again and again.

He had met the girl in the course of his employment as a messenger. It was the third job he'd had that year. Jobs held no value, they were all around, provided the person who applied knew that he would have to move on as soon as the man he was replacing came back from the service. He never waited for that to happen. When he became bored enough he quit.

Her name was Erma, with an *E*. She had been standing behind the cosmetics counter at D.J. Healy when he came in with a stack of order forms and had directed him to the manager's office. His collegiate good looks appealed to many different kinds of women; he knew by the way her professional smile stretched a couple of notches at the corners when she spoke to him that she was his to take out for the asking, and probably to bed. She was a thin blonde with a nose that tilted up like Myrna Loy's. She told him she had applied to the department store hoping to model fashions, but she was an inch too short. Since she couldn't see a future making tracer bullets at King Seeley's she took a job squirting perfume on fat women from St. Clair Shores, rich Grosse Pointe women doing their shopping mostly at Lord's and Gately's. All this he had found out over a plate of veal served San Francisco style at Lelli's. He found her loathsomely boring. If he weren't sensitive about being seen too often alone at movies—the fifth-column shrink at the Light Guard Armory had asked him, in a tone that suggested curiosity rather than routine, if he was a homosexual—he would have made some excuse and taken her home. Now they were walking among the patrons trickling out of the baroque interior of the Michigan Theater, she clinging to his arm, he fishing in a pocket of his pleated civilian slacks for his keys. It was a warm June night, late but not long past dark on the extreme western edge of the Eastern Time Zone. Big Band blare spilled out the open windows of cruising cars, scattered fireflies struck blue-green sparks in the dark between streetlamps. Now and then Erma switched her hips to a snatch of "In the Mood" or "Song of India." He bet she was a jitterbug. He hadn't taken a girl dancing since before Pearl Harbor. He considered it improper to expend so much energy in wartime to no good result.

"Someone told me once I looked like Taylor. I didn't believe her." He watched her out of the corner of his eye.

She leaned away from his arm to squint at his profile. "You

were right." She huddled back in. Her chunky heels made an irritating clacking noise on the sidewalk.

He probed. "It could have been worse. She might have said Humphrey Bogart."

"He doesn't look so bad. I thought he was handsome in *The Roaring Twenties*. He wore pretty suits and he wasn't as short as Jimmy Cagney. Anyway I don't see why all the girls like Robert Taylor. Van Johnson is much better looking."

"I can't picture him."

"He was dreamy in *The Human Comedy*. Piles and piles of wavy blond hair. You're blond, aren't you? It's hard to tell with all that stuff you put on."

He resisted the impulse to smooth back his hair. He never put on a hat when he was wearing civvies. "I only go to war movies."

"Oh, this was about war. It all took place in a small town, and the war kept coming and taking people away. I think small towns are quaint. My uncle and aunt used to have a cabin on Houghton Lake and we'd stop in small towns along the way and have a soda."

He wondered if her uncle and aunt hoarded ration stamps.

"Where should we go now?" she asked. "Sammy Kaye's playing at the Eastwood Gardens. I love Ishkabibble."

"Ishkabibble's with Kay Kyser." He unlocked the door on the passenger's side of his Nash and opened it for her. "Don't you have to be at work early?"

"Tomorrow's Saturday, silly. Don't tell me you're running out of steam." She swung into the seat, flashing a Coppertoned calf with a seam drawn up the back with eyebrow pencil. At least she didn't hoard nylons.

He slid under the wheel and checked his hair in the rearview mirror. It looked glossy black under the domelight.

"I've been on my feet all day. I'll take you someplace for dessert."

"Carl's?"

"Closed by now." He punched the starter. "Roma's Cafe stays open late sometimes. Depends on who's there."

"Roma's, then." She commandeered the mirror to touch up her lipstick.

chapter eight

Restaurants in general aspire to be more than they are. Roma Cafe—"Roma's" popularly, the possessive case assigned by mass mutual agreement—aspired to be less. Its name and location, in the 3400 block of Riopelle north of the Eastern Market, home of sow's ears, fresh goat meat, and dead fowl with the feathers on, suggested an old-fashioned Italian eatery. The red-and-white-checked tablecloths and basketed Chianti bottles suspended from the ceiling managed to capture the flavor of an unprepossessing establishment where a family of four could get in and out for under fifty dollars. In reality there were cases of Mumm's champagne in the storeroom, boxes of imported squid packed in dry ice in the walk-in refrigerator, and even a superficial total of the prices on the menu customarily handed to the head of each party resembled a bid for a defense contract.

The restaurant's history was the history of Detroit in the twentieth century. It had been in operation since 1907, had seen the city evolve from the Stove Capital of the United States to the world's premier automobile vendor, and witnessed the laying of the first course of bricks on the first skyscraper downtown. Theodore Roosevelt had dined there in 1916 after delivering his famous "Damn the mollycoddles" speech at the Detroit Opera House. The next year the proprietors had hosted a party for the doughboys of the 31st Infantry before they shipped out for France. Walter Reuther and Richard T. Frankensteen, bruised and bleeding from the "Battle of the Overpass" with Harry Bennett's Ford Motor Company strikebreakers, had wolfed down plates of pasta in the kitchen at the exact moment the Ford goons were celebrating their victory with red wine and calamari in the dining room. Rallies had taken place there to elect William Howard Taft and Woodrow Wilson, and campaign workers in straw hats and armbands reading REPEAL THE EIGHTEENTH AMENDMENT had drunk smuggled Canadian whiskey and huddled around a Philco Cathedral radio set brought in to monitor the FDR landslide in 1932. Caruso and Garibaldi lived still in frames on the wall behind the bar. The Caruso was signed. General MacArthur fell two inches shy of covering the faded rectangle where Mussolini's likeness had quietly been removed on the Day of Infamy.

Carlo, the maître d', had been in residence since shortly after Roma opened, working his way up from busboy to wine steward in a little over eighteen months—a performance that lost some of its shine upon consideration that he was a cousin of one of the proprietors. The final leap, from silver cup to reservation stand, had taken twelve years, and was accomplished only upon the death of the original maître d', who had held that position in the second oldest restaurant in Florence from 1872 until he fled to escape execution for murdering his brother-in-law in a vendetta. Some customers, knowing only part of the story, mistook Carlo for the vendetta killer, but this was understandable. His predecessor, whose photograph in a silver frame decorated the wall beside the stand, had been a mild-looking white-haired fellow with ruddy cheeks and a cherub's smile, whereas Carlo was lean and sallow with iron gray in his brushed-back hair and a five-inch scar on his right cheek where a tumor had been removed. He never smiled, the surgery having damaged the nerve that worked the required muscles, and his unblinking stare had silenced the bluster of many a would-be diner who claimed his reservation was lost. Very few people knew he sent most of his salary to his sister in Sardinia, that he attended confession three times a week, and that he hadn't missed a Sunday Mass at Most Holy Trinity in thirty years.

Max Zagreb, who was one of those who knew, asked Carlo if he had a table for four. It was a polite question; the restaurant was nearly empty at that hour. The stragglers that remained were nursing last sips of coffee before going home to empty apartments and sullen families.

"The burners should still be hot." Carlo snapped his fingers. A waiter in a knee-length apron separated himself from a group surreptitiously checking wristwatches and came their way.

"Frankie in?" Zagreb asked.

The maître d' uncorked his lidless stare. "Signor Oro is dining in his private room. I'll ask if he's receiving visitors."

"Make sure he says yes."

Seated in a corner booth under a framed print of *The Last Supper*, the four detectives glanced at their red leather menus and folded them at the same instant, like a precision drill. "Veal parmigiana?" asked the lieutenant.

Canal said, "Double order for me. Two jugs of Dago Red."

"One jug. We're working." Zagreb handed the menus to the waiter.

"I'll just have the chowder," said Burke. "My gut's on end again."

McReary said, "In that case I'll have your veal, too. Getting the shit stomped out of me in a bar always brings out my appetite."

Canal wiped each of his protruding eyes with a corner of his napkin. The condition was the result of an overactive thyroid and they tended to water at the end of the shift. "You're just compensating for missing out on that leggy barmaid at the Ladybug."

" 'Compensating'?" Burke was still a little pale from the morgue.

"His wife bought him a subscription to *Reader's Digest.*" Zagreb peeled off his hat and smoothed his hair back from his bulbous forehead.

"Hey, I'd rather whack off to her than that picture of Betty Grable you got in your wallet," McReary told Canal.

"It's Alice Faye."

The waiter left, and returned with a basket of bread and a pitcher of ice water. While he was pouring, a young couple came in the front door. The young man spoke briefly to Carlo, who shook his head. After some fumbling the young man produced a pair of crumpled bills. They vanished, and Carlo snapped his fingers. The girl was pretty, not much more. Her date was good-looking and knew it. He reminded Zagreb of a hundred good-looking young men he had seen hawking Pfeiffer and Luckies on billboards. The lieutenant wondered why he wasn't in uniform. A waiter led the couple to a table behind a post and Zagreb forgot all about them.

"Signor Oro will see you now."

Zagreb looked up from his bread slowly; an act of will in a situation that would have made most men jump. He hadn't seen Carlo approaching, had not noticed that he had ever left the reservation stand to consult Frankie Orr. Life was mystifying. Burke and Canal and McReary clattered through it like junkwagons, making noise and drawing attention, and they became plainclothes detectives. Carlo the swarthy Sardinian could make himself invisible in a roomful of redheaded Irishmen, and he became a headwaiter.

"Tell him I'll be there when I finish my meal."

jitterbug

"He's going home soon."

"It's a free country. If he doesn't mind us dragging his guinea ass out of bed and down to the basement at Thirteen Hundred."

Carlo's unblinking stare was his only response. Then he was gone.

Canal grinned. "Just for a second there you sounded like Father Coughlin."

"I got a thing against making appointments with cheap crooks."

"So how long you going to let him boil?"

Zagreb smeared butter on his hunk of bread. "Just till I finish this."

"Miss the uniform, I guess."

McReary dunked his own bread in his glass of water. "Zag knows he's safe. There ain't enough dicks to go around till they hang Hitler."

Burke said, "Going back to uniform don't scare me. I don't want Carlo spitting in my chowder."

When the lieutenant ate the last of his bread, the others pushed back their chairs. "Just Canal," he said. "I don't want to give the little greaseball a coronary."

"He'd have to have a heart to begin with," Burke said. But he reached for his bread.

The room, normally reserved for large parties, contained Frankie Orr, seated in the middle of the long, empty table, and Tino, his bodyguard and sometime driver, pretending to be a piece of furniture in a corner. A tattered green, red, and white flag from some forgotten Italian campaign decorated a mahogany-paneled wall lined with portraits in frames of olive-skinned men in stiff collars with oiled hair and studs in their ties. Tino, a product of a Sicilian coastal village where sailors had docked for six hundred years, was fair-haired and blue-eyed, with roses in his cheeks and a beautiful mouth, curved like a violin. He had a twenty-inch neck and the muscles of his jaws stuck out on either side like barbells. Zagreb knew he carried an army .45 automatic in an underarm holster and that he used it to snuff out candles at outdoor wedding receptions on Belle Isle. His permit to carry a concealed weapon was signed by Governor Kelly; one of several services requested by his employer in return for helping to end a milk drivers' strike in Port Huron. Two arrests, petty theft and assault with intent to do great bodily harm less than murder, no convictions. Zagreb liked Tino. He had bought his widowed father a house in Sterling Heights and had been among the first to present himself for recruitment at the Light Guard Armory after Pearl Harbor—catching hell from Frankie, who had pulled a senator out of bed to see that the paperwork was torn up. The bodyguard wore an American flag pin in his lapel and bought war bonds every payday.

Francis Xavier Oro, a Brooklyn tough imported by the late Sal Borneo to save Oro from street retribution following his acquittal on a charge of garroting a man to death aboard the New York elevated railway—hence the sobriquet the Conductor—had put on weight since Prohibition, but retained the slick good looks of a movie gangster. Streaks of silver highlighted the glossy black waves of his hair, and his teeth—straightened, bleached, and bonded—shone blue-white against his sunlamp tan when he chose to smile, which he seldom did when the police were present. His brows were plucked, his face close-shaven by a barber, and the nails on the fingers he was wiping with a moist warm towel provided by the waiter were pared and buffed, although never polished. The fit alone of his dark suit bespoke its two-hundred-dollar price tag, and a conservative striped necktie lay quietly against his white shirt. He had abandoned flash after the lesson of Al Capone and Lucky Luciano, who had gone to prison more for the showiness of their lifestyle than the charges the government had trumped up against them. Rumor had it Frankie had been more than peripherally involved in the killing of radio commentator Jerry Buckley in 1931. Uncorroborated testimony by one witness before a grand jury had accused him of slashing the throat of a disloyal employee in a downtown restaurant the same year.

Orr put down the towel, picked up a knife, and pried open a mussel on a plate mounded high with them. A boneyard of empty shells lay on a platter at his elbow. "Max Zagreb," he said without looking up. "What the hell kind of a name's that?"

"Yugoslavian. What kind of name's Orr?"

"Oro. If I wanted to go by what the newspapers call me I'd of put it on my citizenship papers."

"The State Department wants to yank your citizenship, I heard."

"The State Department's got its hands full rounding up Japs to send to Manzanar."

"They'll run out of Japs." Zagreb put his hands in his pockets. "I hear Mussolini hangs mafiosos six at a time. Right on the dock when they're deported from America."

"Mussolini's got his hands full, too. You a citizen, Lieutenant?"

"I was born here."

"I would of been if I'd had a say. It's a great country. You know I came here with forty-eight dollars in my pocket? Now I own two hotels and I'm negotiating for a quarter interest in the Hazel Park track. The streets really are paved with gold."

Canal said, "You just have to scrape off the shit to get down to it."

Orr looked up at the big sergeant. The Sicilian had heavy lids with blue veins in them. He spoke to Zagreb. "The invitation was for one. Barney Google's crashing the gate."

"This isn't a friendly call." Zagreb was looking at Tino, who had come out of his slouch. The bodyguard met his gaze but stayed where he was.

"I guessed that. That's why I didn't offer you a mussel." The racketeer sucked the meat out of the shell he'd opened, washed it down with red wine from his glass, discarded the shell, and reached for another. "If this is about the strike at the Packard plant, I'm not in that line of work now. It's unpatriotic in time of war."

"We'll let Roosevelt handle that one," Zagreb said. "This is about ration stamps."

"If you're short on red points I can make a call."

"Somebody's been killing old people for their stamps. Grabs them from behind and cuts them open and leaves them to bleed to death while he goes through their hoard."

"That's anti-American."

Canal swiveled his eyes. "That's one I didn't expect from the Conductor."

"I meant hoarding. Depletes the stores when they cash them in. Everybody suffers, especially our boys overseas. You ought to make this guy Citizen of the Year."

Zagreb said, "We don't have one of those. I guess we'll lock him up till he rots instead."

"I was kidding, of course. I don't like amateur crooks. They fuck up the average."

"You could help take this one off the street. We're burning a lot of gasoline on him that should be going to submarines."

"I'm all ears." He held up an open shell as if he were listening through it.

"He's got to be laying off those stamps someplace. You own

the black market. You'd know if you were buying more from one person than one person ought to have to sell."

"I'm an honest businessman who loves his country. I donated a car to the scrap drive, a Lincoln. Repeat what you just said and I'll take you to court."

"We're all friends here," Zagreb said. "Right, Tino?"

Tino said nothing.

"This is horseshit." Canal leaned on his big hands on the table. "You own a roadhouse up on Square Lake, B-girls and gambling. I got a friend with the Oakland County Sheriff's Department owes me a favor. It's a big enough favor to make him forget how much the county prosecutor wins there every month. You got six betting parlors on Gratiot alone, a whorehouse on Cass, and the pinball concession on the West Side. I ain't swung an axe since Repeal. I need the practice."

Orr had to lean over to look at Zagreb. Red spots the size of poker chips had appeared on his cheeks. "There's a leash law in this town."

The lieutenant kept his hands in his pockets. "You forgot numbers."

"I didn't forget numbers," Canal said. "I was saving them for last. We ain't had a good bum sweep in five years. Your runners could get swept up for vagrancy, by accident of course. We'll kick them loose as soon as you vouch for them, but them little paper bags they carry might get lost in Property. No big deal, I guess. How much dough can you carry in one of them little bags?"

"Who's this Polack working for, himself or the department?" Orr picked up another mussel.

"I ain't a Polack. I'm Ukrainian."

"Fucking communist."

Canal took his hands off the table. Tino took a step away from the wall. Zagreb patted the big man's arm. Canal relaxed.

"The sergeant's a Republican," Zagreb said. "Anyway, the commies are our friends now. The common enemy, you know?"

Orr got open the shell, looked at the meat inside, then laid it on his plate. He tested the point of the knife against the ball of his thumb, then laid the knife down too and reached for the moist towel.

"I'll ask some questions around," he said. "I can't promise anything."

Zagreb said, "That makes two of us."

chapter nine

After leaving Roma's, Max Zagreb said good night to the others and went back to his office at 1300 Beaubien. There was no one waiting for him in the two-room apartment on Michigan Avenue, and he didn't feel like going back and listening to dance music from the Oriole Ballroom. He sublet the apartment from a marine whose last address was in Sydney, Australia, depositing his rent the first of every month in an escrow account at the National Bank of Detroit. On the same day he made his monthly mortgage payment to Detroit Manufacturers Bank to maintain the two-story house he'd moved out of on Rivard last December. His wife's complaint, he remembered as he shuffled through the photographs of the slashed and bloated corpse that had surfaced in Flatrock Monday, was that he never discussed his work.

The office had even less of the personal touch than the apartment, but at least it was supposed to be that way. His Academy class picture, just another stamped-out face in an oval among three rows of them, hung crooked between a war map and a bulletin board shingled three-deep with FBI wanted circulars, most of them featuring espionage suspects. A Stroh's beer case stuffed with files stood atop a scratched green file cabinet—overflow from the drawers—and a black Royal typewriter with a wide document carriage occupied a metal stand next to his yellow oak desk, a scrapyard of arrest forms, stacks of copies of the *News, Times,* and *Free Press* turning orange, and unwashed coffee mugs serving double duty as paperweights. There was a coffin-shaped Airline radio with a police scanner and a steel wastebasket bearing a label reading WARNING—VOLATILE MATERIAL that he had inherited from the room's former occupant, who had appropriated it from the Chrysler tank plant before shipping out to England. Someone had pasted a cutout of Betty Boop to the inside of the frosted-glass door, then tried to remove it with a scrub brush, leaving only the huge eyes and chronic pout. Something about it reminded him of the KILROY WAS HERE cartoon on the sidewalk in front of the house where Anna Levinski was killed. He'd thought about finding a brush and finishing the job, but had decided against it. A little reminder couldn't hurt.

Aside from convincing him that the Levinski woman had been Kilroy's second victim, the details of the Flatrock case were no help. The victim, Ernest Sullivan, was a retired Corktown bartender, reported missing three days before by his daughter, who after the body was discovered insisted she knew nothing about unredeemed ration stamps. Neighbors and merchants in stores where he shopped reported seeing fistfuls of stamps bound with rubber bands whenever he took out his wallet, but added that he seldom used them, paying for non-ration items with cash. No wallet was found on the body, and the local police assumed the motive was robbery. Details of the autopsy were a close match with Dr. Edouard's in the Yegerov killing and Zagreb's own observation of the corpse in the Levinski case. All three victims had been sliced open lengthwise like watermelons.

Zagreb laid the file atop the debris on the desk, thumbed down to the folder marked LEVINSKI, and looked through the contents, setting aside the crime-scene and autopsy photos, which were useless to anyone but a student of geriatric anatomy. Again he fingered the scrap of newsprint he had used to make an impression of the pen scratches on the varnished top of Anna Levinski's lamp table. The photographer, who had done his best, had succeeded only in confirming what they'd already guessed, despite the many angles he had used in shooting the table and the chemicals he had used to treat the negatives. The script matched samples from grocery lists Mrs. Levinski had written, and the rest of "Hamtramck" and part of the house number proved she had recorded her address on something—shortly before she died, if the fresh ink stains on her hands were any indication. No pen had been found containing ink to match, and no recent documents on which she had written her address. He couldn't help thinking that the reason she had been writing, and the fact that the killer appeared to have taken the pen and document with him when he left, were central to the solution. He wondered if she was ordering something. Posing as a salesman was one way to get inside a strange door.

OST.

He said it aloud: "Oh ess tee."

The photographer had been unable to coax any more letters out of the other part of what she had written; the pictures had nothing to add to that part of the paper in Zagreb's hand. He produced another fold of newsprint from his inside breast pocket, his makeshift notebook, spread it out on the corner of the desk, and made a list:

MOST

HOST

GHOST

POST

POSTER

ROSTER

NOSTRIL

After that he went blank. None of the words helped. He re-folded the sheet and returned it to his pocket. Maybe something better would occur to him when his brain was fresh. He wondered if Walters, the Hamtramck detective who had presided over the initial investigation, had had any luck canvassing the neighborhood for witnesses. He called the Hamtramck PD, but got only a desk sergeant who told him Walters wouldn't be in until 8:00 A.M. tomorrow. Zagreb's Wittnauer said it was ten past one. He rang off without saying good-bye.

He walked back to his apartment. He'd let the others have the car and his own vehicle, a 1939 Plymouth coupe, was in storage. The garage fees were less than he would have spent on gasoline and oil and tires even if he had the ration tickets, and between his rent and the mortgage payments on a house he was no longer living in he had barely enough left to buy cigarettes and groceries. Anyway, he did some of his best thinking when he was walking. Just now he was thinking that for all the good his thinking was doing the City of Detroit he might as well enlist in the navy. No one expected you to use your brain when you were swabbing a deck.

At Fort he stopped and waited for the light to change, he didn't know why. There were no cars in sight, not another person on the street. If it weren't for the lights he saw in several of the buildings, he might have thought a blackout was in effect. He wondered if the end of the war, if it ever ended, would bring back the city's nightlife, or if people would grow accustomed to early evenings, cheap novels printed on coarse paper, and necessities doled out by a stern bureaucracy. Already the days of neon lights in Cadillac Square and weekend jaunts to Windsor seemed part of a past so remote it might have been something described to him by his grandfather.

While he was waiting he shook a Chesterfield out of the pack and rattled the remaining contents. Only two more. He couldn't remember if there had been another unopened pack in the carton that morning or if this were the last. He glanced at the Cunningham's on the opposite corner, willing it to be open. The CLOSED sign was in the door. There was a light in the display window to discourage burglars, beyond which he could see part of the magazine rack and, tantalizingly, rows of crisp cigarette cartons in front of the pharmacy counter. He sighed and returned the unlit cigarette to the pack. He needed one to put himself to bed, another to wake himself up in the morning, and a third with his coffee.

He looked again at the drugstore window. The light had changed, but he'd lost interest in it. One of the glossy magazine covers in the rack was partially obscured behind a Revlon lipstick display on an easel in the window. All he could read were the last three letters of the magazine's name: OST.

He recognized the typeface and the distinctive style of the cover illustration. There was no need for a closer look, but he crossed the street and stood in front of the window, leaning close and cupping his hands around his eyes to block the glare from the corner streetlight. From that angle he could see the entire cover. It featured a Norman Rockwell painting of a gang of half-dressed boys running away from a pond with a NO SWIMMING sign prominently displayed. It was the July issue of the *Saturday Evening Post.*

chapter ten

He shaved off the disappointing moustache first thing Sunday morning. Taylor hadn't worn one in *Bataan,* and the clean look shouted America, drowning out cries for Hitler's toothbrush and Tojo's graying chevron. While his hands were occupied with the razor, Father Coughlin came on WJR and he was forced to suffer through the bombast. He had once listened avidly to the fiery pastor of the Shrine of the Little Flower in Royal Oak, only to tune out when Coughlin broke with FDR and denounced him as anti-God.

He was a great admirer of Roosevelt. The economy was of no interest to him, and First Lady Eleanor's efforts to raise the status of American Negroes left him unmoved, but the "Day of Infamy" speech on December 8, 1941, had made him a disciple. He'd seen and heard the speech in a newsreel at the State and gone directly from there to the Armory to sign up. His subsequent rejection had only reinforced his conviction that the president was surrounded with traitors.

One of these was U.S. Attorney General Francis Biddle. It was Biddle who had resisted his chief executive's order to intern all 600,000 German aliens registered in the United States. Biddle's move to round up 125,000 Japanese-Americans was hardly conciliatory. The first man, the man he'd seen buying oranges in the Eastern Market with cash from a wallet stuffed with unredeemed ration stamps, had looked a little like Biddle in a picture he'd seen of the attorney general with Roosevelt in *Liberty.* He'd followed him down to the river, waited for a young couple dressed up for a concert at Ford Auditorium to pass, then moved in from behind, cut him, and tipped him into the water, reaching down to grip the fat wallet, effectively allowing the old man to fall away from his hoard. It was all over in three seconds.

He rinsed, toweled off, and stepped through the open bathroom door to change stations on the tombstone-shaped Philco that came with the apartment, but there was no war news and he turned it off. He hadn't been able to add a flag pin to the *National Geographic* map since Pantelleria. He hoped the troops weren't bogged down in trenches. World War I movies, obsessed with rows of tin-hatted doughboys wallowing in mud behind coils of barbed wire, depressed and disillusioned him. They pushed the pacifist party line by making soldiering as unromantic as ditch-digging.

He ran a finger down the radio guide he'd torn from the *Free Press* and taped to the top of the sideboard, stopping at the selection he'd circled in pencil:

9:00 P.M. (EDT)
NBC-BLUE: HOLLYWOOD PLAYHOUSE—JOHN GARFIELD, GUEST.

Garfield was an actor he'd liked in *Air Force.* He'd played a G.I. who at the climax hoisted a hefty fifty-caliber machine gun to his hip and chopped down a Japanese Zero for strafing a buddy in a parachute; Taylor couldn't have done it better.

He looked at his wristwatch, a waterproof Hamilton in a brass case with a shatterproof crystal, approved by the U.S. Navy. Then he switched on the fan in front of the open window, as if moving the sluggish air around would make the twelve and a half hours go faster. The fan, gleaming aluminum with a cast-iron base and a housing shaped like the nacelle of a B-17, whirred and lifted the loose end of the radio guide. He glanced around, located the Modern Library edition of *Mein*

Kampf on the coffee table, and laid it atop the rectangle of newsprint. Hoping to understand the mind of the enemy, he'd struggled through the first twenty pages, then put it down and gone to see *Hitler's Children* instead. The movies and the radio were his principal sources of information. At times he thought they spoke to him directly, in coded messages tailored to him alone. The newspapers were all anti-FDR, and so pro-Nazi. He looked forward to the trials after the war.

He kept most of his personal items in the cheap maple sideboard there in the living room, the bedroom being too small to contain a proper dresser. He opened the top drawer and removed the gleaming metal sheath from beneath a stack of shirts. It was fourteen inches long including the handle, nickel-plated steel with a mirror finish. When he grasped the bayonet, the blade slid free with almost no effort. It was unplated; naked steel darker than the sheath and not as shiny, but the edges were blue where they sloped down from the vane. He spent hours each week whetting them against a stone worn round at the edges like soap. He could shave with the bayonet if he so chose, could cut paper with it. A 1916 patent date was engraved next to the serial number on the underside of the hilt.

The weapon had never been issued. He'd bought it from an army surplus store in Ypsilanti with money he had stolen from his mother's purse when he was eleven. She had not missed the money. She never kept track of the amounts she got from men, or how much she spent on liquor. An undersize youth, malnourished and hollow in the chest, he had bought the bayonet to defend himself against her rages, but he hadn't been able to get to it when she seized him and with the help of one of her men friends stripped and chained him to his bed as punishment for removing all the pictures of his father from the family album and refusing to tell what he had done with them.

That was near the end. After three days a suspicious neighbor broke into the apartment while his mother was out and found him spread-eagled naked in a wallow of his own feces and urine. The police and juvenile authorities were waiting when she returned from the liquor store. After several sessions a psychiatrist had declared her incompetent to stand trial and she was committed to the Ypsilanti State Hospital for the Criminally Insane.

There had been only three pictures of his father in the album: a wedding shot in the old style, the couple looking glum with the name of the studio embossed in silver script beneath; a sepia-tone service photo, stern face, dress tunic, and cap; and a sawtooth-edged snap of him grinning at the camera, stripped to the waist and kneading a sponge, one foot propped up on the running board of his new 1928 Hudson.

The snapshot no longer existed. His son had torn it and the wedding photo into tiny pieces and flushed them down the toilet. It had been the only evidence that his father hadn't died at Château-Thierry. He'd told that story so many times and with such detail that he found himself believing it for long stretches, could see the smoke and shreds of canvas and plywood splinters and feel the heat as he described them. Before he had stopped displaying it on a wall, he had told people the bayonet was his father's, a trench weapon he'd carried to defend himself in case his plane was shot down over enemy territory. The real story, that his father had left him sitting in the auditorium of the Grand Circus Theater to get a candy bar, didn't tell as well. He had sat through three showings of a Felix the Cat cartoon, a creaky travelogue on Tahiti, a *March of Time* newsreel about revolutions in Argentina and Brazil, and the feature, *Hell's Angels*, watching Ben Lyon and James Hall shoot down countless Germans from their fragile biplanes for the love of Jean Harlow, and then an usher had glared a flashlight in his face and a policeman took him home. That night, while his mother finished off a bottle of vodka in the kitchen, he had hung on to the sides of his bed, barrel-rolling and turning Immelmanns in a sky filled with choking smoke, triggering his Lewis gun while the brute faces of the enemy contorted and dissolved behind sheets of cleansing flame.

"Hi."

He hilted the bayonet with a click and returned it to its drawer. The girl was standing in the bedroom doorway, wearing the shirt he'd had on the night before. The makeup she'd substituted for nylons started above her knees and ended at the insteps of her bare feet. She looked as if she'd been wading in muck.

"Is the bathroom free?" she asked. "I have to make a winky."

He hesitated. For a moment he'd had no idea who she was and what she was doing in his apartment. Then he remembered. It had been easier than getting rid of her.

"Just a second." He went past her through the open door into the bathroom, snatched the wallet photo of Robert Taylor from the frame of the mirror, slipped it into his hip pocket, and stepped back out. "Okay."

On her way past she smiled and skated her nails across his bare chest. "Have to be somewhere?"

"Yes."

"Church?"

If he said yes again she might want to go with him. "I'm working today."

She looked back at him from the bathroom door. "On Sunday?"

"Sundays are busy sometimes. The post office is closed."

"You should get a better job. There are lots of openings with the war and all."

"I just started this one."

She pulled a pout and drew the door shut. He heard her chunk down the seat, then a trickle of water into the bowl. It made him want to vomit. He always ran water in the sink when someone else was in the apartment.

He took a shirt out of the drawer and put it on. In the bedroom he selected a necktie from the rack inside the closet door, inspected his uniform quickly to see if it had been disturbed—women were nasty little snoops, he should never have taken her back to the apartment—tied a quick Windsor, and opened the drawer in the nightstand. His father's service picture was there, in a silver frame. He didn't keep it out because the uniform was infantry. It didn't go with the aviation death he'd drafted, and anyway he didn't like to think of his father wallowing in the trenches like Lew Ayres in *All Quiet on the Western Front.*

Or a boy stretched out naked in his own filth.

Straightening his tie with the aid of the mirror above the rack, he thought about last night in Roma's. He'd wondered about the two men who had passed his table on the way to the private room at the back of the restaurant, the big one and his smaller friend, who seemed to be leading the way. They dressed similarly, in cheap dark suits. He was pretty sure they were policemen. Later, when they'd come back and collected their two companions and moved toward the door, walking four abreast rather than breaking into two groups of two like ordinary diners, he was sure of his assumption. There was something familiar about the leader, his tired face and large forehead; he thought he'd seen his face in a newspaper photograph. It made him think of his father. Not that they looked anything alike, and when he thought about it, tried to pull it apart, the similarity went away.

He took his zip-front jacket off its hanger—two-tone worsted, brown with cream-colored sleeves—shut the closet door, and went back into the living room. The girl, still clad in just his shirt, was standing in front of the sideboard. She had the second drawer open. He could see what was inside from across the room, the jumble of pasteboard squares, some loose, others held together with rubber bands.

"You sure have a lot of ration stamps." She turned to smile at him. The smile stayed, even when she saw his face. She really was criminally stupid.

part two

Let Me Off Uptown

A sparrow shit on Dwight Littlejohn's head at work and he thought, *go shit on a white man's head, I ain't no better off than you.*

The rafters were full of the little bastards. They flew in through the bay doors, which were never closed, built their nests under the galvanized roof, and hatched youngsters who might never know what it was like to live outdoors. He only thought about them when they shit on his head, though. It happened often enough he didn't bother to take off his beanie and slap it against his knee anymore. The last time he'd done that the foreman had yelled at him, said he was holding up the line, what was he, a fucking yellow saboteur? So he thought, what the hell, the birds weren't doing anything to him the whole white world hadn't been doing for nineteen years.

Dwight Littlejohn worked in the longest room in the world. That was official, according to Ripley. He didn't like to think about it, and was grateful that his job confined him to one section of the L-shaped building at Willow Run. The section stood in what had been a cornfield before the eminent-domain lawyers swept in like SS shock troops and pounded industry up the ass of rural Michigan with sledgehammers stamped U.S. GOVERNMENT PROPERTY. He didn't like to think that the Liberator plant was the longest room in the world, because when he put down his riveting gun and climbed out of his coveralls and into his 1932 Model A with the rumble seat stuck open perpetually (just like the doors to the plant), he drove home to the smallest room in the world, elbowed in as an afterthought under the slope of a leaky roof in one of a row of saltbox houses on Cross Street in Ypsilanti.

The plant was a hangar-shaped building one mile long, with two 150-foot-wide bays through which the unfinished airplanes—or ships, as they were entered into the log—were shunted, acquiring their aluminum skins, wings, rudders, hydraulics, thousands of miles of insulated wiring, machine guns, and cockpits as they went. Albert Kahn, the genius architect behind the art deco wonders of the Packard and sprawling Ford River Rouge plants, the Fisher Theater, and the buildings that housed the Detroit *News, Free Press,* and police department (not to forget Rose Terrace, the elegant Grosse Pointe mansion where Edsel Ford died), had envisioned a straight tube into one end of which loose parts were shoveled and out the other end of which rolled gleaming bombers gassed up and ready to level the cathedrals and mosques of the Old World the same way Henry Ford and son had flattened the barns and farmhouses and forests that had stood on the site for a century. But Kahn had died a few months into the project. Less artistic heads had reasoned that the inconvenience of crossing county lines with one piece of construction outweighed aesthetics, and so the building was bent in the middle, obliging the cigar-shaped fuselages to turn a corner heading into the stretch. It was still plenty long enough for the drones who had to walk a mile just to get out into the parking lot.

Dwight had been working there since January, when he and his brother Earl drove up from Eufala, Alabama, to go to work for the defense industry, as Earl liked to put it; Dwight told people he screwed airplanes for a living. That was when they'd fucked up the rumble seat, jammed a hinge or something tying Grandpap's ancient ironbound trunk behind the seat of the coupe. The main building was still under construction then, and whenever there was a pause in the shrilling of the drills and rivet guns, the clatter of clawhammers rushed in to fill it. For all he knew, they were working on it still. For sure they had begun pouring slab foundations for additional buildings. The first center-wing fixture went into production less than nine months after clearing had begun on the land; in the time it took to make a baby, the Fords had turned a cluster of farms and wooded lots into a factory, complete with its own airport for flying out the finished product.

He worked in Center Wing Vertical Assembly, Department 936, punching rivets into a fifty-five-foot section of steel and aluminum that when he had first seen one reminded him of the inside of a Westinghouse refrigerator, all ribs and racks and gleaming metal. Now it reminded him of nothing, because he'd stood in front of thousands of the bastards and punched millions of little button-shaped pieces of iron into them. From there the center section went to Assembly, where they were attached to the fuselage and the outer wings were added, expanding the span to 110 feet. After acquiring flaps and ailerons, engines, propellers, and a coat of camouflage paint, the finished B-24 bomber took on fuel and was flown to its destination, either in the United States or England, by female and male pilots of the Ferry Command in Romulus. He bet the Krauts and the little yellow fuckers in the Philippines shit when they looked up and saw the shining tidal wave coming their way.

But aside from such patriotic deviations the finished airplanes meant nothing to Dwight, who almost never saw one. He was concerned only with filling the little holes with rivets. The holes were made by the man who stood next to him with an electric drill. They had worked side by side for five months and had never spoken a word to each other. The other man was white except for his cherry red neck, and Dwight was black on both sides of his family going back to before the Civil War, which was still being fought in Alabama, and apparently in Kentucky, too, where the fellow who worked the drill was from; he'd overheard him talking to another Kentuckian in the locker room. The man's name was Boyd. Since he wasn't openly hostile, Dwight had ceased to think of him. The little holes were more significant, and since the fellow never missed making one Dwight had no reason to think of him at all.

It was the loudest place he'd ever worked. Against this solid wall of high-pitched whines, whomping drill presses, pinging hammers, and constant shuddering rumble of the great unfinished engines of war moving down the conveyors, he looked back on the noises of his previous employment as silence. All the air horns on all the packet boats and all the cursing of his fellow dockworkers bucking bales of cotton off the barges on the Chattahoochee didn't answer. The place stank of oil and raw metal and rubber and sweat, but he didn't smell these things anymore and wondered sometimes if his olfactory sense had sustained as much damage as his hearing. Already his friends who didn't work at Willow Run complained when he chose a table too near the jukebox at the Forest Club; when they made the selection he could scarcely tell the woodwinds from the brass. But hearing was overrated. The job could have his as long as it continued paying him more in one week than his entire neighborhood in Eufala had made in a month.

He could do without having his head shit on, though. The symbolism was just too heavy.

When the whistle screeched, signaling the shift change, Dwight Littlejohn stripped off his goggles and stopped work on his five hundredth bomber that month. His replacement passed him on the stairs to the catwalk without greeting—he, too, was white—and stepped into the hole inside the coil of electrical cord Dwight had just vacated. Time elapsed between the last chatter of the rivet gun on the nine-to-five shift and the first on the five-to-one: forty-six seconds.

"Hey, buddy, mind?"

Dwight, standing at the time clock, looked around for the owner of the piping tenor, then down. He'd learned not to grin when he saw a diminutive version of himself, scarcely three feet tall, in coveralls scaled down to a child's size; the dwarves hired to climb inside the wing assemblies to buck rivets and seal fuel cells didn't appreciate amusing their full-size coworkers. Dwight gripped the little man under his upstretched arms, lifted him, and held him while he slid his time card into the slot and pulled down the handle.

"Thanks." Back on his feet, the dwarf hurried toward the catwalks with a rocking gait, dripping with dignity. Dwight figured there were tougher breaks than being born black.

Earl was already at his locker and dressing for town. He had on pearl gray peg tops belted just under his sternum and was tying a tie with silver saxophones on a bright blue field. At his brother's approach he grinned a gold-toothed greeting into the mirror inside the tin door. "Why so late, Gate? Take the slow freight?"

"Some of us wait for the whistle." Dwight peeled off his coveralls and slung them into his own locker. "Who's punching out for you?"

"Wash Adams. I covered for him last month when he was biffing that secretary he thinks looks like Lena Horne."

"They all look like Lena Horne when you been staring at Pratt and Whitneys all day."

"Don't they just? I'm meeting Liz for the early show at the State. See you at the Forest later?"

"Only if you can see all the way to Cross Street. I'm bushed. I guess you're taking the car."

"I'd drop you, but I'm late already. You can ride the cat-tle car."

"You're so good to me." The last time he'd taken the defense workers' trailer-bus he'd gotten sick on monoxide.

"You can stand it. I'm an old married man." Earl snapped his fingers.

His brother separated the key to the Model A from his ring and gave it to him. "You act like you're still dating."

"We are, Jackson, we are."

There wasn't much resemblance between the Littlejohns. Dwight was built low to the ground and solid, Earl lanky and tall. Earl spent God only knew how much of his pay on hair straighteners, with qualified success; his hair was black and glossy where he smoothed it back from his temples, but the forelock insisted on curling. It made him look less like Billy Eckstine than a dusky Frankie Sinatra. Dwight's hair, tightly coiled, clung to his head like a helmet and at nineteen al-ready showed faint traces of gray. People often assumed he was the older of the two. He was three years younger than Earl, but had closed that gap emotionally long before they left Alabama.

Dwight disapproved of his brother intensely. However, whenever Earl's flippancy got him in trouble, in bars and park-ing lots, it was Dwight who waded in, fists pumping like pis-tons, to clear the way for the other's escape. Similarly, he had opposed Earl's decision, on the strength of ten days' familiar-ity, to marry a girl he had met at the Forest Club in the com-pany of her friends from school; but when the wedding took place at the Second Baptist Church, there was Dwight, got up in a rented tuxedo with extra blacking on his workboots to con-ceal their steel toes, handing Earl the ring. The couple married six weeks before Dwight found out Elizabeth was a fifteen-year-old bride. She had altered the date on her birth certificate to apply for a marriage license without her parents' consent. It had cost Dwight two hundred dollars, all the money he had managed to put aside after two months working at Willow Run, to persuade Earl's angry in-laws not to have his brother arrested for statutory rape. But then he usually got the shit beat out of him in those bars and parking lots, too. At times like those he felt old enough to be Earl's father.

He watched his brother shrug into a suit coat whose hem swung almost to his knees, then tug on a matching fedora with a red feather in the band and smooth the brim between his fingers. The brim was at least six inches wide. "Holy shit."

Earl struck a model's pose, hand on hip. "What you think? It's a zoot."

"It sure is. Where'd you get it?"

"Clayton's. Well, the suit. I had to go to Higgins and Frank for the hat. Keep the sun out of my eyes, you know?"

"What'd it set you back?"

"Twelve bucks."

"I meant the suit."

"Hundred and forty."

"Holy Christ."

"It came with two pairs of pants."

"It ought to come with a running board. Where'd you get the money?"

Earl tipped his head back to look at him from under the brim. "You ain't the only one sets something aside."

"Every dime you ever had you spent on something that wasn't worth a nickel. You steal it from Elizabeth?"

"You know how long it'd take Lizzie to make a hundred and forty cleaning people's houses for ten bucks a week? Every other Friday I hand her my check, she sticks it in the bank and gives me back five to walk around with. She makes Henry Morgenthau look like Santa Claus."

"She know you took out a hundred and forty to buy that clown suit?"

"*Zoot* suit. Cab Calloway wears one. Anyway, I took out two hundred and fifty."

"What the hell for?"

"Hold your horses." Earl dug deep into the suit coat's right side pocket and came up with a box two inches square, covered in blue velour. He snapped it open under Dwight's nose with a flourish. The tiny diamond caught the overhead trough lights with a blue glint.

"Is it real?"

"It better be, I got it at Lord's. Quarter of a carat. Three hundred smackers."

"You said you took out two hundred and fifty."

"I put down a third. I never got Lizzie an engagement ring. She'll shit. See, that's why I bought the suit. I can't wear that bag from the Salvation Army when we step out for our anniversary."

"You only been married three months."

"Three months today." He clapped shut the box and returned it to his pocket.

"What about the other ten bucks?"

Earl looked at him with pity. He had started growing a pencil-thin moustache that didn't make him resemble Duke Ellington in the least. "Cat, you can't walk around this town on no five bucks."

Dwight remembered his beanie, took it off, and was about to toss it in after his coveralls when he noticed the fresh brown-and-white stain and remembered. He went over to a fifty-five-gallon drum currently serving as a trash can and dropped it in. When he returned to his locker, Earl had the skirt of his baggy suitcoat hiked up in back and was using both hands to stuff something under his belt between his kidneys.

jitterbug

Dwight knew it was the nine-inch section of shifting cane from a Hupmobile his brother had rescued from a scrap-drive pile in Eufala and had been carrying ever since they came to Michigan. It was made of hard rubber and ended in a ball weighted with lead and made a handy blackjack.

"You got to get out of Sojourner Truth," Dwight said. "You just might be able to pull that skull-buster out from under all that flannel before some redneck blows a hole through you with a Frontier Colt."

"What, and move in with you in that attic? Anyway, everything's jake there now. I just got so used to packing it the suit don't hang right without it."

"Right, and the Klan didn't shut down Packard for promoting niggers over whites."

"Just till Franklin D. ordered them back open. We got friends in Washington, little brother." He made a gun with his finger, fired it at Dwight, and swung on down the row of lockers, the metal taps on his saddle shoes clicking like Western Union. Dwight slapped Old Spice on his face and wondered if he should ask Elizabeth where Earl got the money.

chapter twelve

Good-bye, Arsehole of Democracy."

"That's *Arsenal*." This voice held less conviction.

"Tell that to my piles. You could stack coins on the sons-abitches."

"Thanks. I'll pass."

Dwight didn't take part in the conversation, if it could be called that. The exhausted workers aboard the trailer-bus didn't seem to be speaking with any expectation of receiving a response. The bus, provided by Greyhound on a contract with the Ford Motor Company, consisted of a tractor cab towing a long trailer with windows that reminded Dwight of nothing so much as the livestock carriers in his home state. The laborers who rode in it referred to it as the cattle car. It stank of the same smells that permeated the plant, with additional contributions from the musty upholstery and the leaky exhaust system. Dwight had made sure to board early enough to get a window seat; not because he cared to look out at the raw, turned earth of an industrial complex under perpetual construction or the rows of drab tents sheltering those workers and their families who couldn't get into the Willow Lodge dormitories, but for the fresh air. The last time he rode in the bus the fumes had given him a forty-eight-hour headache.

He braced himself with both hands on the seat in front of him as the driver, physically separated from his passengers and thus indifferent to their comfort, spun the wheel and bucked up over the ruts between the two-track dirt road and the blacktop. An arc of remote noise came through the windows, the harsh coughing of a machine gun being tested at the Gun Butt. It was difficult to imagine a sound more foreign to farm country; but then he found it almost impossible to picture the place as it must have been before the bulldozers and earthmovers came through. He seldom took this route when he drove himself, but he should more often. The tents and dormitories, the plywood trailers that served as transition between them, the wet laundry drooping from clotheslines strung between the trailers and the bumpers of parked Model T's made him feel better about his little room under the eaves in Ypsilanti. True, it wasn't as comfortable as his brother's neat one-bedroom house in the Sojourner Truth project in Detroit, but on the other hand he hadn't needed the army and the state police to help him move in.

Loneliness was the worst of it. He had never made friends easily, and separating himself from the few he'd had back home hadn't been difficult. Women weren't impressed by him on first acquaintance. He'd had sex with only one, and that relationship had lasted only until she took up with the son of the owner of a Piggly Wiggly who allowed the young man use of the delivery van. Later, when the Klan smashed out its windows and scratched NIGGER all over its surface, she'd come back to Dwight, who by then had bought and fixed up his Model A. He told her he wasn't interested. That's when she said that dating him was like going out with an old man and she had a better time in bed on her own.

It didn't hurt as much as she'd intended, as he'd suspected that was the case. When his and Earl's father had hopped a freight to Florida in 1938, it was Dwight, aged fourteen, who quit school to go to work on the docks to support himself and his brother and his mother, who'd been dying of some drab disease for as long as he could remember. She'd asked Dwight to make the sacrifice for his brother, who was the hope of the

97

family; good-looking, outgoing, a charmer who cast his spell over everyone he met, even some white people. There was no telling how far someone with Earl's gifts might go with a high-school diploma. Dwight did as he was asked without complaining. He hadn't any friends in school anyway and the subjects weren't challenging. So he put in twelve-hour days and went home and did Earl's homework. Earl did the rest, charming his teachers into loose interpretations of his answers on his finals, and their mother got dressed and left the house for the first time in months to attend the commencement. Dwight had to admit his brother looked far better in a mortarboard and gown than he ever would have. After the ceremony he stood back while their mother handed Earl an envelope containing three hundred dollars she'd gotten from selling an antique dining-room set that had been presented to her grandmother by the mistress of the cotton plantation where she worked, on the occasion of her being set free. Earl spent most of the money on whores and his gold tooth. The rest went to the doctor who dosed him with mercury to cure his clap.

Four years later their mother finished dying. The house was rented. The Littlejohn brothers sold the contents and invested the money in a stake for the trip to Michigan. The war was on, Ford Motor Company was offering a dollar an hour for defense workers, and Eufala was already a ghost town; every man and woman under the age of fifty was going north. US 23's two-lane blacktop was a jam of cars and homemade trailers with mattresses and luggage lashed on top. At night the pilgrims gathered into camps, complete with open fires and piles of dirty diapers soaking in galvanized washtubs. It was like *The Grapes of Wrath,* only with portable radios tuned in to the news from Europe and the South Pacific, Jack Benny, and the *Make Believe Ballroom.*

That first night, conserving their resources, the brothers had shared a can of pork and beans heated over their fire, then used the can to make coffee with water drained from the Model A's radiator. While Earl sat on the running board talking about looking up a pretty "high yeller" girl he'd seen riding in the backseat of a Terraplane loaded with boxes and duffels, Dwight stood sipping the bitter stuff from the can and had a flash of what the housing situation might be like around Detroit. Both the government and the Ford Motor Company had promised to provide adequate shelter; but Dwight was a child of the Depression and a Negro to boot, and had not grown up trusting to the compassion of big business and elected authority. Before he left, their father had told them of the time he had been thrown down the steps of the local Nash dealership for asking about the price of a used sedan after he hit a number, and one of Dwight's earliest memories was of a cross burning in a neighbor's yard. He had seen the flames reflected on the wall of the room where he and Earl slept and thought the house was on fire, but when he woke his brother he told him to stay in bed and keep away from the window. The next day the sheriff had driven up to the house next door in his big Cadillac touring car, and before noon the people who lived there, another colored family, had packed up their rattletrap truck and rolled out. The charred stump of the wooden cross remained in the front yard until the weeds grew up around it and then the landlord came out to get the place ready for the next tenant.

Dwight's worst fears were confirmed long before they got to the plant. Tents, dilapidated trailers, and tar-paper shacks—converted chicken coops, for chrissake—crowded the landscape on both sides of the four-lane divided concrete highway, begun in November 1941 and dedicated an astonishing eleven months later. During that time, nothing had been done to house the workers who would be commuting along that stretch. Afterward, federal surveyors were sent to lay out housing projects, only to be evicted forcibly by security men employed by Harry Bennett, Ford's iron right hand, and their stakes torn up and flung away. To alleviate the problem, federal authorities went outside Ford jurisdiction and established a housing project for Negro workers in Detroit, christening it Sojourner Truth after the heroic freedwoman who had helped to establish the emancipation movement. But the site chosen was in a white neighborhood, predominantly Polish, and in the face of fierce resistance Washington announced that the houses would be occupied by whites. A month later it reversed the decision. Black workers and their families pulled in and began unloading furniture and luggage from cars and trucks with plates from Mississippi, Kentucky, Louisiana, and Georgia.

On the last day of February 1942, a white mob armed with knives, bricks, and baseball bats smashed windows and pulled colored residents from their homes and beat and slashed them, swelling the local hospital population. Police brass, the fire marshal, and city officeholders came to the scene with megaphones and broadcast news that the policy had changed yet again: Negroes were banned from the project. The mob dispersed. Fifth-column infiltrators operating in Detroit fed the news to Berlin. Axis Sally interrupted her program of Bing Crosby and the Andrews Sisters to announce mellifluously over the air that American morale was so bad gangsters had to be brought in to put down the rioting in the streets.

Apprised of this development while addressing the Daughters of the American Revolution in New York, Eleanor Roosevelt repaired to her room in the Algonquin Hotel and without pausing to remove either her fox stole or her white cotton gloves, telephoned her husband at the White House.

Within twenty-four hours, a presidential order arranged for a thousand federal troops to be mobilized in Detroit. There they were joined by three hundred Michigan State Police and 450 Detroit police officers, who stood by while colored families moved their belongings into Sojourner Truth.

But there was a long waiting list by the time the Littlejohn brothers got to Michigan, and Dwight and Earl spent their first January north of the Mason-Dixon under a square of canvas procured from Fox Tent and Awning. They got their heat from the same one-burner Coleman stove they used to warm the cans of Campbell soup they ate for breakfast, lunch, and supper. Three months had passed since Dwight had moved into his attic room, but he still avoided the aisle containing the red-and-white cans at Kroger's.

The opportunity to leave the tent had coincided with Earl's wedding, which had moved his brother up to the top of the list of defense workers waiting for a house in Sojourner Truth. It was still a white neighborhood, and Dwight worried about Earl in that environment, but not as much as he worried about Elizabeth. She was a pretty girl, with delicate features—island, he assumed—and although her bearing and natural serenity made her seem far more mature than she was, he hated to think of her walking outside the relative safety of the project to shop or see a movie with a girlfriend. He was a little in love with his sister-in-law, and although he would never say it aloud, thought that she could have done a good deal better than his brother.

The trailer-bus let him out twelve blocks from his house. He walked along the tree-shaded street, carrying his black lunch pail and trying not to think about anything. One thing you had to be in Ypsilanti was alert.

He had to pass a corner bar, and as he drew within sight, he saw that three or four men were lounging in front. The sixth sense of a lifetime—well, of a race—told him they were young and white before he could see either of those details. Thought of crossing the street occurred; it always occurred, and he always rejected it. The bastards could beat the shit out of him but they couldn't make him go out of his way. He was twenty yards away when he smelled the beer on their breath.

Passing them now, gripping the handle of his lunch pail hard enough to imprint the waffle pattern on his palm. The unbreakable steel Thermos inside made a good weapon. Taking it out and carrying it by its neck would have been like asking for trouble, but he could still swing the kit and kaboodle if he had to.

He didn't have to. The conversation—it was about the war, something to do with Sicily—stopped, he found himself walking through a hurricane eye of silence, feeling little beads of sweat pop out on the back of his neck. Then he was past them and somebody said something about Eisenhower and somebody else said, Eisenhower, shit, he's one of *them,* and Dwight let out his breath. He hadn't realized he'd been holding it.

He paid thirty dollars a month for his room at the very top of a two-story house that represented no architectural style in particular and had very little going for it apart from a new oil-burning furnace and middling-good water pressure. Neither the local building inspector nor the county tax authorities had been notified that the owners, a couple in their sixties with a grown son in the VA hospital in Ann Arbor, were taking in boarders. The bed was a reasonably comfortable single on an iron frame, shoved up under the slope of the roof so that he had to bend double to get into it, and avoid sitting up abruptly when his alarm clock rang. He had a reading lamp—really just a bulb with a funnel shade, suspended from a stringer— a stack of magazines, *Life, Popular Mechanics,* and *National*

Geographic (the African issues, for purposes of masturbation), and a Philco Transitone that got uncommonly good reception in that high spot, especially at night, when you could swear Fatha Hines was right there in the room. It was loads better than a soggy tent, except when it rained and he had to dig out his collection of battered pots and empty Maxwell House cans to catch the leaks.

The room depressed the hell out of him even when skies were clear. He wanted his own house. That was the reason he had left Eufala, gone along when Earl dangled the incentive of a life of plenty and city lights in the form of a full-page ad in the classified section of the Montgomery paper headed FORD WORKING FOR VICTORY and featuring photographs of men and women, many of them colored, working at the "War Bird Powerhouse" in Willow Run. For Earl, a dollar an hour meant zoot suits, a gold tooth, and juke music every night. For Dwight it represented freedom from a life rented from people who owned things, a chance to own things himself. His Model A was the first thing he'd ever bought and paid for, and it had taken him the better part of a year haunting junkyards for parts and crawling in and out from under its chassis with the tops knocked off all his knuckles and rust particles in his eyes to get it running. At forty bucks a week minus withholding—more when he put in overtime—he'd figured he could save enough to manage the down payment on a house at the end of two years. A place he could paint any damn color he pleased, and where he could pound nails to hang pictures anywhere he wanted without having to answer to some landlord. It didn't have to be Rose Terrace. Just a thousand square feet of siding and foundation to prove he was a better man than his father.

He'd failed to figure in Earl, though. The two hundred he'd had to pay Elizabeth's parents to keep his brother out of prison had pushed back his timetable six months. And when he turned off the radio and unscrewed the bulb in the lamp and set aside his *Life* with Joe Stalin on the cover, he couldn't sleep for thinking that Earl's hundred-and-forty-dollar suit and three-hundred-dollar diamond ring were going to push it back further yet.

chapter thirteen

Anita . . . Oh, Anita . . . Say, I *feel* something!"

"What you feel, Roy? The heat?"

"No, I feel like blowing!"

"Well, blow, Roy, blow!"

And Roy Eldridge blew, taking the trumpet to heights only visited before by the divine Louis. Then the brumping brass section came in behind Anita O'Day's husky contralto, leader Gene Krupa hurled himself into his trap set, walloping the bass like the naval fleet pounding Corregidor. The little wooden dance floor thudded under the feet of the jitterbugs, the boys in their canary yellow zoots playing leapfrog with the girls in their plaid skirts and bobby sox. Just like the Oriole, only there the dancers were white and the band was live. But the Wurlitzer was cranked up all the way, knocking dust down from the rafters and plaster loose inside the laths. If you closed your eyes you could see the line of golden horns pointed at the ceiling and the pretty girl swaying behind the microphone, giving you a flash of garters and white panties when she shook her skirts. "Let Me Off Uptown."

The Forest Club was jumping, especially for a weeknight. Saturdays there would be a local band, not quite Chick Webb but close. Dwight preferred the juke. It left money in his pocket that otherwise would have gone into the cover, and the music was just as good on somebody else's nickel, although to his taste there was a shortage of Sidney Bechet and McKinney's Cotton Pickers. He didn't think that jazz was served by pushing it through three times as many instruments and adding strings.

In any case he seemed to be in the minority. All these welders and riveters were determined to get as much out of their time away from the plants as their paychecks would support. The music wasn't even loud compared to the decibel levels they were used to. Some of the young men probably didn't work in the factories, were just waiting to be called up; Dwight knew them by the wild glaze in their eyes and their molar-exposing grins. There wouldn't be much dancing in North Africa.

He asked the lean, chestnut-colored youth in the red jacket behind the bar, plainly too young to be serving alcoholic beverages, for a gin ricky, paid for it, and moved off to an uninhabited spot where he could hear the music without distortion. The room was indistinguishable from many of the white clubs in town, if you didn't figure in the Oriole and places like that; the rosy light over the bar and the pink-and-green shifting neon of the juke threw the exposed pipes into shadow and gave the bare brick walls a kind of dangerous ambience, like that movie *Algiers.* Charles Boyer might have felt right at home, sticking out his lower lip and talking about "Ze Casbah." Right before one of these tough fuckers whose families moved north right after the Emancipation Proclamation slipped a blade between his Gallic ribs.

Not that it was that kind of place. Located in Paradise Valley, the city's most staunchly colored section, the Forest Club complied with most of the statutes enforced by the State Liquor Control Commission since Repeal, which included a ban on illuminated beer signs, batwing doors, and anything in writing referring to the bar as a "saloon"—bad memories of the sodden times that had given birth to the Women's Christian Temperance Union and the eighteenth Amendment.

There was even a yellowed bill, framed and forgotten on the wall above the back bar, reminding customers that it was unlawful to consume alcoholic beverages in a standing position. For all Dwight knew the law was still on the books, but even when there were vacant stools at the bar he'd yet to witness anyone connected with the establishment admonishing a drinker to find a seat.

He looked around in vain for anyone he knew. Most of his acquaintances worked at Willow Run, and he didn't get into town too often, by choice. Detroit was a pretty good old place, ugly as a ticky old hound dog but just as friendly, if you knew just where to scratch it. Its Negro population was well ensconced, the grandsons and granddaughters of freedmen and runaway slaves who had reversed directions on the Underground Railroad to Canada under Lincoln, and he didn't feel as out of place as he'd feared. Most of the hostility, in fact, came from the scions of these old families, who looked upon the wartime newcomers as uncouth country cousins who threatened to upset the balance of eight decades; Dwight's drawling speech had gotten him more than his fair share of rudeness from black merchants in town. The rest came up with the rednecks, newcomers themselves who had never before ventured any farther from their scrabbly little farms and flyblown hamlets than it took to do business with the local moonshiner, and couldn't get used to the idea that Jim Crow didn't travel.

He could handle, or rather avoid them all right, and the worst he got from belligerent members of his own race was short change and the occasional bottle of milk that had started to turn. The reason he stayed out of Detroit was it was an excellent place to spend money. Dwight was his father's son, his brother's brother. Saving didn't come naturally to him, and so he had to ride herd on himself all the time. That was a little less difficult in Ypsilanti. Ypsilanti was the dullest town this side of Eufala: neighborhoods of Victorian and Queen Anne houses and a three-block business section of hardware stores, family bars, pot-roast restaurants, and a great marble mausoleum of a bank with solid-oak tellers' cages inside built to repel John Dillinger. The whole place might have been dug up by the roots anyplace between there and Alabama and transported by flatbed up 23, complete with rednecks. In Ypsilanti the challenge was to find something worth wasting one's money on. He didn't regret his choice of places to live.

But even Dwight got the awfulest kind of lonely. The thought of spending another evening like last night, stretched out on the bed in his little narrow coffin of an attic room leafing through magazines with the radio on, made him feel bleak. He'd hoped he'd run into Earl in the Forest Club, or someone he knew from Willow Run. Instead, alone in this room full of strangers and loud music, he felt as isolated as if he'd stayed home. He resolved to finish his drink and catch the last bus. His brother still had the Model A.

"What's the matter, Jackson, shoes nailed to the floor?"

He blinked. He'd been off in the middle ground, looking right at Earl coming his way through the crowd without seeing him. His brother had on his hundred-and-forty-dollar suit with what might have been a pink shirt—it was difficult to judge colors in the Forest Club—and Elizabeth was with him.

"Hello, Dwight. Where you been keeping yourself?"

He told Elizabeth hello. He knew the question called for a clever answer, but he was not a clever man. He only regretted it when he was in her presence. She was a striking girl, more handsome than pretty, in a way that would only improve with age. He liked her regular features and wide-set eyes, her ginger coloring, her hair cut short after the fashion established by women who wanted to avoid snagging it in the machinery of the defense plants, although she was too young for such employment. In her platform heels and yellow calf-length dress with padded shoulders she was as tall as Dwight and could pass for twenty-one anywhere in town. He liked the way her face shone when she greeted her brother-in-law. She genuinely liked him. She pecked him on the cheek and he smelled the brief light citrus scent she wore, clean and pleasant. She was wearing the ring Earl had bought her.

"Ain't you heard, sugar?" Earl said. "Dwight's working undercover for the eff bee eye. Dyes his hair yellow and puts flour on his face and goes to Bund meetings. Got him a teeny little camera in his belly button. He don't answer to nobody but old J. Edgar hisself, or maybe Pat O'Brien."

Dwight smiled; indulgently, he hoped. Elizabeth punched her husband's shoulder. "You let your brother be. It wouldn't hurt you to stay home some nights."

"Maybe when I'm as old as old Dwight." He tipped up his glass. Dwight caught a sharp whiff of pure grain alcohol. He hated vodka. It was their father's drink.

"Through with the car?" he asked.

"Tomorrow. We gots to get home tonight."

"Put oil in it? It burns oil."

"You know I don't know nothing about that." Earl was bouncing to the "One O'Clock Jump." "Let's dance, sugar."

"I can dance with you anytime. I want to dance with your brother."

"I don't think they got the minuet on the juke."

Dwight said, "He's close to right. I can't jitterbug."

She opened a little clasp purse and thrust a nickel at her husband. "Find something slow."

"Wayne King? Sammy Kaye?"

"Try Dorsey," Dwight said. "I'm not dead."

"These Detroit boys going to string me up." But he took the coin and moved off.

Alone with his sister-in-law, Dwight took a long pull at his ricky.

"Can I have a sip of that?"

"I might be arrested for contributing to the delinquency of a minor."

She pouted. He handed her the glass. She sipped at it, made a face, and handed it back. "Too much Coca-Cola."

"I'm not a big drinker."

She shook her head, smiling. "Sometimes I can't believe you and Earl are related."

He couldn't think of anything to say to that, partly because the same thought had crossed his mind many times. The manic Harry James record came to an end. In the silence he took another drink and said, "Congratulations on your anniversary."

"Oh, that. That was Earl's idea." She twisted the ring. "I told him we couldn't afford it."

"I guess it cut into your savings."

She looked up at him quickly. Then a new record dropped down and a trombone started playing "I'm Getting Sentimental Over You." Dwight glanced around, found a horizontal surface for his glass, and took her hand. The floor was crowded, for which he was grateful. No one knew you were a bad dancer when there wasn't room to show it.

Elizabeth's hand in his was cool. He held it loose for ventilation, because he knew his was moist. The feel of the small of her back against his other hand gave him butterflies. He hadn't danced with a woman since the Piggly Wiggly episode. This close he could smell the warmth of her skin beneath the citrus scent. He wanted to press her on the subject of where Earl had gotten the money to buy her the ring, but he was afraid it would spoil the moment, end the dance; and that would likely lead to a scene between him and his brother. Maybe the question hadn't really startled her, as he'd thought. Maybe she was surprised at him for prying. He resolved not to bring it up again pending evidence. And he despised himself for his cowardice.

The music stopped in the middle of a phrase. There was a burring among the crowd. Dwight and Elizabeth separated, craned their necks, but from where they stood they could see neither the entrance nor the jukebox, whose plug had obviously been pulled. He wondered if it was an air-raid drill.

Somebody read his mind, because a deep male voice with gravel in it announced, "Simmer down, boys and girls. We ain't Japs or Germans. We want all the women over here and all the men lined up there along the bar. Now."

Robbery, thought Dwight; but as the crowd began to migrate in two directions he spotted the blue uniforms. Half a dozen policemen were in the room, holding their nightsticks in both hands across their thighs. All of them were white. The one with the words was a sergeant with thick sloping shoulders and a carpet of blue beard covering the lower half of his face, like a gangster in an editorial cartoon. Dwight saw his kind every day on the line: knob-knuckled Poles whose grandfathers and great-grandfathers had turned the iron-hard soil of tenant farms in the Balkans for generations. Their fathers had come over when Henry Ford started paying a dollar a day to build Model T's in Dearborn, and when the plants were filled had fanned out to fill the positions nobody else wanted. Boxer. Garbageman. Cop.

"Dwight."

He blinked at Elizabeth. He'd forgotten for a moment she

was there. Her face was pale beneath the ginger. He smiled and put a hand against her upper arm, giving her a little push. "It's all right."

She stood her ground, but the swell had started. Bodies came between them and he turned toward the bar, where a ragged line of men in bright party clothes had begun to form. He looked for Earl but couldn't find him.

"Come on, boys, come on. You-all can shuffle faster than that." The big sergeant stood in the middle of the floor, bouncing the end of his stick against a square palm. He had a big purple vein on the left side of his forehead and a fat neck that rolled like an inner tube over the edge of his buttoned blue collar.

A younger officer, skinny as twine, with sad eyes, walked along the line of patrons, touching with his stick those who were facing him instead of the bar. "Hands on the bar! Lean!"

Dwight obeyed before he got to him. "What's the trouble, Officer?" he asked over his shoulder.

"Shut up."

Then came the frisk. A pair of officers working from opposite ends of the line patted down each man from armpits to ankles, not neglecting to pull back the cuffs of their jackets and run a finger around inside their collars and inspect the occasional hat. Whenever a switchblade or a revolver came to light, the owner was torn away from the bar and shoved stumbling into the arms of the officers by the door, who handcuffed him and took him out. Red lights throbbed against the door whenever it opened. Dwight guessed a van.

"Well, what have we here?"

Dwight risked a peek halfway down the bar. He recognized the bulbous end of the Hupmobile shifting cane sticking out of an officer's fist. He couldn't see Earl for the line of men leaning between.

"What's the matter, Rastus, lose the rest of the car?"

"I take that out to keep folks from driving it off." This was Earl's voice.

The big sergeant closed the gap between himself and the bar in two strides, swinging his nightstick in a short underarm arc. There was a loud grunt, ending in a wet whimper, and Dwight saw the back of his brother's oversize suit coat as he sank to his knees. The other officer, the one who had found the weapon, caught him by his collar and dragged his sagging body across to the group in uniform. The toes of Earl's saddle shoes made black skid marks on the floor's varnished surface. Dwight heard a woman's cry from the other side of the room, quickly stifled. Either Elizabeth had caught herself or one of the other women had silenced her. The unspoken rule was not to draw attention to oneself.

The officer working from the opposite end of the bar got to Dwight. He had never been frisked. The thoroughness of so swift an operation astonished and humiliated him. He felt that this stranger, whose breath stank of some deep corruption that reminded him of his mother, knew all his physical secrets. He knew his crotch was damp with perspiration and hoped it wouldn't be mistaken for urine. His wallet was squeaked from his hip pocket, gone through, and thrust back. He'd heard bills crackle and was pretty sure the man had palmed some of his cash.

"That's the lot," someone told the sergeant; Death Breath, Dwight guessed.

"Stamps?"

"Not enough in the place to throw a barbecue."

"Shit."

"Close the joint?"

"What for, listening to white bands?" The sergeant raised his voice. "You niggers can relax now."

There was movement along the bar. Dwight turned around. While he was being frisked, four more white men had entered the room, all in civilian suits. Two were big, one of them bigger than the sergeant, with scary eyes, bulged like in a cartoon. Dwight, who had an instinct about such things, looked to the smaller pair for the leader. One looked too young even to be a policeman. He decided on the other one, and congratulated himself when the Polack sergeant went up to him to report. He walked that way.

"Where you headed, skate?" murmured one of the men at the bar. "That there's the Four Horsemen."

"Yeah? Where their horses?"

He had never heard of the Four Horsemen. All he saw was a group of white men in cheap suits a size too large in the coats to make room for their underarm rigs and gray felt fedoras too shaggy for summer. The one the big sergeant was talking to didn't appear to be listening; his tired gaze roamed the room restlessly and he had his hat pushed back to keep the smoke from the cigarette in the corner of his mouth from parking itself under the brim. He had a large brainy-looking forehead. The tired gaze lighted on Dwight. He jerked his chin in that direction. Turning, the sergeant spotted the colored man approaching and stuck out his stick. Dwight almost ran into it. "That's as far as you come, Rastus."

"My name's Dwight."

The sergeant's neck swelled. Instinctively Dwight changed his tone.

"I don't want no trouble, boss. I just want to axe about my brother. The one in the zoot suit?"

"Call Mr. Keen." The sergeant had a mean grin, all bottom teeth with black between them. "Tracer of Lost Persons, you know? Your mammy hear you on the rah-dio."

"Which zoot?" asked the man with the forehead. "All you boys dress like circus wagons."

"He had him a Hupmobile stick in his pants. Your men done took him."

"Concealed weapon, Lieutenant."

"My old man had a Hup," said the lieutenant. "That's an uncomfortable thing to carry around."

Dwight said, "He lives at Sojourner Truth."

The lieutenant dropped his cigarette and ground it out. "Got a job, has he?"

"Willow Run. Me, too. Today's his wedding anniversary," he lied.

"You'll have to give him his present at the jail."

"Can I bail him out?"

"That's up to the judge. You'll have to wait till he's arraigned."

"Can I ask what's this about?"

"Curious nigger, ain't you?" The sergeant was grinning still, but there was danger in it now.

"We're looking for ration stamps. Lots of ration stamps. You read the papers?"

"No, just magazines."

"We're looking for a killer. He kills old people for their ration stamps."

"He colored?"

"Tonight's the coloreds' turn. Last night it was the wops. Tomorrow it'll be the Polacks, or maybe the Belgians. We ought to have this one wrapped up in twenty-three days. That's how many groups we got in this town. Any more questions?" He thumped the bottom of a pack of Chesterfields and speared one between his lips.

"Hits 'em over the head, do he?"

"Guts 'em like a perch, why?"

"It ain't Earl. All he gots is that Hupmobile stick."

"The law discourages that, too." The lieutenant thumbed the wheel of a Ronson, tilted his head to bring the end of the cigarette to the flame. "That okay with you?" He blew a plume, snapped shut the lighter. When Dwight said nothing he nodded. "Good. On account of we wouldn't want to do anything that didn't meet with your approval."

Dwight thanked the cream-colored fuck for the information and went to find Elizabeth.

chapter fourteen

The turnkey Dwight spoke to in Visitors, a
Wayne County sheriff's deputy with wire-rimmed glasses and
wisps of colorless hair like corn silk combed across his scalp,
ran a finger down a list of names on a clipboard suspended by
a string from a nail in the wall and told him he didn't have any
Earl Littlejohn in the population.

"What's that mean, he ain't here?"

"What it means."

"*Was* he here?"

The turnkey looked at him, opened the top drawer of his
gray steel desk, still looking at him, slapped a folder bound in
shabby mahogany-colored cloth onto the desk, and snapped it
open. He turned a page, moving his lips as he read, then closed
the folder and returned it to the drawer and punched it shut.
"Somebody came and got him last shift."

"What, bailed him out?"

"Somebody from downtown. I can't make out the signature."

"What's downtown?"

The turnkey sighed. "Police headquarters." When Dwight
didn't react he said, "Thirteen hundred Beaubien. Want me to
draw you a map?"

"I don't live in town."

The man sighed again and gave him directions. Dwight
stopped listening after two turns. The damn city was laid out
like a wheel downtown, but whoever had designed it had lost
interest after a few blocks and changed it to a grid. Police

headquarters seemed to stand somewhere in the no-man's-land between. He went out and asked the first colored person he saw, an old baldy with a white moustache, dressed in overalls and sweeping a concrete stoop belonging to the building next door. The man said, "Hell, boy, you're standing smack-dab in front of it."

Dwight looked up at the city block of granite with arched windows marching the length of the ground floor. The weasel in the jail had wanted to get him lost.

"Where can I find the Four Horsemen?"

The old man scratched a clump of white whiskers under his chin. "Well, war's all around. You don't gots to go far to find famine, nor pestilence neither, comes to that. I ain't seen Jesus."

Dwight thanked him for the information he could use and walked around to the front of the building, which was all stairs to the entrance. He had on Earl's old suit and one of his brother's more conservative ties, gray-and-black rayon with a musical clef printed on it. Even with the belt buckled just under his sternum the pants were too long and he'd had to turn up the cuffs, which Elizabeth had insisted upon ironing so they'd look natural. He'd slept on the old couch in their living room after staying up late saying soothing things when she expressed her fears about Earl in police custody; fears he shared without admitting it. The key to the Model A had gone with Earl, and Dwight had had to call two cab companies before he found a driver who would accept a fare to Sojourner Truth. He'd risen after just two hours' sleep to catch the bus downtown, only to find his sister-in-law already up and in the kitchen cooking him breakfast. He hoped Earl appreciated her. He couldn't remember a morning in Eufala that didn't find their mother still in bed while Dwight and Earl made coffee, often using yesterday's grounds because she was too sick to visit the market. It had been this way even when their father was still around, his nights out tending to crowd noon of the next day.

It made Dwight's cheeks burn to ask again for the Four Horsemen, but the sergeant behind the front counter, who looked like Churchill, didn't blink. "Fifth floor, Racket Squad." He jerked a nicotine-stained thumb in the direction of the elevators.

Dwight vaguely remembered hearing that Detroit Police Headquarters was designed by the same man who had laid out the Willow Run plant, but he couldn't see much of a family resemblance between that utilitarian barn and the corridor where he stood waiting for an elevator to come get him. The marble floor needed mopping and wax and there were gum wrappers and cigar bands swept up like drift snow against the golden-oak wainscoting, but even the casual squalor of the police couldn't cloud the Roman Empire authoritarianism of the architect's vision. He was aware of the dirt under his nails and the fact that his shoes needed polishing. He suspected it was part of the plan that he felt like a flea in a cathedral.

By the time the brass doors shuttled open he had been joined by two officers in uniform, both over six feet and two hundred pounds. They took up most of the car, the stench of their cheap aftershave lotion was inebriating. He was relieved when they got out on the third floor, without ever having given any indication that they knew they weren't alone. Dwight felt invisible now, and decided that was an improvement.

Another marble-and-wainscoted corridor greeted him on five, lined with oaken doors with frosted-glass panels, one of which bore gold letters spelling out RACKET SQUAD. He opened it against the pressure of a pneumatic closer and let it sigh shut behind him. The room beyond wasn't much larger than an ordinary office, with a portion sacrificed besides for a corner cubicle whose walls fell four feet short of the ceiling. The linoleum floor was none too clean, littered with the inevitable scraps of paper and scarred with orange cigarette burns. The windows were heavily gridded, filmed with tobacco smut, and under the buzzing fluorescents stood too many desks, each with its swivel captain's chair, uncomfortable-looking ladder-back for visitors and suspects, and typewriter table bearing a machine with visible belts and gears, unreplaced since before Armistice Day.

At one of the machines sat a bald man in shirtsleeves, chattering away impressively with all his fingers. He didn't look up until the bell rang, at which point Dwight was startled when he recognized the youngest of the four detectives who had entered the Forest Club the previous night. Without a hat on the man had just a brief fringe of red hair and looked much older. He had freckles on his scalp.

The man looked at Dwight with no recognition. He picked up a smoldering cigarette from an old burn groove on the edge of his desk, took a drag, replaced it in its groove, and sat back. The fan on his desk, battered stainless steel with a cast-iron base, gnawed at the smoke, but hadn't the power to shred it, much less stir the stagnant air in the room. "Help you?"

"I'm looking for the lieutenant."

A bald head tilted toward the cubicle. "That's his office."

Dwight went over there. The gold lettering on the frosted glass read LT. M. ZAGREB. He raised his fist to knock.

"He's out now," said the man at the desk.

Man let him walk all that way.

"Know when he'll be back, boss?"

"Later."

"Can I wait?"

"Free country."

Dwight sat on a ladderback chair next to a desk with a nameplate that read SGT. S. CANAL. The swivel stood in front of the square plaster post that held up the ceiling. There was a hair-oil stain on the institutional green paint where the back of the sergeant's head came into contact with it when he leaned back in his chair. Above the stain, yellowed Scotch tape held a sheet of ruled notepaper with a penciled legend printed in round upper- and lowercase letters, as by a child:

> There is more law at the end
> of a nightstick than in all
> the courts in the land.

Feeling more out of place than he had since coming to Michigan, Dwight folded his hands in his lap and concentrated on making himself invisible. A long minute crawled past before the typing resumed. After a while the monotonous rhythm became its own soothing kind of silence, against which he heard the sounds of other life in the building coming up the ventilation ducts and through the open transom over the door. Telephones rang, Lowell Thomas's voice recited a long list of unpronounceable Russian place names on a radio snarling with static. An overloaded metal file drawer boomed shut—office artillery. Dwight looked up at the big electric clock, calculating how long he could wait for an interview that might take ten minutes. When he'd called in to the plant pleading family emergency he'd promised to try to make it in by eleven. He had fifty minutes if the buses were running on schedule.

After twenty minutes a man came in whom Dwight remembered from the Forest Club. The second biggest of the four men in plainclothes, he was the best dressed and the oldest-looking—forty anyway, with a tired posture that suggested his custom shirt was the only thing holding him up.

The hair on the backs of his hands was as coarse as wire. He spotted Dwight right away, but didn't look his way again even when it was clear he was discussing the presence of a stranger with the young bald man at the desk. They spoke in low murmurs, lost under the high ceiling and the purring of the inadequate fan. Two or three minutes of that, and then the newcomer sat down at a desk by the windows and picked up a telephone and started dialing. His conversation this time was louder, he had a bad connection. He asked who was running at the fairgrounds, listened, then placed twenty dollars on Betty Blitz's nose. After that he made another call, less comprehensible from his end of the conversation. The other man continued typing, scraps of life elsewhere in the building drifted into the room, and Dwight wallowed in the conviction that he didn't matter.

He had, he reasoned, ten minutes' grace, and was planning his exit and his route to the nearest bus stop when the hall door opened and the man he now knew as Lieutenant Zagreb entered, accompanied by the big goggle-eyed plainclothesman who from the process of elimination Dwight identified as Sergeant Canal. The lieutenant looked small in his companion's presence, compact in the same black suit he'd had on the night before and gray winter fedora. He was in fact six inches taller than Dwight; his large head, like a brainy scientist's in a movie with a Nazi kidnap plot, contributed to the illusion. He paused before the bald man's desk and spoke with him quietly for thirty seconds. Dwight had risen at his entrance, and a glance in his direction from the bald man told him he was being talked about once again, but Zagreb never gave him a glance, and after a moment walked straight to his cubicle and unlocked the door and went in and closed it behind him.

Sergeant Canal hung his hat on the hall tree by the door to the corridor and came over and sat down behind his desk. He looked it over as if to determine that none of the objects on top had been moved, slid open the belly drawer and looked at its contents. He shut it and swiveled his eyes toward Dwight.

"You can go in."

The inside of the cubicle smelled of dry dust and pulp paper, musty like old magazines. Zagreb was sitting behind a wooden desk heaped with papers and curled file folders, his face illuminated eerily from below in the reflected light of a banker's lamp with a green glass shade. The shade had a crack, and Dwight stepped to one side to take the jagged blade of white light out of his eye. Lighted that way and with his hat off, the lieutenant's head above the eyebrows looked as big as a world globe.

"Your name's Dwight?"

It took Dwight a second to nod. He'd had no indication he'd been recognized from last night.

"You don't look much like your brother."

"I thought we all looked alike." He tried to smile.

No reaction. "You're new to Detroit."

It was a statement, but Dwight answered it as if it were a question. "Yes, boss. We come up from Alabama in January."

"How do you like our winter?"

"I expected it be cold. Didn't know summer'd be so hot, though."

"You've been to the jail, I guess."

"They said somebody done took Earl away."

"He's in an interrogation room downstairs. We wanted to ask him some questions."

Dwight said nothing. After a little silence Zagreb switched off the desk lamp and sat back. His suit coat slid open, exposing the cherry handle of the revolver in his underarm holster. "Take a seat."

The only other chair was stacked with newspapers. Dwight

lifted the stack, looked around for a horizontal surface, and transferred it to the floor. It was a wooden chair with arms, not as uncomfortable as the one in the squad room.

"Where do you live, Dwight? You don't mind if I call you Dwight."

The lieutenant's tone hadn't changed. It wasn't unfriendly, but it wasn't as friendly as the words. Dwight said it didn't make any difference to him. "Ypsi," he said. "I got me a room."

"You learn fast. There are hillbillies living there a year who still say *Yip*-see. You smoke, Dwight?" He plucked a fresh-looking pack of Chesterfields out of his shirt pocket.

"No, sir, I never got the habit."

"Too bad. I read in *Reader's Digest* it's good for your system. Kills germs." He stuck one between his lips and snicked open his lighter. It wouldn't fire. He found a match and used an old scar on the edge of the desk to scratch it. "Fucking Ronson. Lost my Zippo. You read *Reader's Digest,* Dwight?"

He wanted to say this was bullshit. "Just the jokes."

"You read magazines, though. *Saturday Evening Post*?"

"Sometimes. When can I take Earl home?"

"That depends on your brother, Dwight. Right now he's refusing to answer our questions."

"What questions? All he done was get himself caught carrying around a old Hupmobile stick."

"We're holding him for treason."

Dwight's blood went to his feet. He couldn't say the word and didn't think he ever had. It shamed him that his first thought was, Jesus God, what's Earl gone and got himself into now?

He was aware Zagreb was studying him closely. He didn't bother trying to put on any sort of face. He didn't know which one the lieutenant was looking for.

"We haven't charged him yet. That'll bring in the FBI, and

we're not ready to give him up. We opened his locker at Willow Run. Plant security's cooperative, we didn't have to get a warrant. We've applied for one to search his house. If we find there what we found in his locker, we'll have no choice but to notify the feds."

Dwight felt drained. The son of a bitch was making him ask. "What'd you find?"

"Ration stamps."

"Everybody gots ration stamps."

"Everybody doesn't have a shoebox stuffed full of them."

"Hoarding ain't against the law."

Zagreb stabbed out the cigarette in a dirty bronze ashtray. It was only half-smoked. His face looked tired and pale under the great brow.

"Rationing only went into effect this year," he said. "That's not long enough for one man to have hoarded as many as we found in that box. He stole them, Dwight, and he's selling them on the black market. Treason in time of war's a hanging offense, Dwight. No appeal."

chapter fifteen

I need to ask a favor," Dwight said.

"Ask, Dwight," Zagreb said.

"Stop calling me Dwight."

Zagreb blinked. "You said it didn't make any difference."

"You weren't talking about hanging my brother then."

"You prefer 'Mr. Littlejohn'?"

"I wouldn't answer to it. Nobody ever called me that. I just need to ask you to stop saying Dwight every time you open your mouth. What I mean is, there's only two of us here. I think I can figure out who you're talking to."

"That sounds just a little bit uppity, Dwight."

"I guess that's Mr. Ford's fault. We all the same on the line."

The lieutenant might have smiled then, or he might not have, and it might or might not have meant amusement. You never could tell with white men.

"Okay, Dwight. I mean okay."

Dwight relaxed a little. He didn't know if he'd scored a point or lost one. He was a little surprised to find out he didn't care. He didn't care about catching the bus either. "Now what's this shit about treason?"

"One of those Washington words. You won't find it in the city code. I'm as patriotic as the next guy, but J. Edgar's got special agents coming out of his ass and I'm just a street cop with a wartime staff you could carry in your hip pocket. I'm only interested in clearing up a string of murders. You read about it? That's right, you don't read newspapers." He jerked his chin in the direction of the stack Dwight had removed from the chair.

The *Detroit Times* was on top. Dwight leaned over and picked it up. The banner read 'KILROY' KILLER STILL AT LARGE. The story had bumped the war news to a spot below the fold. There was a drawing of a man's head, a blank oval with a question mark where the face should be. It looked old-fashioned.

"That's a headline they run when they've got nothing new to say," Zagreb said. "That fucking Hearst. Diddles Marion Davies and then instead of smoking a cigarette like anyone else he picks up the phone and tells his editors to write news stories without any news in them. The fucking Krauts just wiped out an entire town in Czechoslovakia. The whole thing, right down to the last wooden shoe. Don't bother looking for it there. It's in the second section."

"I don't think they wear wooden shoes in Czechoslovakia."

"Who gives a shit? Not Hearst, that's for sure. Anyway, you can see what I'm up against. If I don't close this one, I'm in a landing craft on my way to some little shit island in the South Pacific. I'm a coward, Dwight." He made a face. "Sorry, forgot. I'm a coward. I'd rather buy bonds."

Dwight folded the paper and laid it in his lap. The cop still thought he was a dumb nigger, acting at him that way. "My brother ain't perfect. He blows with the first wind. He ain't no killer, though. What's this Kilroy?"

"Not a thing. Somebody drew one of those cartoons on the sidewalk in front of the house where we found the second victim. Forensics is pretty sure it was there before the murder. It'd been rained on once. We haven't had any rain in over a week. It's catchy, though, isn't it?" He lit another cigarette.

"It's nice to see someone sticking up for his brother. It doesn't explain all those ration stamps in his locker."

"Ask him."

"We did. We are. Earl's not as smart as you. He'd rather swallow that gold tooth of his than tell us the day of the week."

Dwight had a cold ball of clay in the pit of his stomach. Zagreb knew it. He leaned back, turned up the volume on a wooden cabinet radio perched on the radiator, listened for a moment to a male dispatcher who sounded like Fred Allen at the end of a long programming day, then turned it back down and leaned forward, resting his forearms on the heap on his desk. When he spoke again it was in a tone Dwight hadn't heard from him.

"Earl's not the man we're looking for. I've got a theory about him. We're keeping it out of the papers, so if you tell anyone you'll be sorry you ever left Mississippi."

"Alabama."

"What do I know? I've never been south of Toledo. The point is if I'm right and it gets out and this piece of shit goes underground, I'm going to haul you off the line and take you to a certain hotel room in Paradise Valley and turn you over to Sergeant Canal. You've met Sergeant Canal?"

"I seen him."

"He's pretty hard to miss. There's a rumor going around that big guys are gentle slobs. Sergeant Canal hasn't heard that rumor."

He figured it was time to shuffle a little. "I thinks I understands, boss."

"Good. Now save that Amos and Andy shit for Marcus Garvey. I grew up in a mixed neighborhood. I'm not your everyday ofay."

Dwight was impressed in spite of himself. Not many ofays were aware of the term.

"My theory is this dickhead got into the house on that second kill by posing as a guy selling magazine subscriptions. The victim, a woman, filled out some kind of form before she died. One of the things she wrote was what I think were the last three letters of the *Saturday Evening Post*. The house was in Hamtramck. You know about Hamtramck?"

"Polack town."

"Ukrainians too, but the woman was Polish. Polacks hate niggers worse than Russians. I don't know why. Maybe they just need somebody to look down on the way they've been looked down on by the Irish, who were looked down on by everybody else. Great city, Detroit. We've got so much hate we decided to export it, and that's how we're going to win this war. Where was I? Oh, yeah. Polacks hate niggers. There's no way in hell your brother talked himself into that woman's house. I don't care if he was giving away free kielbasa and a stack of polka records."

"So how come you're holding him?"

"You keep forgetting those stolen ration stamps."

Dwight lost his temper. It was his saving grace that when that happened his blood pressure dropped and so did his voice. Otherwise he'd have been beaten up and thrown into the Chattahoochee years ago. "Go ahead and charge him, then. Don't keep handing me this treason shit. You hang everybody that finds some way to get around rationing, you'd have to duck your head every time you walk under a streetlight."

Zagreb flicked ashes into the mounded-over tray. "He's a colored man caught in a felony. You think Hearst is going to waste an inch on him if we string him up or send him to the Milan federal house for twenty years?"

The room got quiet. The chattering of the typewriter outside, and the drone of a male voice on the telephone, came in over the partition. Dwight crossed his legs, the first time he had ever done so in a white man's presence. "What's the deal?" he asked.

"Ever hear of Frankie Orr?"

"The gangster?"

"A little history lesson, Dwight; no extra charge." This time he didn't apologize for condescending to call him by his Christian name. "Orr's Sicilian born, but he didn't stay there long enough to pick up the language. Grew up in New York City, ran numbers, tended bar, bounced drunks with a sawed-off baseball bat for the Five Points mob. That was Capone's old outfit. How old are you, Dwight?"

"Nineteen."

"I'd've thought older. This was during the dry time, I don't guess you'd remember it much. Anyway, Frankie got himself into some heat when he used a piece of piano wire to strangle another guinea to death on the New York Elevated, which is why they still call him the Conductor. Old Sal Borneo— he headed up the Mafia here in Detroit—took him on as a favor for his greaseball friends back East. Lucky us. We've got him down for the Jerry Buckley killing in '30, no evidence, the Collingwood Massacre in '31, no evidence, and the murder of Joey Machine in '35. No evidence. Am I going too fast?"

Dwight shook his head.

"Good. I get excited when I start talking about Frankie. He's my favorite subject after gonorrhea. Let's see, the murder of Joey Machine. Which after Old Sal died peacefully in his sleep put Frankie in charge of what the papers like to refer to as all illicit activities in the Motor City. We know he spearheaded the drive to take over the slot machine action in the Midwest after Repeal, and everyone who runs a legitimate bar between here and Indianapolis knows you don't install a jukebox without Frankie's friendly seal on the back unless you want your place firebombed and your female customers raped in the parking lot.

"Well, now it happens we've got us a little war. FDR's signature wasn't dry on the Rationing Act when Frankie bought a warehouse in Toledo and started stocking it with butter and eggs and meat and gasoline, barrels and barrels of gasoline; strike a match within two blocks of the place and you could invite everyone in the forty-eight to the barbecue. There isn't a farmer or an oilman in the country won't tell you he can get a better price from Frankie Orr than he can from the War Department, and you don't have to wait for the check to clear on account of he deals in cash."

"The American Way," Dwight said. He'd never known a cop to be so gassy.

"Hey, the country started with a hijacking. We didn't pay for that tea. It's not all greed, though. The government's been trying to deport Frankie for years for violation of the Mann Act, you believe it? Transporting women across state lines for immoral purposes. Pimping charge. He needs the money for his defense fund. The price of congressmen has gone up like everything else since the New Deal. But he's learned from his past mistakes. Every one of his black marketeers turns in enough ration tickets and stamps to justify a healthy volume of customer traffic. Sure, there's counterfeiting—anyone with a cylinder press and a decent engraver can dupe them off, and you'd be surprised how much goodwill you can buy from investigators with a refrigerator full of meat and a set of tires—but he does a lively trade fencing stolen stamps. That's where your brother comes in, and where Kilroy comes in."

"What makes you think Earl's doing business with Orr?"

"He's got to. If he went to anyone else, and that party didn't go to Orr, we'd have found both of them strung up by now in the Buhl Building with blowtorch tans. That American Frankie isn't. Competition gives him hives."

"Maybe Earl's saving 'em to use for himself."

"If he did, he could throw a block party every day for a month. He hasn't been in town long enough to make that many friends."

Dwight had run out of arguments, not that it mattered. He'd guessed the worst the moment the lieutenant had told him about the ration stamps. "What do you want from me?"

"Not a damn thing."

Dwight waited. Zagreb finished his cigarette in silence. He put it out, dislodging a couple of butts from the pile, which he ignored. He took a swollen nine-by-twelve manila folder from the belly drawer, unwound the string that held the flap shut, and tipped its contents out onto Dwight's side of the desk. There was some change, a cheap gold-plated tie clip with an Old English *E* on a blue enamel background, a worn leather wallet, and a key attached to a Bakelite tag bearing what was left of the name of a used-car dealer in Montgomery, half–worn away from handling. Dwight recognized the tag, and the key to his Model A.

The lieutenant dug through the mess on the desk until he found a pad of preprinted forms, which he filled out with a fountain pen and signed his name. He tore off the top sheet and thrust it at Dwight.

"Take that to Interrogation Three. It's on the third floor. You might want to stop at a White Tower on the way home. We didn't touch Earl, but we didn't feed him either."

"You're letting him go?" Dwight reached for the sheet.

Zagreb pulled it back. "He was never booked. We could've got what we want out of him eventually, but I don't have the stomach for it these days. Why break bones when you can talk civilized to his brother?"

"I don't know nothing."

"We know. But you will. We're holding on to those stolen tickets, and if we don't hear from you in march time with something we can use, we're tying up the box and sticking a stamp on it and sending it to Washington."

"But what do you want?"

"Names. A name. Earl's black-market contact will do to start. We probably know it, but if we can link him to an actual transaction we'll have leverage."

"Who you after, Frankie Orr or Kilroy?"

"We'll settle for both." Zagreb moved a shoulder. "Call me a hoarder, I'm greedy. We talked to Frankie. He says he doesn't know who Kilroy is any more than we do and I believe him, but if we can apply some pressure and get him to put his boys to work and smoke the son of a bitch out, I'll be satisfied. Deal?" He waved the release form as if it were a bonus check.

"I'll talk to him. I can't promise nothing. Earl was born with a lie on his lips."

"I'll take that chance, Dwight. I can afford to. Earl's the one stands to lose."

Dwight took the form, scooped up the items from the envelope, and distributed them among his pockets. He pushed himself out of the chair, using the arms. He'd gained a hundred pounds since sitting down, and he hadn't come in feeling light. When he didn't turn right away to leave, Zagreb lifted his eyebrows.

"How you know I don't know nothing?" Dwight asked.

"We got your address from Personnel after we kicked in Earl's locker. We searched your room this morning. No stamps, no corpses under the bed. Speaking of which, the bed hadn't been slept in. You take your sister-in-law home last night, Dwight?"

"Go to hell."

All the playful animosity went out of the lieutenant's face. He aimed his finger at Dwight like a gun. "Everybody gets one," he said. "That was yours. Now get your black ass out of my office."

chapter sixteen

For a time after Dwight Littlejohn left his office, Max Zagreb sat doing nothing. His hands took out his cigarette pack, but he looked at the heap of coffee-stained butts in the bronze ashtray and his stomach did a slow turn. He returned the pack to his shirt pocket, turned up the volume on the police-band, then after a minute or so realized he wasn't taking in a word of what he was hearing, and turned it off.

He felt exhausted and vaguely ashamed of himself. He looked at the smooth, characterless face of Police Cadet Zagreb in the group photograph hanging crooked on the wall and couldn't think of a way to explain to him that serving the citizens of Detroit meant bullying the Dwight Littlejohns who came to it. The Earl Littlejohns were halfway to hell already. But he wasn't bothered so much by his parting words to Dwight as he was by the fact that he wasn't bothered more. That was how Inspector Brandons happened.

"McReary!"

The typewriter stopped chattering. The door opened and the bald officer leaned in.

"Hear anything yet from that Lieutenant Walters in Hamtramck?"

"Not a thing. Want me to call him?"

"I'll do it." Zagreb lifted the receiver, found the number on the mustard-stained list he kept next to the telephone, and dialed. McReary was still standing in the doorway. "What."

"You really kicking Littlejohn?"

"Small fish. Bait."

"What'll you tell those newspaper assholes when they ask if we've made any arrests?"

"Why don't you let me worry about that?"

McReary shook his head. "I'll never be a lieutenant. How do you know when you're making a mistake?"

"Make plenty."

The officer left. When Walters finally came on the line, Zagreb heard syrupy music in the background. It was too early for *One Man's Family*. Maybe the scrawny albino had a weakness for Fred Waring.

"I never heard whether your boys turned anything on that house-to-house," Zagreb said.

Violins simpered through a perplexed pause on the other end.

Jesus Christ. "Anna Levinski," he prompted. "Someone cut her open in your jurisdiction?"

"Oh, right. I thought you'd have that tied up by now." Paper crackled. "Levinski, Levinski. Okay." A chair squeaked. "This ain't as simple as it would've been a couple of years ago. Back then everyone was driving like a bat out of hell, foot traffic stood out. It's a busy neighborhood, shortcut to just about everywhere, and everybody's shank's mare now. Also all the housewives are working in the plants."

"You said that before." He suspected Walters was bored and wanted someone to talk to.

"Talked to a Henrietta Wolocek." Walters spelled it. "She's at three-oh-one-two Dequindre, next block. Widow, sixty-two. Neighborhood snoop, spends more time in her front window than the silver star she got when her boy went down on the *Arizona*. Saw a bunch of people she didn't know on the street the morning of the murder. We checked out the meter reader, he was a substitute, regular guy called in sick. Guy in a blue pinstriped suit knocked on the door of the house across the street and was let in. Talked to the homeowner there, want his name?"

"Later."

"Pinstripe's an adjuster with NBD, came there to inspect the property. Owner wants to refinance his mortgage. It checked out at the bank."

"What else?"

"Nothing. The usual mix of strangers in a hurry, suits and coveralls and military uniforms. Needle in a haystack. Maybe you got the personnel to run them all down. I sure don't. Send the report over?"

"Yeah. Thanks, Walters. Good work."

"Always ready to help. Especially when it's the Four—"

Zagreb hung up.

"McReary!"

McReary leaned in.

"Where's the Yegerov file?"

The bald officer stared at the pile on Zagreb's desk. "I think you've got it, Zag."

"Shit."

He spent the next quarter hour looking for it. As long as he was at it he did a general housecleaning, glancing at and tossing obsolete memos into the wastebasket, finding room for the files he didn't need immediately in the cabinet and the beer case on top of it, and shoveling the rest into the catchall drawer at the bottom of the desk. When he had a relatively clean work surface he spread open the file on the murdered dry cleaner. Except for the autopsy report, which matched those of Anna Levinski and Ernest Sullivan as to cause of death, there was nothing in the Yegerov case to link it to the others. He was not a hoarder, had a record of using the scanty number of stamps issued an aging widower with no dependents regularly. Few friends, none close, no known enemies.

Zagreb would have kicked the case back to Brandon except for the fact that if he laid any of the postmortem shots on top of any of those in the other two files and held them up to the light, all three ghastly incisions lined up. He was no great hand at homicide, but had sat in on enough investigations to recognize a brushstroke when he saw one.

He came to a photostat of the ledger page into which Yegerov recorded his business activities on the day he was killed. The old man had used Yiddish as a kind of shorthand, but Zagreb hadn't lied to Dwight Littlejohn when he said he'd grown up in a mixed neighborhood; his smattering of Balkan tongues, Gaelic, street-nigger, and kike served him more often than any classical student's knowledge of Greek and Latin. The cleaner had taken in several dresses, three suits, one blue and two brown, and a wedding gown. In a separate column he had recorded amounts paid for the items that had been reclaimed. The lieutenant turned from the photostat to the inventory of items found in the shop by police officers after his body was discovered. No wedding gown, but the gown had been brought in first thing that morning, cleaned, pressed, accepted, and paid for the same day. The dresses and one of the brown suits were still in inventory. The blue had needed pressing only and had been reclaimed and the transaction noted. Zagreb looked for the other brown suit in Yegerov's ledger and found it, identified as "Anz, brn, ink," with something illegible scribbled between the last two words. He slid his finger over to the transaction column. There was no entry.

Could be nothing. The cleaner was getting on, he had put in a long day, and when the garment was reclaimed he might have forgotten to record the event. But it was the only lapse on the sheet. A brown suit had been dropped off to have an ink stain or stains removed and the suit was not in the shop.

He was puzzled also by the nonsensical scribble following

"Anz, brn." *Anzug* meant suit of clothes. The thing after
"brn"—brown—didn't even look like letters. It might have
been a doodle, except the neat characters and figures in the
columns didn't suggest a doodling kind of personality.

"McReary!"

This time Canal opened the door. "He's taking a shit. Want
me to tell him to wipe up and get moving?"

"I need his eyes."

"I got eyes enough for us both."

"I mean a younger set. Well, take a look at this."

The big sergeant had to swivel his shoulders to get through
the door. He picked up the sheet and held it close to his face.

"If you can make it out, I can translate," Zagreb said. "If it
doesn't make sense it's Yiddish."

"These are Cyrillic letters."

"What's that mean?"

"It means it ain't Yiddish. It's Russian."

"Yegerov was a Russian Jew. You read Russian?"

"My grandfather was a Cossack in the Imperial Guard. I got
cop in my blood." He looked at it again, then put it back down
in front of Zagreb. "It says 'uniform.' "

chapter seventeen

The war was stalled.

He glowered at the American flag pin skewering the fly-speck identified as Pantelleria on the war map in his living room. It had been there for a week, with no new pins to join it, and it was looking stale.

He was impatient, and not a little put out. Since that pin had gone up he had struck three times in support of the Allies, who as far as he knew were sitting around some bomb-blasted villa swilling wine from the cellar while the Axis raped its way across Europe and the South Pacific.

To be truthful, he shouldn't count the dry cleaner, who so far as he knew was not an enemy to victory, or the girl. They were just pawns, whom he had been forced to sacrifice to preserve the secrecy crucial to his success. The point was he had been *doing* something, and he felt betrayed.

Turning away from the map, he viewed the apartment with his objective eye. The small gateleg table where he took his meals looked naked without the oilcloth. He had used it to wrap the girl's body, stitching up the ends with a stout needle and fishing line he had made a special trip to Woolworth's to get. While he was out he had looped a two-inch length of cotton cord over his doorknob, which upon returning he'd been gratified to see had not been dislodged.

After that he'd decided not to press his luck. He'd stayed in the apartment the rest of that day, through the night, and until the following evening, when his landlady left the house in her blue worsted suit and white pillbox hat and white gloves and took her big Buick out of the garage and burbled away toward her twice-weekly night of euchre and dandelion wine with friends in Sterling Heights. He'd waited another half hour, just in case she forgot something and came back, then went out to his Nash parked on the street and pulled it up the driveway and around to the back door. Up the stairs and back down, his stiff bundle across his shoulders in a firemen's carry. The Nash had a big trunk, compensation for the fuel it wasted in a time when gasoline meant men's lives.

He was about to heave his burden inside when someone came walking along the sidewalk whistling. He froze, unwilling to make a noise that might tempt investigation; then as the whistling grew louder, he spotted the narrow cupboard built next to the back door to shelter the electric meter. If it was the Edison man, he'd run out of time to throw down the bundle and slam the trunk lid on it. It was a cool evening at the end of a day that had been trying to rain since morning. He had on his two-tone zip-front with the bottom of the right slash pocket cut out to give him access to the bayonet in its scabbard inside his dungarees. He shifted his load, freeing his right hand to reach down and grip the cold slippery steel.

The whistling began to fade. It was just a stroller after all. He laid the bundle on the floor of the trunk, closed the lid, and climbed behind the wheel. The starter ground a long time before it caught. He made a mental note to have the motor looked at. He might need the car in a hurry someday. The enemy was all around.

He kept well within the wartime speed limit. He considered it liberal anyway, but he was under special pains to avoid breaking any laws. He slowed down for yellow lights, rolled to a complete halt at stop signs, signaled all lane changes and turns. He passed two police sedans and remained invisible to both. Rather than encouraging him, however, his success filled him with contempt. Did they expect the fifth column to run through red lights and fly swastikas from their radio antennas? There were times when he felt he was fighting alone.

He took the new expressway west. The four-lane sweep of white concrete made him proud. While squadrons of American and RAF bombers pounded holes into the medieval roads and cart paths of Europe, American surveyors and engineers were building a network of shining highways, blasting tunnels through mountains and slashing straight lines through cornfields and pastures for the speedy transport of men and matériel to plants and embarkation points, filling the charged air with the oatmeal smell of wet cement and the acid stench of poured steel. Eleven short months from groundbreaking to ribbon-cutting, reducing the travel time between Detroit and Ypsilanti from an hour and a half to twenty minutes. He swept past teams of yellow earthmovers with their headlamps on, planing hills for yet more ramps and overpasses, convoys of canvas-covered trucks carrying soldiers from Selfridge field and the National Guard camp in Grayling to the Light Guard Armory, lines of cars driven by defense workers on their way to and from their shifts. The buzzing of the rumble strips under his wheels vibrated up through the soles of his feet like a steady charge of low-grade electricity.

He had not had to use the bayonet on the girl. Her neck was slender, the bones that protected her throat thin and hollow like a bird's. He had barely felt them crunching beneath the pressure of his thumbs. He'd stared without expression into her congested face, bending her without effort backward over the open drawer of the sideboard and the ration stamps inside. After he'd stripped her body of his shirt and dressed her in her own clothes, he'd noticed her nails had left a row of small semicircular cuts on his wrists, but he'd poured iodine on them and could wear long sleeves until they finished healing. He'd resigned himself to the fact that the war he fought offered no Purple Hearts, no medals of valor—only the satisfaction of having done his part.

He exited the expressway near Willow Run and followed a country road in transition, a narrow ribbon of raw earth alongside a lane of freshly poured concrete lined with yellow cones, to an intersection, where he braked and for a time studied his choice. At length he downshifted and turned right, toward a stand of woods where no lights shone, away from the farmhouses that had so far withstood relentless industrialization. The road was barely wider than the car, walled on both sides by hardwoods and evergreen scrub, dense enough to double the noise of his bubbling exhaust with its own echo. He used the brake once only, when his headlights caught the glass green glow of a pair of eyes in his path. The deer, a young spikehorn buck, froze for a moment, then found its legs and vaulted up over the bank into the cover of the trees. After that he proceeded slowly, moving at scarcely more than an idle. The atmosphere inside the car became airless. When he rolled down the window on the driver's side, the ratcheting of the crickets drowned out the sound of the motor.

He congratulated himself upon his discipline. Every atom of him wanted speed. He longed to jettison his load and turn around and fly back to the city. He hated the country. It was an alien place without measure or right angles—sloppy, random, out of all order. Civilian life at its most blatant. He despised its anarchy. He thought the greatest punishment that could be handed the enemy was under way: the bombing and mortaring and bullet-clobbering of its buildings and monuments, the reduction to rubble of its mitered walls and stately streets, the laying open of its civilization to the slathering gluttony of nature. He had spent the spring of 1940 listening to Edward R. Murrow's descriptions on the radio of London beneath the bombs with every light in his apartment blazing, exactly as if he had tuned in to some crawler of a Halloween story on *Lights Out,* or the Orson Welles broadcast of *The War of the Worlds*. He gave no thought to the bodies under the debris, but to the survivors who after the raids had to go about their business stumbling over piles of shattered architecture, the streets they knew transformed into something at the base of some hideous irregular mountain in Idaho, or someplace equally hideous. That was how he had felt walking out of the Light Guard Armory, having been denied his escape from the horrifyingly disordered life outside the military. Only destiny had spared him then, steering him toward his new quarters and the uniform left behind in the closet by its former occupant.

At last he came to a clearing. Really it was only a break in the monotony of the forest where an old fire had burned several acres, long enough ago for a new growth of grass to have covered the char, but recently enough that no new scrub had sprung up. He stopped, set the brake, and turned off the lights and ignition. He sat absolutely still for five minutes, possibly longer; it was too dark to read his watch even had he allowed himself that luxury. He considered it a further test of discipline as much as a safety measure to determine that he was indeed alone in a spot where traffic was infrequent, at least at that hour of the evening. How many cars or pedestrians might visit it after he left, or what they might discover, interested him not at all. Crickets ratcheted, a nighthawk signaled to an accomplice with a short, reedy whistle like a tentative teakettle. Mosquitoes whined in through the open window. He was pricked numberless times but let them feed, not even moving to smack at them, although that was his first instinct. A soldier without repose was a casualty in the making.

Finally he popped the glove compartment, retrieved his

black rubber flashlight, and got out to reconnoiter. He directed the beam downward, turning it on only intermittently, memorizing what he saw in its light to avoid tripping over roots and burned stumps in the dark. When he was satisfied of his choice he went back and opened the trunk. Holding the end of the flashlight in his mouth, he drew the bayonet from its sheath and sawed through the stitches he'd taken in the oilcloth to prevent incriminating particles from collecting inside.

The sound of a distant car reached his ears like surf. Noise traveled at night, you could never tell for sure how close it was or if it was approaching. Moving quickly now, he scabbarded the blade, switched off and laid the flashlight inside the trunk, and hoisted the girl's body free of the cloth. Rigor mortis had made it easier to handle than when he had wrapped it. Using the firemen's carry he retraced his steps a few yards into the clearing, ducked his head, and flung the corpse forward. It made little noise landing. The girl had weighed barely a hundred pounds.

He drove another quarter mile before he found a place to turn around, and he didn't use it. Instead he continued until he came to the next crossroads, where he executed a neat, unhurried Y and headed back in the direction he'd come. Before he reached the spot where he'd dumped the body, he passed another car going in the opposite direction. In the beam of his lights he saw a pair of faces, pale and elderly, a flowered hat on the passenger's side, a fedora with the brim turned up all around on the driver's. They didn't look like a couple that had discovered a corpse. Obligingly he stepped on his dimmer switch, taking his high beams out of their eyes. When he passed the clearing he didn't turn his head.

He felt his heart growing lighter with each mile he put between himself and that patch of woods. He'd heard it was the same way for men returning from the front, though the identical territory had filled them with fear going in the opposite direction. He grinned his Robert Taylor grin when he quit the gravel road for the entrance ramp to the expressway. By the time he saw the lights of civilization reflected on the belly of the overcast he was positively giddy, whereas normally he disapproved of the target they made for enemy bombers. He was an indispensable defender of an invincible country. He turned on the radio, caught the last five minutes of an episode of *Suspense* starring Ray Milland and then all of Lowell Thomas, who hinted that something was about to happen in a place that sounded a lot like Sicily. He laughed out loud. He felt as if his night's activity had actually freed things up. He was Admiral Halsey, standing on the bridge with the sea wind in his face. He was George S. Patton peering through binoculars from the open hatch of a Sherman tank.

He had changed back into his prized brown oxfords in the car. In Romulus, ten minutes outside the Detroit city limits, he stopped for gas at a Red Crown station, and when the attendant took his dollar and went back into the office for change, he bundled the new pair of tennis shoes he'd worn into the woods inside the newspapers he'd spread on the Nash's floorboards—the name KILROY shouted at him from the crumpled surface—got out, and pushed the bundle well under the surface of the trash in the bin that stood next to the air hose. He couldn't be sure how clear were the footprints he'd left in the woods or what kind of regionally unique dirt he might have tracked into the car. A good commander protected his flanks.

chapter eighteen

The first thing Dwight saw when he entered Earl and Elizabeth's living room at Sojourner Truth—the first thing *anyone* saw—was the big Zenith radio in a walnut floor cabinet with fluted corners and a big old Buck Rogers dial in the center, all aglow, with a Tigers game washing out of the tapestry speaker. It was the most ornate thing in a small room with celery-colored walls, prints clipped from magazines and mounted in cheap Bakelite frames, and secondhand furniture, albeit clean and decked out with homemade slipcovers and Elizabeth's unfussy doilies pinned to the worn spots. Dwight wondered how many payments were left on the radio and if any Earl made had come from the couple's savings.

Earl was sprawled on the studio couch in peg tops and a sleeveless undershirt, with blue-and-yellow argyles on his long bony feet. A forest of Pfeiffer bottles had sprung up on the Sears & Roebuck coffee table, polished to a high gloss by Elizabeth and protected by a crocheted mat with silver thread. An open bag of New Era potato chips squatted on the floor in a litter of crumbs and pieces.

On the radio, Pete Gray, one-armed outfielder with the St. Louis Browns, hit a long foul off Dizzy Trout, a 4-F pitcher with Detroit. If the war went on another year they'd be using blind shortstops. Steve O'Neill called for a time-out and went out to talk to his flat-footed hurler.

"Where's Elizabeth?" Dwight had let himself in when there was no answer to his knocking.

Earl stood a bottle up in his mouth, set it down empty among the others on the table, and belched loudly. "Work."

"I thought she only cleaned houses Tuesday and Thursday."

"She got another house. This keeps up she'll hire on help. Just like Henry Ford."

Dwight could tell when his brother was drunk. "Ain't you got the afternoon shift this week?"

"I got a hour. Shit!" Gray sent a grounder between Joe Hoover's legs and ran to first. "Son of a bitch is a cripple, you know."

"I know. They called him up when Walker went in."

"Wonder who we got to declare war on before they call up a nigger."

"Mars, probably."

"Got me a double sawbuck riding on this game."

"What's the score?"

"Six-two St. Louis."

"Say good-bye to Alexander Hamilton." Dwight lowered himself into the rocking chair. He'd filled in for a sick-out on the midnight to 4 A.M. to make up for missing his shift yesterday and he was exhausted. He felt as if he'd been dragging his bones behind him in a gunnysack. "Earl, where you getting the money?"

"Get me another beer, will you? Grab one for yourself. I told Lizzie to pick up a case on the way home."

"Too early for me. What about the money?"

"You know about the money. You bailed me."

Dwight hadn't told him the terms under which he'd taken him from police custody. His brother hadn't slept in jail and the lights in the interrogation room hadn't let him. By the time Dwight saw him he was punchy. "You doing business with the guineas?"

jitterbug

"Listen to him. 'Guineas.' You never saw a Eyetalian in your life."

"How many you seen?"

"I look like George Raft? I do my own selling. No partners."

"Where you steal the stamps?"

"My brother, you be surprised how many folks right here in the neighborhood don't lock their back doors."

"You a burglar now, Earl? Dress up all in black and fuck with grappling hooks, shit like that?"

"I just walk through doors. Folks got no imagination, you know it? They all of them keeps their stamps the same places: dresser drawers, cookie jars, ceegar boxes. You going to get me that beer?"

Dwight got up and went into the kitchen, a narrow box painted cheery yellow to make up for the lack of a window. It had a two-burner Hotpoint gas range and a Servel refrigerator that banged the wall behind it when it kicked in and purred like a lion at feeding time. There were two bottles of Pfeiffer inside. Fuck it. He found the opener, a giveaway advertising job, in a drawer and pried the tops off both of them. He brought one out to Earl and sat down in the rocker and took a swig. The cold beer tasted better than breakfast. Good enough anyhow to make him decide never to drink another one in the morning.

"Mr. Ford ain't paying good enough, I guess," Dwight said.

Earl drank his beer and said nothing.

"Elizabeth know?"

"She does now. I heard everything you're going to say from her. Hey, hey!" York and Bloodworth retired the side with a double play.

"Where you selling 'em, Earl?"

"Why, you want in?"

"I want you out. I made a deal with the cops."

Earl turned his head for the first time since Dwight had entered the house. His eyes were bloodshot and he hadn't shaved since leaving police headquarters.

"This is federal shit you're mixed up in," Dwight said. "Don't you care who wins this war?"

"What's the difference? Whoever wins, we lose. Things won't change for you and me, little brother. We still be black. And they still be on top."

"And you be busting up rocks in Kansas when Shirley Temple's a old lady."

Earl thumped down his bottle and stood up. He caught his balance on the arm of the sofa and reached to hook his shirt off a floor lamp. "Let me know how the game comes out."

"Where you going?"

"Anyplace else."

"I'll drive. They won't let you on the bus. You're too drunk."

"Just don't talk." Earl gave up trying to button the shirt straight and left it open.

Dwight kept his mouth shut in the car. His brother looked out at the scenery. Stopped for a light at Grand River, Dwight watched a pedestrian, blond and lanky in a blue work suit with company patches on the sleeves, start across. When the STOP sign swung up on the pedestrian signal he picked up his pace, then caught sight of Dwight's face behind the windshield. He slowed to a stroll.

"Fucking redneck." Earl reached over and punched the horn button.

Dwight actually saw the man flush to the roots of his fair hair. Almost clear of the car when the horn blatted, he spun on both heels, retreated two steps, raised both fists so high over his head Dwight could see the scabby, unwashed flesh of his elbows, and brought them down on the hinged hood, popping loose the latch on one side and making twin egg-shaped dents he could see from behind the windshield.

"Step on it, Dwight! Run the fucker down."

He advanced the hand throttle, expecting the man to dodge when the car lurched forward. But he'd forgotten to downshift when he'd stopped; the frame clunked, the motor coughed and died.

The man's face now was purple. He lunged along the left side of the car. Dwight punched down the lock button just as he seized the handle. He wrenched the floor lever into first and tromped on the starter. The motor ground, ground, caught, ground, ground, ground, caught and held. Dwight let out the clutch and pushed down on the throttle. The man's hand was still on the door handle, and Dwight felt the jolt when the Model A shot forward, yanking the man's arm straight out from the socket. In the rearview mirror a moment later he saw a lanky figure standing in the traffic lane with legs spread and a middle finger thrust skyward.

"You got to move faster than that, little brother," Earl said.

"Any faster and I'd of run right over him."

"What I said."

Dwight looked over at his brother. He couldn't tell if Earl was serious. He hadn't been able to tell much of anything about him since they'd come north.

"Look what the wind blew in. You boys thirsty so early?"

Beatrice Blackwood was behind the bar of the Forest Club, mixing Bloody Marys in a big pitcher. Her ingredients were lined up along the bar's glossy varnished surface: a fifth of Smirnoff's; Tabasco in a quart jug, available only to wholesalers and professional furniture-strippers; four small cans of Del Monte tomato paste; a fifth of Teacher's; a jar of hot peppers; a pint of Old Grand-Dad; and a tall stainless-steel container filled to the rim with liquefied tomatoes, blended from scratch.

"Born thirsty, sugar. Highball for me, rye and Vernor's. Strawberry milkshake for my little brother." Earl swung a leg over a stool cowboy fashion.

Dwight slid onto the next stool. "Coffee, if you got a pot on."

"It's percolating. Hold on till I get this right."

Beatrice was a tall Jamaican, fine-featured and light-skinned, with blue-black hair permanent-waved over to one side like Lena Horne's, and she prided herself as a mixologist, fussing with her pourers and siphons like an artist with his brushes. Ordinarily, Dwight liked to watch her measuring out her portions with a jigger and an eyedropper, pouring sea salt and cayenne pepper into her palm, dusting it into the pitcher, and stirring the contents with a long-handled glass spoon. Today, those fine details only irritated him. For distraction he looked around the room, which seemed smaller by daylight, the naked pipes and old-fashioned exposed wiring shabby in the extreme. The jukebox dozed in the corner, uselessly garish when not engaged in its purpose. The floor hadn't been swept of last night's litter. Cobwebs hammocked in the rafters.

"I needs that drink, darling. Dwight and me just fought the Battle of Gettysburg all over."

"Who won?"

"Come in here on our own legs, didn't we?"

She used a funnel to empty the pitcher into a big Mason jar, screwed on the cover, gave it three vigorous shakes, and put it in a boxy Westinghouse refrigerator with the compressor coil on top. Then she cleared the clutter from the bar and mixed Earl's highball. A two-gallon blue enamel coffeepot stood with its lid rattling on a hot plate on the back bar. She wrapped a bar rag around the handle and poured Dwight a cup. "You want a nail in it?" she asked.

"Just some cream."

She added cream from a container in the refrigerator and set the thick white china cup and saucer in front of him. "Who's buying?"

"Shit. I done left my roll at home." Earl sipped his drink.

Dwight got out his wallet. "What's the damage?"

"For you, eighty-five." Beatrice showed her brilliants.

He laid a dollar on the bar and told her to keep the change. She rang it up in an old-fashioned brass register and slipped a nickel and a dime into her apron pocket. "I hear I missed some excitement the other night," she said.

"Just a roust," said Earl. "Cops won't stop till we're all on our way back to Africa."

She fitted a cigarette into a jade holder and lit it off a slim matching lighter. She was the only woman outside the movies who Dwight thought looked natural smoking that way. "I heard they were looking for that Kilroy character. What you think, colored?"

"They thought that, they'd turn out every joint in Paradise Valley." Earl drank. "They'd take a torch to the whole fucking street."

"What's Dwight think?" She was smiling at him.

Dwight concentrated on his coffee. He was shy around Beatrice. He could never tell if her interest in him was genuine or if she was making fun of the new kid. She was ten years older, and she'd been around. He knew she'd worked the streets, both here and in Jamaica, and the rumor was she kept her hand in when rent time came around. Even if it turned out she liked him, he doubted he measured up.

"I think it don't matter what I think," he said.

"I bet you got a theory. You're the thinky type." She put an elbow on the bar and rested her chin in her hand. Smoke coiled out of the cigarette in its holder clamped in the corner of her mouth. Earl, who never missed an episode of *Terry and the Pirates,* referred to her as the Dragon Lady when not in her presence.

Dwight said, "My theory is he's going to step in a hole and the cops are going to fill it in."

"That's the cops' theory."

"No, that's their plan. It ain't the killing, they don't care about that. It's the stamps. That'll bring in the feds. They'll bury the guy if it means using the army and stretching the war out another year."

"You called it right the first time," Earl said. "It don't matter what you think."

Beatrice said, "It makes sense to me."

"That's 'cause you think he's talking about Kilroy."

"Oh. Forgot. You got a call."

Earl grinned. "Count Basie looking for a road manager?"

"If he was, I'd take it. I got a big heart for that Joe Williams. My, my." The smile stayed in place. "Gidgy wants you to call him."

Dwight said, "Who's Gidgy?"

"Search me, little brother. I never heard of the man. It was a mistake, sugar."

"I make a lot of those." She came up off her elbow, tapped ash into a tin embossed L&Ms tray on the bar, and touched her hair with a slim hand with red-lacquered nails. "Freshen that cup, Dwight?"

He looked at the Burma-Shave clock. "Better not. I got to get Earl to the plant."

"Soon's I take a leak." Earl drained his glass, hopped off the stool, and took the narrow sloping hallway to the rest rooms in back. He was whistling "Let Me Off Uptown."

"War effort getting along without you today?" Beatrice scooped up Earl's glass, mopping up the ring with the bar rag in her other hand. Her every movement was as graceful as a dancer's.

"Even Henry Ford gets a day off now and then." He drank the last of his coffee. "I can't remember if you got telephones in back."

"Seems to me we do." She turned her back to plunge the glass into the soapy water in the double sink.

"Who's Gidgy?"

She rinsed the glass thoroughly. "I don't know him any better than your brother."

"I believe that," he said.

She wiped the glass dry with a clean towel, placed it bottom side up among the others on the back bar, and turned to retrieve her cigarette and holder from the ashtray. Her eyes were mahogany-colored. "God decides the order, Dwight. If He meant for you to be the big brother He'd have had you born first."

"I just asked who's Gidgy."

She shrugged a padded shoulder, turned away, and looked over the collection of posters and framed pictures crowding the wall behind the back bar, searching with the concentration of a librarian looking for a particular book among stacks she saw every day. Finally she came to a framed newspaper clipping, brown and spotted, with a photograph of ten colored men in hats, cloth caps, and pinstriped suits, lined up against what looked like one of the wainscoted walls at Detroit Police Headquarters. The headline read TEN QUESTIONED IN NEGRO RACKETS WAR. She pointed to the third man from the left, standing with his hat in front of his face.

"That's Gidgy," she said. "He's just as camera-shy now as he was in '31."

chapter nineteen

Gunther Lenz approached his father with caution. The old farmer—he was eighteen years older than Gunther's mother, having buried his first wife in Bavaria before shipping to the U.S. in 1909—was seated on the front porch in his hardrock maple chair, drinking his thick bitter coffee and scowling at the trainlike profile of the Willow Run plant on the horizon, backlit by the setting sun. His mood, always subject to sudden change, was never good when his thoughts rested on that architectural non sequitur in the midst of farm country. He had been in negotiation to buy a fine virgin wooded section for clearing and planting when Washington condemned it out from under him to make room for an employee parking lot. Baldur Lenz was the son of an old Prussian Junker, whose features, hewn out of straight-grained *Nordwald* and decorated with a white imperial, glowered out of a tinted photographic portrait in an oval frame in the dining room, and his sympathies in the current war were clear. He called the president "Rosenfeld," blamed the surrender of Berlin on Jewish betrayal, and bore a hideous pattern of wormlike scars on his back from having been pulled into a field by hooded men in March 1918 and horsewhipped for his Germanism. Gunther looked with dread upon the day he must explain to his father that he had registered for the draft, and when called intended to serve. Right now he only wanted to ask a favor.

"You fix that post like I told you?" was his father's greeting.

"Yes, sir. I took it out and sank a new one. It was all rotted."

Standing on the ground in front of the porch he tried not to look up at the old man, nor down at his feet either. At eighteen he was aware of the power of the word *sir,* but also of the self-loathing it cost him to use it.

"Sink that wire good and tight? I didn't buy good seed corn to feed the damn deer."

"Yes, sir." He didn't point out that the ongoing construction at Willow Run had frightened away all the deer for a generation at least. That would have turned the conversation in the wrong direction. "I thought I'd go into town tonight, if I can have the truck."

"Got holes in your shoes? Put in newspaper."

"I'm going to Detroit, not Ypsi."

"What's in Detroit?"

"I'm taking Susan to the Michigan."

"What's wrong with the picture show in Ypsi?" His father had gone to see a movie only once since *The Jazz Singer.* He claimed the English came too fast for him to follow, but Gunther suspected it was the price of the ticket that kept him away. He'd bought one suit in his life, which he wore to funerals and meetings at the grange hall, and had stopped going to ball games when the price of hot dogs went to fifteen cents.

"Jimmy Dorsey's playing live at the Michigan. Susan likes to dance."

"She a jitterbug?" He pronounced the word in the tone he reserved for Jews and FDR.

"No, sir."

He worked his mouth around his false teeth. His eyes were pale blue in a thicket of sharp creases that went all the way down to his chin when his face showed any expression at all. The irises were barely distinguishable from the whites. They were still fixed on the bomber plant. "What's the picture?"

"Lady of Burlesque."

"Sex show?"

"Pa, it's Barbara Stanwyck."

"You got four acres of corn to plant tomorrow."

"I'll be home early. There's a curfew."

"Put gas in it."

Gunther thanked him and went inside to clean up. He put on his suit, brushed his hair straight back, and teased forth a lock to form an apostrophe above his right eye, like Clark Gable. He couldn't do much about his square jaw and beefy neck, which had German farm boy all over them, and wished he had the confidence to carry off a silk scarf tucked into an open shirt collar, Ronald Colman style. His mother paused in the midst of setting the table to kiss him. Her face wore a perpetual worried look these days. She shared the secret of Gunther's draft registration, and had a brother in the marines, whose infrequent letters she couldn't share with the family for fear of arousing Baldur's ire. She had a beaten-down quality that filled Gunther with sympathy and contempt.

The Model T truck stood in a bare patch of lawn, the grass long since killed by spilled oil from the crankcase. He advanced the spark, inserted the crank, being careful to align his thumb with the rest of his fingers to avoid breaking his arm, and wound the motor into life. By then his sweat had begun to attract mosquitoes; quickly he threw the crank onto the floorboards, swung into the driver's seat, and slipped the clutch to lose the voracious insects in the slipstream. The night air felt cool on his face when he cranked open the windshield. It was heavy with the scent of turned earth and spread manure. He wondered if it smelled different in France and Italy.

Susan Moller lived in one of Ypsilanti's oldest houses, a spike-gabled Queen Anne on a quarter acre lot, once painted in a rainbow of pastels but now white with gray trim. A new six-foot board fence, not yet whitewashed, stood between it and the house next door, nearly as old but recently divided into apartments to take advantage of the housing shortage among workers at Willow Run. Susan's father was the latest in a family line of area pharmacists going back to the Civil War.

She met Gunther at the door in a salmon-colored party dress with a white lace shawl over her bare shoulders. She was nearly as tall as her escort, but had formed the habit of standing with her head thrust forward to divert attention from her height. Tonight she wore her black hair pinned up. It struck off blue halos under the porch light. He helped her up into the seat, then slid in beside her and let out the clutch. Despite gas rationing he'd left the motor running. He hadn't wanted to work up another sweat cranking it.

The Michigan Theater was an art deco palace in downtown Detroit, illuminated from below with searchlights like a church steeple and crusted over with gilt cherubs and bunches of grapes inside. The local band opening for Jimmy Dorsey onstage was good but derivative, playing a medley of familiar hits in imitation of the styles of the various famous orchestras that had recorded them. A temporary dance floor had been erected over the pit normally occupied by house musicians before the main feature, and a few couples were taking advantage of it. Most of the five thousand seats were filled with patrons conserving their energy for the star attraction.

The curtain rolled down on a spirited version of "Song of India." Five minutes of murmuring conversation, anticipatory coughs, and suspenseful silence, then the unmistakable tootling of Jimmy Dorsey's clarinet began the opening lick to "Contrasts," the band's theme; and as the brass and the rest of the woodwinds came in, the curtain rose on a cushion of music and thunderous applause. All the props used by the previous band had vanished, replaced by two rows of white music stands with the initials JD intertwined in gold on their faces.

The footlights and overheads flared off shining brass, white dinner jackets, glistening hair oil. Jimmy Dorsey, jug-eared and amiable, stood several yards back from the microphone on its stand as if unwilling to monopolize it, waving his clarinet like a baton when the reed was not actually in his mouth. The dance floor began to fill. By the time Bob Eberly and Helen O'Connell swept out from the wings to sing "Tangerine," there was barely room to maneuver. Gunther and Susan danced to "Amapola" and "Green Eyes," but when Ray McKinley on drums laid down the rumbling beat for "Cow Cow Boogie," Gunther acquiesced to a plea from a skinny caricature in a Michigan letterman's sweater to cut in. Susan loved to jitterbug, and his feet were too accustomed to busting clods to keep up.

The movie program started on schedule, disappointing those who wanted the music to continue. *The March of Time* caught the president fishing at Warm Springs, showed Alice Faye and Phil Harris loading gear and personnel aboard a ship carrying a USO troupe to Pantelleria, and presented an "Arsenal of Democracy" feature on the bustling defense plants in California, New Jersey, Indiana, and Michigan, the sound track lost beneath applause when the audience recognized River Rouge, Willow Run, and Dodge Main. A Popeye cartoon followed, then the main feature, *Lady of Burlesque.* The movie, based on a murder mystery purportedly written by Gypsy Rose Lee, the stripper, failed to charm Gunther. He guessed who the murderer was thirty minutes in and found the subject matter about as sexy as a Playtex ad in a magazine. On the way home he argued about it with Susan, who found it difficult to be critical of anything from Hollywood.

They made up, and as she snuggled in close to him he left the expressway and took the back roads. The hour was early. He knew of a clearing where they could be alone. She made no protest as he turned off the tree-lined road and bucked up over the natural berm. As he drew the brake, the truck's lights fell on a dark patch on the ground fifty yards ahead, which lifted in a sudden, ragged cloud like a pile of dried leaves struck by a gust. The movement, and the harsh cacophony that accompanied it, startled Susan, whose nails dug into his biceps.

He patted her hand. His own heart was fluttering, but he made his voice calm. "It's just crows. They must have found something."

"What?" Her grip hadn't relaxed.

"A deer, probably. Someone hit it and it crawled off there and died." As he said it he remembered how long it had been since he'd seen a deer so close to Willow Run. He reached for the door handle.

She didn't let go. "Don't get out."

"I'd better take a look." Gently he pried her fingers loose and opened the door and stepped down.

A low ground mist smoked in the beams from the head-lights. The bed of pine needles and last year's leaves was damp. He hoped the moisture wouldn't ruin his only good pair of shoes. Above him, the crows had perched in the trees, where they found courage to harangue him noisily. He smelled decayed flesh then, saw what the birds had been feeding on. He had just enough presence of mind to remember his date and step outside the light to vomit.

part three

Is This Trip Necessary?

chapter twenty

Crazy Henry, looking shockingly frail in a full-dress tuxedo and butterfly collar too large for his wattled neck, entered the dining room of the Book-Cadillac Hotel on the arms of his wife Clara and Harry Bennett. Mrs. Ford was dressed all in black for her martyred son Edsel and the men had satin mourning bands sewn to their sleeves. It was obvious that Bennett and Clara were supporting the eighty-year-old patriarch of America's number one automotive family between them; if they were to let go of his elbows he would collapse into a pile of brittle bones on the steps leading to the dais. Even his small sharp eyes, set deep beneath the mantel of his great bony brow, had taken on the luminescent quality of a wandering mind. He did not look like a man who had assumed complete control of his company in the wake of his son's death.

Nor had he, despite the claims of an army of press agents employed by the head office in Dearborn. Harry Bennett, bowlegged and short-coupled, had been calling all the shots from his office in the Ford Service Department since before Edsel Ford ascended to his paper presidency, and in the presence of Henry's failing health and weakening faculties had acquired authority unprecedented in the history of the one-man firm. It was Bennett who during the labor troubles of 1932 had ordered machine guns to be installed on the roofs of the Ford family residences at Fairlane and Gaukler Pointe. It was Bennett's strikebreakers who beat up Richard Frankensteen and kicked Walter Reuther down the steps of the Miller Road overpass for distributing union literature in 1937. The fortunes of the world's oldest and most famous manufacturer of automobiles—and now, of battleships and bombers—lay entirely in the hands of a man who didn't know a carburetor from a chafing dish, and who could barely sign his own name to the deliveries of pornographic films he ordered by the case. Despite expensive tailoring, in evening dress he put Max Zagreb in mind of a midget wrestler at a formal wedding.

The dining room, paneled in hand-rubbed walnut and inlaid with marble and gold, had been transformed overnight with red-white-and-blue bunting and fanciful representations in pen and ink of Churchill, FDR, and Stalin looking with grim determination to the East. Even a blindfolded Justice had been inducted by way of a banner strung behind the dais, draped in Old Glory and directing squadrons of Ford B-24s and companies of Chrysler tanks with her sword. The martial atmosphere extended to the chandeliers, whose crystal pendants looked like bunches of bullets. Max Zagreb saw the spectacle for what it was and yet still felt his dick growing hard. By the same token he found it easy to sneer at Edward R. Murrow's lump-throated descriptions of stiff-upper-lip Brits defying Goering's Luftwaffe from the London Underground, but difficult to keep his chest from swelling with allied pride whenever he heard "The White Cliffs of Dover."

He was there under orders. Mayor Jeffries had directed Commissioner Witherspoon to accompany him to the black-tie event to raise money to equip GIs with gas masks on the improved design, and the commissioner had in turn issued one of his infamous memos "requesting" inspectors and better to attend. However, when a chicken-pox epidemic claimed several members of the department brass, lieutenants and even some sergeants had been pressed into service. Some of Zagreb's ambitious peers had rented full-dress outfits. He had selected his best blue suit and the black knitted necktie he wore to civilian funerals, and was gratified to observe a number of overweight precinct commanders struggling with their cummerbunds every time they got up or sat down.

It occurred to him, as the head table took shape, that a German potato-masher lobbed in that direction would deprive the Home Front of most of its generals. In addition to Henry, laboring to mount the steps to the platform with the help of his party, fellow auto pioneer Walter P. Chrysler, Liberty ship builder Henry Kaiser, and William Knudsen, former General Motors chief and now head of the federal Office of Production Management, and their wives had gathered behind a floral centerpiece the size of a washtub. Zagreb thought it symbolic of the new style of mechanized warfare that the only two warriors he recognized were Ford and Knudsen, and Knudsen only because he was decked out in the beribboned uniform that went with his special commission as a lieutenant general of the army. There wasn't a Sergeant York or a T. E. Lawrence in the bunch.

He was seated at a large round table covered in white linen with a midget version of the head table's centerpiece blocking his view of the diners opposite him. A miniature American flag surrounded by the French tricolor, the British Union Jack, and a forest of less recognizable pennants grew out of the pot, which he was willing to bet would go to the lucky guest whose ticket bore the magic number. He hoped it wasn't him. The incentive of bringing home such a prize had gone with his wife, and if he contrived to forget it, someone was bound to be offended, and he would retire a lieutenant. Preparing for disaster, he surveyed his neighbors for the face of someone who would accept the gift of his good fortune in the spirit in which it was not intended.

The pickings held little promise. To his right sat a buxom woman with blinding white hair creamed and cooked into indestructible waves, with lace at her throat, silver-rimmed glasses, and so much powder on her liver spots it fell in a cloud to her dress every time she turned her head. If she accepted the centerpiece at all it would be to present it to a servant in lieu of a raise. Her escort, a pale bald man with a severe white fringe and thick glasses in heavy black frames, appeared to be withering inside his tuxedo. His starched shirt might have been the only thing preventing him from sliding under the table. He was nothing more than a fixture between the woman and the party with whom she was conducting an animated and powder-scattering conversation, the thin, well-preserved widow of an auto pioneer who had been dead since Coolidge. The widow's severe tailored suit and plain silver jewelry did not suggest a love for flowers.

The man on Zagreb's left was an unescorted shrimp in an unpressed gray suit ten years out of date. He wore a heavy ingot class ring, University of Detroit, and slicked his muddy brown hair back Valentino style from a Greek face, all nose and pink rounded knob of a chin. He caught the lieutenant looking and hoisted the water pitcher in front of him, lifting his eyebrows in a silent offer. When Zagreb shook his head, the man filled his own glass.

"I don't know what's wrong with me these days," the man said. "I'm drinking water the way I used to swill hootch. I guess all the fun went out of it after Repeal."

Zagreb nodded, then decided comment was required. "It's better for you, though. Water."

"It's overrated. Alexander and Genghis Khan conquered the known world on wine and fermented mare's milk. They say Attila preferred to drink plain water from a wooden cup while his men guzzled wine from goblets, but that was politics. He died of a hemorrhage brought on by alcoholic poisoning."

"Are you a historian?" He was mildly interested.

"Only by default. I was a newspaperman until the news I covered became history overnight. The Twenty-first Amendment put more people out of work than the Eighteenth. Connie Minor." He set down his glass half-empty and held out his hand.

Zagreb took it. "I thought I recognized you. We met once, sort of. Max Zagreb."

"I know. I've seen your picture in the paper. I don't remember us meeting, though."

"It was in the hallway outside the Ferguson-O'Hara grand-jury room. I was in uniform then. I testified right after you."

"That was four years ago. I'm surprised you remembered."

"You were a celebrity. Everybody in town read your column."

"Everybody in the country read my column. I was syndicated in four hundred newspapers. Then liquor became legal, and I couldn't get a job as copyboy. When I testified I hadn't been inside a city room in six years."

"What are you doing now?"

Minor grinned a bitter grin. "I write advertising copy for a hardware chain."

"Is that bad?"

"Not if you like writing about chain saws."

"I thought maybe you were covering the dinner."

"I've still got a couple of friends in the business. One of them couldn't make it. You ever chum around with hardware salesmen? A couple of conversations about Stanley hammers and you'd stick up an old lady for her ticket to some musty fund-raiser."

"Still feel that way?"

"You have to have a reporter's eye," Minor said. "People are the only entertainment not affected by wartime shortages. I'd duck a ball game to watch Old Henry decomposing in public. What do you think, Lieutenant, does Harry Bennett still suck his eighty-year-old dick?"

Zagreb glanced toward the head table, at Ford sitting behind his untouched plate, staring out into the emptiness of the room above the heads of the assembled guests, and bouncy, red-haired Bennett shadowboxing for the benefit of Mrs. Chrysler, who appeared to be listening politely to a story from his pugilistic past. Clara Ford broke off her conversation with Henry Kaiser to lift her knife and fork and cut up her husband's breast of veal (four points per pound).

"I kind of didn't hate him the one time we met," Zagreb said. "He was talking about that silly-ass castle he built out by Ypsi, full of secret passages and lions and tigers in cages. He was like a kid with a wad of money."

"Tell that to Reuther."

"Reuther's a Red."

The waiters, wearing gold jackets and white cotton gloves, arrived with the meals for the table. Zagreb's veal looked underdone. The peas were khaki-colored and came from a can.

Minor used his fork to separate the lumps from his mashed potatoes. "I'm glad I'm not rich. Can you imagine shelling out fifty bucks a plate for crap like this?"

"I guess some of them thought they were buying gas masks for the boys."

"Most of them wouldn't know what one was if they put it on their plate. If one of those boys showed up on their doorstep without a uniform they'd turn the dogs loose on him. The men are here to make deals and the women just want to get the prewar chiffon out of mothballs before someone kills Hitler." Blackening his meal with pepper, he grinned again, this time sheepishly. "I'm kind of a Red myself."

They ate for a few moments in silence. Minor gave up trying to make a dent in the veal, pushed his plate away, and refilled his glass from a fresh pitcher. "Well, take a long look at them," he said. "That's history up there in those cartoon shirt boards. Maybe the last time the men whose names hang outside their factories will all be gathered in one place. They hung motors on buckboards and drove them out of barns straight into the twentieth century, taking the country with them. Some of them still have grease under their nails. In five years their sons will be running things—business-school grads who think a screwdriver's something you drink."

"That was the idea, wasn't it? Everybody wants something better for their kids."

"Bullshit. If they didn't have to die they wouldn't bother having them."

It was Zagreb's turn to grin. "I can't tell if you love them or hate them."

"Neither can I. That's what makes me so mad at the sons of bitches." He sat back and rattled the ice in his glass. "You're working the Kilroy case." It wasn't a question.

The lieutenant nodded and speared a pea.

"The papers say you're putting the arm on Frankie Orr. Anything in it?"

"Orr runs the black market."

"You really think this guy's selling the ration stamps?"

"He's not using them for himself. Nobody has that many friends. Not even Bob Hope."

"Maybe he's not doing anything with them."

"Then why take them?"

"I don't know. I gave up trying to think like killers a long time ago."

"No good at it?"

"Too good at it. You never know where a thing like that will stop. But I think you're barking down the wrong hole. This guy doesn't give a shit about stamps or money. He's in it for the boot."

"Thrill killer?"

"He doesn't know it himself. He might even have talked himself into believing he's doing it all for a good cause. Jack the Ripper thought he was hosing all the filth out of the East End. You're wasting your time with Frankie. He and Kilroy aren't in the same league. Hell, they're not even in the same sport."

Zagreb slid his knife and fork into his plate and sat back. "Who have you been talking to?"

"How close did I come?"

"You've been doing a lot of thinking like a reporter for someone who claims he isn't one anymore."

"I've made my peace with that. In my day, reporters were the scum of the earth and we knew it. We rolled in it. I got my first job because I was small enough to crawl through a window and steal a picture of a murder victim off the mantel while my partner was talking to the widow on the porch. They're still the scum of the earth, only now they cloak themselves in the dignity of a profession. When the Fourth Estate picks up as many hypocrites as the other three, it's time for all of us to start selling bug-zappers and garden rakes. That doesn't mean the instinct goes away. There were reporters before there were newspapers. Newspapers are just an excuse to ask questions no one wants to answer."

"So this conversation is off the record."

Minor's mouth twisted. "Not at all. It'll be the lead in the next issue of the *Paint-Mixers' Gazette*. I thought all you dicks were good listeners."

"We've got reason to believe Kilroy talks his way into his victims' confidence by pretending to sell magazine subscriptions for the war effort. We're pretty sure he wears some kind of uniform and poses as a veteran."

"It makes sense. Jack Dance once put on a police uniform to kidnap one of Joey Machine's lugs. What uniform?"

"We don't know. He killed a dry cleaner, and there was a uniform missing from his inventory, the record didn't say what kind. We figure the cleaner got suspicious."

"Kind of thin. The country's full of men in uniform."

"We've got a request in to all the area installations for a list of personnel unaccounted for at the times of the murders."

"You think he's genuine?"

"Killing is soldiers' work. Where better for a killer to hide than among killers?"

A waiter came with a tray of ice-cream cups and they stopped talking. Minor declined, explaining that sweets made him giddy. When the waiter left: "I like it better that he's not genuine."

"Why?" Zagreb sank a spoon into his vanilla.

"If he were a soldier, he'd have an outlet. There's nothing like mowing down a line of Japs with a tommy gun if you like spilling blood. My guess is the uniform is more than just an icebreaker. He wears it because it makes him feel good."

"When I was in uniform I couldn't wait to get out."

"You must've wanted it at some point or you wouldn't have joined the department. How would you have felt if they turned you down?"

"I wouldn't've gone around pretending I was a cop."

"That isn't what I asked."

He had some more ice cream without tasting it. "I could get back in touch with the military and ask who's been rejected for service locally."

"You might even get through the list before the war ended."

"Well, since Pearl, say, and before the first killing."

Minor hunched forward suddenly. He looked like Churchill. "Find out who left doing cartwheels and who got pissed and showed it. That'll narrow the field tight."

"How come you're not a cop?" The lieutenant smiled.

"Too short. That's how come I know how Kilroy felt. He started slaughtering old ladies. I bought a typewriter."

Zagreb was still thinking about the list. "Flat feet, heart murmurs?"

"Psychiatric."

"That information's confidential."

"In theory. In peacetime. FDR's run a jump-wire around the Bill of Rights. When was the last time you saw a copy of *Literary Digest* on a stand?"

"It folded."

"It had subscribers and advertisers up the ass. It ran one too many editorials criticizing the administration and Roosevelt closed it down under the Alien and Sedition Act. Call in Hoover. He loves this kind of shit."

"Jesus," Zagreb said.

"There's a war on, you know?" Connie Minor filled his glass from the water pitcher.

chapter twenty-one

Which one, Pasquale?"

Pasquale Garibaldi D'Annunzio Oro—"Patsy" to everyone but his father—stared hard from one of the bolts of fabric to the other, patiently cradled in the arms of two fresh-faced employees in the upstairs fitting room at Harry Sufferin's. He had mixed feelings about the room. He liked its old-fashioned dark mahogany paneling, its framed prints of history's most elegantly appointed gentlemen, its racks of suits in various stages of completion, each one bearing a tag identifying the customer, the clean smells of linen and worsted wool that permeated the walls to the studs. But he found the rows of adjustable male torsos on their iron stands disturbing. At twelve (most people thought he was younger, stunted as he was by the same congenital weakness that allowed him to stand only with the aid of crutches), he knew a little about the underside of his father's business, and the forms put him too much in mind of dismembered corpses.

However, he was more frightened of his father.

The thought of disappointing Frankie Orr by choosing the wrong suit fabric terrified him. He hesitated until even the two assistants started shifting their weight from foot to foot. Only the head tailor, exquisitely attired in lawn shirtsleeves, a roomy vest, suspended trousers, and glistening cordovan loafers with tassles, maintained his serenity in the presence of so much silence. The frames of his half glasses matched his beautiful head of silver hair and he wore his badge of office, a yellow tape measure, around his neck.

Finally the boy pointed at the gray chalkstripe. Immediately he sensed his father's exasperation.

"What's wrong with you? You want your old man to look like a gangster? Look at the gabardine. Feel it, for chrissake. That's how Harry Hopkins dresses. You'd never mistake him for a gun punk. You want me in silk drawers and hand-painted ties like those animals in Chicago. I talk to you, sometimes I feel like going home and kicking your mother in the stomach. When can you fit me?"

The tailor slid a small leather-bound notebook from his vest pocket and turned pages. "Wednesday afternoon?" He peered over the tops of his glasses.

"Tuesday. I'm going to L.A. end of this month. I need the suit by then."

"I've got six fittings Tuesday."

"You got one. Last time you squeezed me in I wound up with an armhole the size of my thumb. If I show up at that Jew cocksucker Benny Siegel's looking like shit I'm coming back here and feeding you ten yards of gabardine and you can wash it down with battery acid. Let's go, Pasquale."

His father offered him no help with the stairs, tapping his hand-lasted shoe at the bottom and glancing at the heavy gold watch strapped to his wrist while Patsy gathered his crutches under one arm and leaned on the banister. He had spent much of his first eight years in examining rooms, and in his dissatisfaction with the results Frankie Orr had concluded the boy was too weak or lazy to use the legs God gave him. He called Patsy's mother a mollycoddler and worse, and when the priest at Sacred Heart refused to grant an annulment had remodeled the house in Grosse Pointe, making the east and west wings self-contained so that the Orrs would never need to see each other except when public social occasions demanded a show of family solidarity. Patsy never knew from day to day in which wing he would sleep that night. He loved his mother while dreading those days when drink made her maudlin and incoherent. His father he feared.

The uninformed passerby might have taken the line of cars drawn up against the curb on Shelby to belong to an official from the War Department, or before the war to a Chrysler road test. The day after Pearl Harbor, suspecting that such luxuries would soon be scarce, Frankie had traded in his three black 1941 Lincoln Zephyrs on a trio of 1942 Airfoil DeSotos in identical maroon. Favoring the elongated profile of the new running board–less designs, and having developed a healthy job-oriented respect for such features as the Powermaster 115-horsepower engine and Fluid Drive Simpli-Matic transmission, he had passed up the Cadillac Sedan DeVille with its comic-book pontoon fenders and the fuel-stingy sluggishness of the Packard Clipper for the low-slung Fifth Avenue Custom town sedan.

Although the sleek look of the concealed headlights and the predatory appearance of the DeSoto's grille—elaborately chromed to resemble the denticles of a grinning shark—appealed to the two sides of his nature, his reasons for selecting the dynamics were practical. From the outside the cars were indistinguishable from one another. With the fore and aft vehicles filled with bodyguards and his own sandwiched between, three drivers hired off the General Motors proving grounds could in the event of pursuit play a high-speed shell game, confusing the chasers as to which car contained the prime target. Since accepting delivery, he reckoned that he had dodged two subpoenas, lost an incalulable number of federal agents assigned to his surveillance, and foiled one assassination attempt. Had he adhered to the poky armor-plated locomotives of Prohibition, he would already be dead or in custody.

Seeing his father's personal bodyguard push himself away from the fender of the middle car and move to open the door to the backseat, Patsy placed his crutch tips on the sidewalk. Frankie's hand, still wiry from his days with the garrote, squeezed his shoulder with a punishing grip.

"Not yet, *imbecille.*"

The DeSoto's motor trembled alive and backed into idle. His father let go.

"How many times I got to say it? Hitler didn't corner the market on bombs. You want some nigger streetsweep to come out and unstring your guts from a lightpole? Get inna car, what you waiting for now?" He gave him a shove.

Patsy liked the feel of the glove-leather upholstery. Frankie had offset the expense by ordering Bedford cloth for the other cars. The smell was smoky gray, like the color of the interior. Since the age of consciousness, the younger Orr had connected odors with colors. The fumes of the stinging ointment his private nurse massaged into the withered muscles of his legs were fiery orange, the aroma of pasta and clam sauce in the kitchen soft saffron. When he was small his mother's smell was pink, like a flannel blanket. More recently it was the copper hue of bourbon. The combination of his father's expensive cologne and his personal scent smelled blue-white, like dry ice.

So cold it burned.

The boy never told anyone he smelled in colors. He was afraid if it got back to Frankie it would confirm his suspicion, already almost a conviction, that his son was without worth. Patsy had always felt that his father had accepted him only on approval, and that the moment he showed himself unequal to the effort he would be turned out—into what, he didn't know, but the thought that it might be even less tenable than life with Frankie Orr filled him with dread. He lived afraid.

They drove through the light wartime traffic with the windows rolled down just far enough to let in air but not bullets, past shops with recruiting posters in the windows and female pedestrians in suits with pinched waists and hats fashioned after overseas caps, heading places carrying briefcases and portable typewriters, past men loitering in doorways and on streetcorners, demonstrably with no place to go; older men mostly, in the wide-brimmed fedoras and sack suits of the previous decade. Detroit had become a city almost entirely devoid of young men. Those who remained, and who had not been judged to hold essential jobs, were by definition substandard, damaged in the chute. The place had the feel of a rummage sale the day after, where the goods still to be seen had been picked over and rejected, awaiting removal to the dump. Outside the smoke and racket of the plants, the Arsenal of Democracy was a dustbin.

The motorcade slid into the curb in front of Carl's Chop House, but no one got out. Frankie produced a gold-and-enamel combination cigarette case and lighter, tapped a Fatima against the case, and lit it. A chain-smoker, he had customized the DeSoto so that there was an ashtray within arm's reach from every angle. Patsy quickly found the atmosphere oppressive, but was unwilling to crank the window down farther for fear of another diatribe. In a little while a broad-shouldered man in a badly fitting suit standing in front of the restaurant opened the front door and leaned in. Then he swung the door wide and Albert Brock came out, walking briskly. Patsy recognized the short, square-built union organizer from earlier meetings with his father and from his picture in the newspapers. He wore sturdy suits made of some stiff material that Frankie would never have allowed in his presence during fittings, wing-tip shoes with thick rippled soles, and white socks. Very quickly he jerked open the door on Patsy's side and got in. He reacted to the boy's presence belatedly. "Does he have to be here?"

"I'm showing him how things work. You got a boy, ain't you?"

"He's away at school. He's not going to push rigs and he's never going to see a set of brass knuckles." Brock spoke slowly, in stark contrast to his actions. He seemed to be experimenting with good grammar. Patsy noticed his manicured nails and calloused palms.

"See, that's the difference between me and you, Al. I ain't ashamed of my work."

"I'm not either. I bounced bricks off the skulls of scab drivers so my boy wouldn't have to."

"That was ten years ago. You wear a tie now, got yourself a big office with wood paneling, a fuckable secretary. I hear you're buying a boat."

"Am I supposed to be surprised you know that? You've got people in every bank in southeastern Michigan."

"I'm just congratulating you on how good you're doing. When I met you you were working two jobs to pay for your own rig, popping bennies like Crackerjacks. You fell asleep anyway, rolled a peddle truck on 23, and got laid up for six months with a busted leg. Did your boss pay your bills?"

"You know damn well he fired me."

"You lost six months' wages and any chance at going into business as an independent. You'd still be in hock for the hospital bill if you didn't run for presidency of the union local and win. Who delivered the vote, Al?"

"*I* delivered the vote, cocksucker! I made speeches in the rain, got my brains beat out by city cops working private security, signed up members standing in snow up to my ass with double pneumonia. I got out of bed six weeks early to do it. My left leg's still a half inch shorter than my right. I didn't see you."

"Let's not fight," Frankie said. "Okay, Barney."

The driver tapped his horn. The car in front skinned away from the curb and the motorcade moved out into traffic.

"Where we going?" asked Brock.

"Relax, Al. If I wanted you in the river you'd be floating. It's almost lunchtime; you want a lot of hungry people looking at a big shot like you sitting in a car with a wanted character like me?"

"For a man on the lam you sure like to stick out. Purple cars, for chrissake."

"Midnight maroon, the dealer said. Anyway I ain't on the lam. I'm out on a writ while my lawyers work out this phony Mann Act rap with the Justice Department. I never ran a whore in my life."

"I guess those cockshops on Michigan and Cass run them-selves." Brock unbuttoned his suitcoat and sat back. He was developing a roll around his middle. "What is it you want, Frank? The pension fund's off-limits, I told you that. That was never part of the deal."

"Well, let that rest. I've got four hundred thousand tires sit-ting in a warehouse in Akron. The market's here. I need trucks."

"You're rich. Call Mack."

"Every time I make a call, J. Edgar Hoover picks up. If I wanted them tires in federal custody, I'd sell 'em to Cordell Hull. I need log entries and bills of lading that'll stand up to a traffic stop. Most of all I need drivers with balls the size of coconuts."

"Lots of luck. The last shipment of those pulled out for England."

"If I trusted luck I'd be rotting in Sacred Heart Cemetery in a ten-grand bronze coffin. I put my faith in my friends." He reached across Patsy and slapped Brock's knee.

"How much you figure to net?"

"Million and a half. I got people to take care of. That's three hundred grand to you."

"Not me. The strike fund. Minus a grand apiece to the drivers. You may have helped put me in, but it's the boys behind the wheels of the rigs that keep me there."

"That's what I like about you, Al. You're loyal. Where can I drop you?"

"At the first light. I'll catch a cab."

"I ain't seen but two this whole trip. There's a war on, you know?"

"There's always a war on, Frank."

It was a busy day.

Their next stop was the Grecian Gardens in Greektown, where they ate lunch in a private room. A police inspector in a uniform crusted all over with gold joined them for baklava and coffee, talked about the war and the Detroit Tigers the whole time, and left with a warm handshake, during which a wad of bills changed hands. Patsy's presence was never acknowledged.

From there they drove out of the city into the wilds of Oakland County to inspect a new line of slot machines in the back room of a roadhouse Frankie owned on Square Lake Road. The place smelled woodsy—deep green to Patsy—full of knotty pine with leafy branches scratching at the windows. The man who ran the roadhouse, small and natty, with greased-back hair and a clip-on bow tie, looked grave. He took them into his office and showed Frankie a stack of 78 rpm records in brown paper sleeves resting in a wooden crate stuffed with straw. Frankie's brow darkened as he read the labels.

They drove fast back to Detroit and braked with a crunch of gravel in front of a crumbling brick building off Jefferson. The place was vast and echoing inside, stinking of fish and the dry musk of rats and stacked with crates and barrels to the rafters. They were accompanied by Tino, Frankie's personal body-guard, his beautiful mouth in a jaw like a concrete pier, who carried the records in his huge hands as gently as a housemaid bringing china to a formal table.

One by one, Frankie showed the records to a squirrel-faced man in a flannel shirt and dungarees while the man's com-plexion went from sunburned brown to watery gray. The road-house was headquarters for the entire Midwestern juke route, an Orr enterprise since 1937. As Patsy understood the situa-tion, the squirrel-faced man had stuck Frankie's manager with a load of Guy Lombardo tunes when the demand was for Glenn Miller, Benny Goodman, Bing Crosby, and the Andrews Sisters. The man stammered an explanation—something about the USO having priority—but by then Frankie had begun dashing the records one by one across the top of the man's head. Patsy didn't think it hurt much, but the employees of the warehouse had gathered to watch, and the spectacle of the squirrel-faced man's humiliation tied the boy's stomach into knots. It was a relief when they left the man sitting on the concrete floor in a litter of brittle black plastic to go back to the office.

The New Deal Recovery Corporation—Frankie had moved with characteristic speed to register the trademark before the dust settled on FDR's special economic congressional session in 1933—operated out of a corner suite on the twenty-first floor of the David Stott Building overlooking Capitol Park. His name appeared nowhere on the lease or in the papers filed with the Securities and Exchange Commission. Even the door to his private office, oiled hickory with a bulletproof steel core, remained blank. Frankie had ordered an electronic lock installed so that no one entered or left unless a buzzer was activated beneath the edge of his desk, a copy of Mussolini's in Rome. Frankie, who hated the dictator for the brutal measures he had taken against the Mafia in Sicily, had nonetheless appropriated some of his more effective psychological tricks. These included knocking down two walls to create a long, nerve-shattering walk from the door to the desk for those visitors he preferred to put ill at ease. Frankie liked to sit with his back to a dazzling west window, against which his features remained a purple blur while he took the measure of the newcomer illuminated in the glare.

Today, still charged up from the scene in the warehouse, he strode across the pile carpet, threw himself into his studded leather swivel, and placed a call to his liquor distributor in Canada, an associate since Prohibition. He seemed oblivious to the presence of his son, who trailed him in on his crutches and sat in an unobtrusive corner. A professional decorator had done the room in ruthless Modern, hanging abstract prints on brushed-aluminum walls and dotting the floor plan sparsely with glass-topped tables and uncomfortable chairs made of chromium and black leather. It reminded Patsy of every waiting room in every brand-new hospital he had sat in while his parents conferred with a specialist in the private office about their son's case.

Frankie was winding up his call when the intercom buzzed.

He hung up, flipped a switch on the varnished wooden box on the desk, and listened to his secretary inform him in her flawless West End accent that three men were there to see him from the Detroit Police Department. Patsy assumed they had come to collect a bribe and let his mind wander. It came back abruptly when his father snapped off the switch and uttered a vile Sicilian oath, something Patsy had never heard him do when they were in the same room, although he had overheard similar sentiments through the occasional wall. Frankie sat back for a moment, one hand covering his chin, the other drumming the desk top. Then he activated the buzzer.

The two plainclothes detectives who entered the room first made a mockery of the hike to the desk, loping across it in three seconds and taking up a position at an angle to the window that forced Frankie to swivel a quarter turn to face them. This put the bright sunlight as much into his eyes as theirs. He got up, drew the cord that closed the drapes, and remained standing with his hands resting on the back of the chair. The visitors were two of the largest men Patsy had ever seen. He was especially unnerved by the one whose eyes stood out from his head like rubber door bumpers, and by his nervous energy; even when he was standing still, his hands continued to open and close at his sides and his entire body seemed to vibrate, like a big engine threatening to shake itself apart if it weren't put to work soon. His companion, older, quieter, with thick mats of black hair on the backs of his hands, represented something altogether more solid and rooted. When he stopped moving it was as if he'd been bolted to the spot for years.

A minute went past before the boy took notice of the third man who had entered quietly behind them. Attired like the others in a black suit and gray fedora, he was slighter and looked much younger, with reddish hair and freckles. He smiled at Patsy, produced a deck of cards from an inside pocket, and throughout the interview executed sleight-of-hand tricks, it seemed as much to amuse himself as Patsy.

"Where's that Polack lieutenant of yours?" Frankie asked. "I thought all you boys went around on the same leash."

"He's too busy to mess around with cheap punks." This from the nervous man with the scary eyes. "And he ain't a Polack."

That seemed to tell Frankie something. The tension went out of him and he circled around in front of his chair and sat down. "This a separate deal, or you figure to split it with the brass?"

The detective who had just spoken rotated his eyes toward his companion and unsheathed a set of teeth with an unhealthy gray sheen. Then he picked up the gooseneck lamp from the desk and slammed it alongside Frankie's head backhand.

Astonished, Patsy belched. His stomach was still tied up from the warehouse and he clapped a palm over his mouth to keep from vomiting. The young detective winked at him. He was still smiling. He cut the deck of cards, transferring the bottom half to the top one-handed.

Frankie, more enraged than injured, started to get up. The older of the two big men leaned across the desk, placed his palm against Frankie's face with a curious gentle movement, and pushed him back down.

"You asked about Zagreb," the man said. "He's changing your bed. He knows how much you like clean sheets. Not like in that shithole in Brooklyn before you sucked your first *capo* dick."

"My lawyers will be waiting downtown. I'll catch a ride back with them. Does FDR know how you boys waste gas? 'Is this trip necessary?' " Frankie was getting himself back. Patsy felt kind of proud.

"Downtown?" The man with the eyes hoisted his brows comically in his companion's direction. "Can I tell him?"

"Be my guest."

The unhealthy gray teeth showed. "This ain't a bust, punk. We're taking you to Niggertown. Ever heard of the California?"

Frankie's smile eroded, and something happened that Patsy had never seen. The pigment paled beneath the natural olive tone of his face, the even finish of his heat lamp–enhanced tan. He jacked the smile back up into place. "Bullshit," he said.

"He's heard about the California," the solid man said to the man with the eyes.

"I ain't some hop-joint snag you can scare with a yarn like that. You boys already bought yourselves a blue-bag beat on Belle Isle. You want to try for 1-A and a free ticket to some pesthole island in the Pacific?"

The solid man shrugged. The movement was like rocks sliding off a mountain. "You're not listening, Frank. All this shit is going to happen anyway if we don't nail Kilroy. That won't make no difference to you. By then you'll be crow meat, just like that girl the sheriffs scraped out of the woods out by Willow Run."

"I told Zagreb I don't know nothing about Kilroy."

"He knows that. He also knows you're the only shop in Detroit without a manpower shortage. It ain't patriotic keeping it all to yourself. We're all of us in the same boat, you know?"

Frankie craned his neck to make eye contact with the man doing card tricks. "What's your story?"

"Me?" The young man shuffled, pasteboards flying between his hands in a blur. "I'm Switzerland."

"What do you say, Frankie?" asked the solid one. "Churchill and Stalin ain't friends, but they got Schicklgruber's nuts in the wringer just the same."

The man with the eyes hadn't spoken in several minutes. He stood twisting the lamp's gooseneck into tortured shapes.

Frankie smoothed back his hair with both palms, adjusted the glistening knot of his tie, and sat back. For a fascinated Patsy, it was like watching a resurrection. "I got ears."

chapter twenty-two

Dwight Littlejohn was being devoured by tigers.

Despite the terror and pain he was lucid. It surprised him that they should start with the feet and work their way up. He'd read somewhere, probably in the *National Geographic,* that big cats went first for the hindquarters, sometimes the entrails; and common sense said the tenderest parts should top the menu. Overthinking things had always been his worst fault; he supposed he'd still be wondering about it when they got to his heart and stopped the flow of blood to his brain.

When the banging started, he thought someone was shooting the tigers. He was mildly sad that whoever it was had come too late. When he realized someone was knocking on his door, he opened his eyes, looked down at the sheet covering him to make sure it wasn't drenched in his own blood, then got up and into his Hudson's Basement robe and slippers. His landlady was telling him he had a telephone call. He followed her downstairs, thinking, shit, tigers. Now he was Little Black Sambo.

It was an old-fashioned wall job in the kitchen with a crank and a separate earpiece. The old woman sat down at the table where her husband was eating breakfast, but the couple remained silent, plainly eavesdropping. Dwight turned his back to them and leaned close to the mouthpiece, sticking a finger in his free ear to block out the racket from the old General Electric refrigerator. There wasn't any way that compressor was going to make it through the war.

"Dwight, it's Elizabeth. Earl didn't come home last night."

"Elizabeth?" His brain was still warming up.

"He's stayed out late before, but never all night. He wasn't with you, was he?" There was hope in her voice.

"I ain't seen him in days, except at the plant. When'd he leave?"

"About seven. He came home and changed clothes and went out. He wouldn't tell me where he was going."

"What clothes did he put on?"

"His zoot suit."

"Did you call the Forest Club?"

"Nobody answered. Dwight, I'm scared."

He looked at the electric clock gurgling on the wall above the pump-up gas stove—7:30. It was his day off. He'd planned to spend it working on his car. "They don't open for an hour and a half. Stay by the phone. I'll start looking."

"Where could he be?"

"I don't know. But he went there from the Forest."

He caught Beatrice Blackwood unlocking the front door. A tall woman built on the Jamaican scale, all legs and long waist, she wore a long summer cotton print dress that outlined her figure to sharp advantage when the sun was behind her and had her hair tied up in a white scarf like a turban. She reminded him of Solomon's Shulamite.

When he hailed her, trotting across the sidewalk, she spun on her platform soles to face him, a razor in her right hand. Recognizing him, she relaxed, palmed the blade back into the handle, and deposited it between her breasts, surely the most desirable sheath in Detroit. "Morning, Dwight. You turning into a morning barfly?" She opened the door.

He grasped the edge and held it for her. "I'm looking for my brother. He here last night?"

"Hell, I don't know. All the nights here run together." She flipped on the lights, went behind the bar, and tied on an apron. "I'll have coffee going in a minute."

"He's missing, Beatrice. No one's seen him since last night."

"Is that a long time?"

"It is for him. He's a fuck-up, but he's always come home to his wife."

"Oh, his wife."

"This ain't one of them phone calls where you say he ain't here. He's in trouble with the cops and maybe the FBI. He's messing around with the black market."

She put as much care into making coffee as she did her mixed drinks, measuring with a tin scoop, cracking an egg from the refrigerator into a small china bowl, and tossing the bits of shell into the percolator basket. "He was in last night. I don't know what time. Early. I didn't see when he left. The place was pretty full."

"Was he with anybody?"

"He came in alone."

"What about later?"

She put the bowl with the egg in it into the refrigerator, plugged in the hot plate, and set the pot on top of it. "I was busy, Dwight. I told you the place was full. I couldn't watch your brother the whole time even if I wanted to."

"Why lie to me, Beatrice?"

She glared at him. The expression on his face changed her mind. She took a cigarette from a box under the bar, lit it off a Camel giveaway lighter, and leaned a hip against the bar. He had never seen her smoke before without the jade holder.

"I'm in this country on a thread," she said. "If everything that goes on in this saloon got back to Immigration, I'd have to quit. After that it's just some time before they arrest me and put me on the next boat. I don't want to be a whore no more, Dwight. Especially I don't want to be a whore in Kingston."

"Do I look like I got connections in Washington? I just want to find Earl."

"For who? You or his wife?"

He hesitated. "That's a dumb question. He's my brother."

"My brother got me into the house in Kingston." She blew smoke, shook her head, and put out the cigarette in a brass tray shaped like a horseshoe. "People think bartenders don't see nothing except glasses that need filling. I've seen you with Elizabeth. Comes a point when three people either have to sit down and talk or one of them has to turn around and walk."

"You don't know what you're talking about." He wondered if she'd come to work drunk.

"Forget I said anything. I closed the place at curfew. I'm still asleep. Gidgy was in last night," she added.

"Gidgy?"

"Gidgy, remember?" She pointed at the man covering his face in the twelve-year-old newspaper clipping on the wall. "He's the Conductor's leg man in Paradise Valley. I didn't see him and Earl together, but Gidgy left early too. Maybe they know each other."

"Where's he hang out, besides here?"

"He runs a record store on Erskine." She gave him the address. "Don't tell him I told you."

He walked past the place twice before he spotted the lettering on the second-story window. It was a walk-up above a narrow lunch counter with three stools and an electric griddle, in the door of which leaned a chef built along the lines of Marcus Garvey in a ribbed undershirt, white ducks, and apron, all indescribably filthy. Dwight found the smell of hot grease nauseating at that hour. The stairs were grubby and creaking, the hallway at the top too narrow for two people to pass. He suspected it had been a long time since two people had had to. A door at the end stood partially open with the legend ABYSSINIA RECORDS AND SHEET MUSIC painted on the yellow honeycomb glass.

The aisle between the oaken bins was even more cramped than the hallway, forcing Dwight to walk sideways to reach the end of the rectangular room. Seventy-eight rpm records in brown paper sleeves stood on edge in the bins, each of which was labeled neatly by hand on three-by-five cards Scotch-taped to the fronts, identifying artists and labels. Billie Holiday and Louis Armstrong were much in evidence, but for every famous name there were several that were unfamiliar: Scrapper Blackwell, Zue Robertson, the Red Onion Jazz Babies. A wind-up phonograph located somewhere in the no-man's-land behind the distant counter was playing Bessie Smith, a version of "Lost Your Head Blues" rendered slightly drunken by a worn-out mainspring. A pile of piano rolls occupied one bin, looking like papyrus scrolls, and a hand-lettered sign informed serious collectors that a selection of rare wax cylinders was available for demonstration upon request. Dwight, whose own tastes ran toward Ellington, Basie, and other mainstream colored orchestras, considered himself in foreign territory. He felt white.

MUSSOLINI INVADES ABYSSINIA bawled the headline on a yellowed copy of the *Toledo Blade* thumbtacked to the plaster wall above the bins.

The tableau behind the wooden counter was a surprise. Framed photographs of varying shapes and sizes filled every inch of wall space, containing likenesses of Walter "Hot Lips" Page, Lena Horne, the Duke and the Count, Earl "Fatha"

Hines, Satchmo, Bessie, and some of the white boys, Tommy and Jimmy Dorsey, Harry James (with Betty Grable on his arm), Benny Goodman, Jimmy "The Schnozz" Durante; smiling broadly (and, Dwight thought in some, drunkenly or worse), unguarded and candid. Bing Crosby, casually attired in a baggy checked sport coat and unmatching dark slacks, laughed at the spectacle of his famous porkpie hat perched on Ella Fitzgerald's elegantly coiffed head. All of the pictures appeared to have been taken in that little cluttered store. Most were autographed. Every bandleader and musician of note seemed to be represented, with exceptions equally impressive by their absence: Wayne King the Waltz King, Fred the Bore Waring of the Pennsylvanians, hammy Sammy Kaye, corny Kay Kyser, Guy Lombardo and his simpering Royal Canadians, the groanworthy Spike Jones. There wasn't a stiff in the display.

"You likes my gallery? I got more I ain't put up. Done run out of wall."

Dwight looked for the owner of the disembodied voice. The counter was heaped high with albums and records, some in sleeves, others naked, with visible chips in the thick Bakelite; he had to stand on tiptoe and crane his neck to see over them. The vista beyond was even more disorganized. Stacks of sheet music, back numbers of *Billboard* magazine, and what might have been mimeographed lists of private record collections consumed most of the floor space, with only a tiny aisle between to allow the occupant egress from behind the counter. The debris had spread like ivy up the sides and across the top of an old rolltop desk in an advanced state of collapse, as if unable to bear the burden. Thumb-smeared envelopes and rolls of paper crammed the pigeonholes, a medieval-looking adding machine with a huge black cast-iron handle rode the surf of paper next to a china saucer with a half-eaten sandwich on it and an empty glass bearing the disreputable-looking remains of buttermilk. Or what Dwight hoped was buttermilk. Even the sandwich looked like a relic left over from a lost civilization.

A mountain of manila envelopes stuffed for shipping had proven solid enough to support the portable phonograph, now coming to the end of its record. A slender black hand at the end of a pink sleeve returned the arm to its prop and threw the brake on the turntable. But for that movement, Dwight might have missed the slight figure sitting in a captain's chair among the detritus. He had on a pink dress shirt with white collar and cuffs, a white silk necktie with a gold clasp to match his studs, and a straw boater tilted away over to one side of his totally bald head, although it would be difficult to picture anyone who looked less like Maurice Chevalier. His legs were crossed in salt-and-pepper trousers, showing six inches of pink-and-black argyle between the cuff of the upper leg and a white suede shoe with a silver buckle. The face behind a pair of smoked glasses was like dark oiled wood, long as an African mask, and bore no trace of a smile. A hand-rolled cigarette smoldered in one corner of his mouth. Dwight recognized the scorched-grain smell. He wasn't a reefer man himself, but the odor was as much a part of the Detroit he knew as pig's knuckles and collard greens deep-fried in bacon fat.

He nodded toward the pictures. "You really know all these people?"

"Customers. I got the biggest collection of race records west of Harlem, and Harlem ain't got some of what I got. That's Johnny Mercer up there in the corner. Steals most of his stuff from old blues tunes. He done bought the whole inventory in '34. I had to shut down for eight months. They comes through town, they stops here. And they all comes through town."

"How'd they find out about the place?"

"Word of mouth. Jack Teegarden come here in '33, right after I opened, walked out a hour later with both arms full of King Oliver and Jelly Roll Morton. After that, you might of thought I was giving away muggles. Ain't nobody buys music like musicians."

"I don't see Billie Holiday."

"Lady Day, she stopped in once, but she looked like shit, wouldn't let me take her picture. And she wasn't looking for music." He changed the subject—slyly, Dwight thought. "What you like? I just got in some Blind Lemon, ain't even un-crated it yet."

"Is your name Gidgy?"

"Depends on what yours is."

"I'm Dwight Littlejohn."

"That injun? You look like a Blackfoot." A bitter little laugh bubbled up from the sunken chest beneath the pink shirt, ending in a smoker's cough. He sucked in hemp and tapped a pile of ash into a Chock Full O'Nuts can perched atop a pile of sheet music on the desk.

"I'm Earl Littlejohn's brother."

"I guess you have to be. Two Littlejohns in one town ought to be related."

"So you know Earl."

"Is that what I said?"

"I'm not a cop," Dwight said wearily. "I ain't with the FBI or the army. I screw airplanes for a living and then I go home. My sister-in-law's worried about her husband. She just wants him back."

"She a pretty woman?"

"What's that got to do with anything?"

"Everything. If she's a pretty woman, he'll come back. It don't even matter if she's a bitch. Man can turn off his ears, but he got to have something pretty to look at."

"She ain't a bitch."

Gidgy went on smoking his cigarette until it was short enough to burn his fingers. Then he tapped it out in the coffee can and laid it carefully beside a row of equally short butts on the side not occupied by ashes. When he got up from the chair it was as if a relief sculpture had just separated itself from a frieze.

"I might need a hand," he said, and opened a door in the back that Dwight had not noticed previously. It was mounted flush in the wall, painted the same drab ivory color, and had neither knob nor handle. Gidgy opened it by pushing it against a spring and letting it pop out, like a kitchen cabinet with a magnetic latch. Dwight negotiated the skimpy path between the stacks of records and papers and followed him through it.

Gidgy said, "I had to satisfy myself you wasn't a spook. You and Earl don't favor each other."

He made no answer to that. He'd heard it all his life. When he was much younger, and vexed over something Earl had said or done, he had comforted himself with the belief that one of them was adopted.

The room, when Gidgy turned an old-fashioned switch to activate the funnel-shaded bulb that hung from the ceiling, turned out to be nearly as large as the rest of the shop, and much more tidy. Vertical rows of wooden crates and fiberboard cartons lined the walls, the wide planks of the floor were swept and bare of clutter. Some of the boxes bore a caduceus, snakes entwined on a winged staff, and the stenciled legend MEDICAL SUPPLIES. A plain wooden table served as a desk with a row of clipboards hung on pegs on the wall above it and a wooden chair drawn up to it. The only other furnishing was a folding canvas cot, where Earl Littlejohn lay snoring, fully clothed, with his back to the rest of the room and the dirty soles of his stockinged feet showing.

"He got a little cokey and decided to fly home," Gidgy said. "I made him drink some laudanum to bring him down, but I guess it was too much with the liquor in him. He been out fourteen hours."

"You gave him dope?"

"I never gave nobody nothing except my dear old mom. He took it for his cut."

"Cut of what?"

Gidgy drew the chair away from the table and folded himself into it. Clearly the effort of moving from one room to another had drained him, or that was the impression he gave. Dwight had never seen a youngish man, not fat, who seemed so fond of sitting. He wondered if Gidgy had TB.

"You know all about me," Gidgy said, "or enough, or you wouldn't be here. Who told you?"

Dwight said nothing.

"Well, I can guess. Don't sweat it, young blood; I likes Beatrice. It don't make no never mind nohow. I'm the biggest employer in Paradise Valley after GM and Ford. I believe I got the edge on Chrysler in this neighborhood. If Earl screws airplanes as enthusiastically as he works for me, we'll be in Berlin by Christmas."

"He's got a job. He don't need you."

"Ain't nobody needs Gidgy. Everybody just wants what he got, same as in '31. Ain't nothing changed, except maybe the lapels." He drew another hand-rolled cigarette and a book of matches from his shirt pocket and lit up.

"Will you help me get him down to my car?"

"I done already helped him into that there cot. He heavier than he looks. I ain't lifted that much since Prohibition."

Dwight found his brother's saddle shoes and put them on him. He rolled him over onto his back and slapped his cheeks. Earl's head rolled from side to side but his eyes didn't open.

"I could give him a whiff," Gidgy said. "Put him on his feet like a wooden injun. Call it a advance."

"I heard you was in the black market. What you doing pushing dope?"

"Wars don't last forever."

Finally Earl groaned. His eyelids twitched. Dwight pried one open and looked at the pupil, but he didn't know what he was looking for. "Earl, you there?"

"Beatrice?" He sounded like a wound-down record.

"It's Dwight. Not Beatrice."

"Give us a kiss."

"Man, I hopes he still thinks you're Beatrice," Gidgy said.

Dwight slapped his brother.

"C'mon, sugar," Earl whined. "What makes your ole heart so hard?"

Talking to him all the time, saying things he couldn't remember later, Dwight got his brother's feet on the floor and his arm across his shoulders and lifted him. Earl made a noise. Dwight thought he was saying something and paused to listen. He was humming "Don't Be That Way." Gidgy started singing along. He had a surprisingly pleasant baritone, good as an Ink Spot. Dwight half dragged, half carried Earl to the door, which had a handle on this side. When he had it open he leaned against the frame with his brother draped across his back, catching his breath. Finally he gathered himself and his burden and lurched on through. He craned his neck to look back at Gidgy, who had assumed his earlier position, legs crossed, one arm hung over the back of his chair, the cigarette smoldering in the corner of his mouth.

"Thanks, I guess," Dwight said. "For not letting him try to fly."

Gidgy lifted a listless hand. "Abyssinia."

chapter twenty-three

He liked rain.

When it fell gently, as it was falling now, hardly more than a mist and invisible when you weren't actually out in it, it softened the edges of the granite and soot-stained buildings and made the streets shine like the Bakelite floors Fred Astaire and Ginger Rogers had danced on before he stopped going to anything but war movies. The brimstone smell that came when the first drops struck the heated concrete and asphalt had gone, replaced by a sweet, tarry odor, like licorice. When he was three he had climbed into the cupboard where licorice drops were kept and managed to devour half the contents of the bag before he was discovered, beaten, and locked naked in the narrow closet under the stairs, where he'd been bitten all over by spiders; but he'd succeeded in hiding five pieces of licorice in his fist, and by doling them out to himself had passed the hours in fear and darkness bearably.

He'd found a black military-style oilskin poncho at Sam's Cut-Rate Men's Clothing, and with it over his uniform and the cellophane cap shield in place he was contented to stand waiting for the streetcar on Woodward, protecting the leather briefcase beneath the poncho. The bench was too wet to sit on, and in any case he preferred to stand when in uniform. He had never seen a picture or a statue of a soldier sitting except on a horse.

He had let one car go by. There had been no one else waiting there when it stopped to let out a single passenger, and half the seats were empty. Aside from the poor hunting, he disapproved sharply of so much electricity being expended on so small a load. Too many people were still driving themselves, and every gallon of gasoline wasted on a frivolous trip involving only one or two travelers in a private vehicle meant another American dead at the front. Just the thought of it made him reach inside the briefcase and grip the handle of the bayonet until his fingers lost all feeling.

Five minutes before the next car was due, a small group began to gather near the bench: a horse-faced young nurse in a cape with a scarf tied under her chin to protect her starched cap, a pair of middle-aged men in Ford coveralls carrying black metal lunch pails, and a couple in their seventies, the man wearing a rumpled brown suit and a corduroy cap and leaning on a bamboo cane, the woman wearing a man's trenchcoat, out-of-fashion cloche hat, and black galoshes with a broken buckle that tinkled when she walked, and holding a black umbrella open over both their heads. He decided to get aboard with this group.

When the streetcar came, he arranged himself at the front of the line without appearing to fight for the position, which for a man in uniform would have appeared rude and drawn too much attention. He boarded first, dropped his token into the box, and took the first available seat on the aisle, next to an elderly man reading a Hebrew newspaper. This gave him a view of the rest of the newcomers as they paid. The nurse, practical woman, had her nickel ready and didn't have to open her purse. One of the Ford workers rummaged through the pockets of his coveralls, muttering. His companion came up with a dime and paid for them both. The old man with the cane climbed up, gathering both feet on each step before attempting the next and leaning heavily on the support bar, then turned around to offer a hand to the old woman, who was stout. He stood with his back to the aisle while she hooked her umbrella on her arm and groped inside a bulky handbag until she found two tokens. She had what looked like a thick bundle of ration stamps inside the bag; the old man's body partially blocked the view. They tottered down the aisle single file and found space for both of them to sit halfway back.

The rain picked up after a couple of blocks. Pedestrians unprepared for a downpour dashed across the street shielding themselves with newspapers and flat handbags, a *Detroit Times* delivery boy stepped inside the doorway at Woolworth's to protect the papers in his canvas sack. A horse hitched to a milk wagon drawn up in front of an apartment building shook its mane and settled in for a miserable wait. The nurse got off and ran into a Cunningham's, more passengers boarded, opening and closing umbrellas and shaking themselves like dogs. The downpour became a deluge. He smirked at the sight of a fat man in short sleeves struggling to raise the canvas top of a sapphire blue Packard. The fat man was soaked to his undershirt, which meant his upholstery was thoroughly saturated. Served him right for not taking public transportation.

Hudson's Department Store hove into view, and as if by an arrangement between Joseph Lowthian Hudson and God the rain stopped. The sun came out, glittering off millions of droplets stuck like diamonds to the plate-glass display windows at ground level and the rows of panes in the multiple stories towering over Salian's jewelry store, the only holdout on the block. The brass-framed revolving doors whirled, propelling shoppers and passersby who had stepped inside for shelter out onto the sidewalk. Every turn sucked at least one new customer into the store. The sight filled him with equal measures of pride and revulsion: pride at the invincibility of a nation whose citizens continued to consume toasters, Palm Beach suits, and poodles in bright ribbons while most of Europe was in darkness, revulsion at this fresh proof of the thousands of Americans who considered news of the war their private entertainment at the end of the day's glut. In less than three weeks the annual J.L. Hudson's Independence Day Parade would trundle down Woodward, the world's largest flag would unfurl its acre of stars and stripes across the front of the huge building, and the hundred maimed and murdered men for each of its forty-eight stars would not mean as much to those Americans as the day off work.

"Are you all right, son? You look flushed."

He turned and stared at the old man in the seat next to his. The Hebrew newspaper was folded in his lap. His heavy Yiddish accent reminded him of the dry cleaner who had removed the ink stain from his uniform. He still felt bad about that. The man had not been a hoarder. But he had caught the young man in a lie, and that made him a hazard. Sometimes the innocent were also the enemy.

He smiled his tentative smile. "I just got out of the V.A. Hospital. I guess I shouldn't have gone out in the rain yet."

"Were you wounded in combat?"

"Yes." He changed the subject. "Do you have family in Europe?"

"My brother and sister-in-law and their children are in a detention camp in Poland. They haven't written in months."

"It's hard to get letters through."

"You boys are doing a fine job," the old man said.

The motorman clanged the bell and stopped the car. The aisle clotted with passengers waiting to get off. The man with the bamboo cane levered himself up and gave his arm to his wife. They had to be married. There was a sameness to the cast of their features that said they'd spent most of the century in each other's company.

He got in line behind them, close enough to smell the stout woman's scent. It reminded him of decaying flowers.

He followed them through one of the revolving doors into Hudson's.

Here there was no war. Although its outward trappings were celebrated like the features of a popular song or movie—men's Kuppenheimer tropical suits, shallow-gorged and pinched at the waist like an officer's uniform, women's rayon pajamas printed all over with bombers in flight, gold-and-enamel pins fashioned after military medals, and the occasional submarine-shaped perfume bottle—the store was an island of peacetime commerce in the middle of a sea in turmoil. The ground floor, which took up the entire city block without walls or partitions, presented a bazaar: lacquered salesgirls behind glass display cases filled with sports shirts and lipsticks, platform-soled floor demonstrators waiting in ambush with atomizers, customers trying on elbow-length evening gloves and hauling around fat children by the hand, as fast as they could waddle. He compared their apple cheeks with the sunken visages of refugee children he'd seen in newsreels, dirty and twitching, their eyes without focus, the faces of little old men and women. Sometimes he felt as if he'd been there, holding them on his lap and giving them chocolate bars from his ration kit.

A squealing as of rats carried his attention overhead, where baskets of currency rode pulleys up and down wires leading to and from the cashier's office, suspended like a gunnery emplacement above the floor. Even Mammon had wings in Hudson's. But for the preponderance of khakis and navy whites among the clientele, time there stood frozen at 1937, when light was showing at last at the end of the long black tunnel of the Great Depression, and Hitler and Tojo were someone else's headache. He wondered how well that attitude would stand up if the Luftwaffe were to drop a bomb shrieking into the middle of the toy department.

He had no difficulty keeping up with the older couple. They

moved among the bustling shoppers, clerks, and swallowtailed floorwalkers like flotsam on a sure tide, neither hastening their pace to accommodate those in a hurry nor slowing it to admire the merchandise on display. He drifted along behind, stopping from time to time to finger a necktie on a rack or read the price tag on the sleeve of a seersucker jacket. He had no fear they'd notice him, as they were oblivious to everything but their own measured pace down the aisle, but he didn't want store security to connect him with the slow-moving pair.

At length they stepped aboard the varnished-oak escalator to the basement, timing the move with the patient calculation of fragile age. He got on several customers later. He had begun to perspire beneath the poncho and regretted bringing it. The forecast had called for steady rain all day long.

The bargain floor was as well-appointed as all the others, yet there was an atmosphere of sad resignation about the place, as if one had come down socially as well as geographically to browse among its discontinued styles, factory seconds, and soiled and damaged merchandise. The crowds were no less dense, but lacked the electricity of those on the upper levels. The ratio of black to white, middle-aged and older to youth, was greater. Their quest was as determined, but there was little joy in it. Wartime prosperity took a heavy emotional toll on those still suffering from the effects of Black Tuesday.

When he alighted from the escalator the couple were examining bath towels. He went over to wander among sheets and pillowcases left from the spring white sale. He was close enough to overhear the stout woman telling her husband she was looking for something with more of a nap.

After a few moments the old man said he was going to look for the men's room. The tip of the bamboo cane thumped the floor in counter to his shuffling footsteps.

That corner was relatively deserted. A table piled with post-season corduroys slashed to half price occupied most of the customers in the middle of the room. The view was blocked by a display of mock windows dressed in last year's curtains. He came around the end of the display, sliding a hand inside the briefcase.

"May I help you, soldier?"

He stopped short. A salesgirl standing on a stepladder smiled down at him from the flouncy valance she was busy threading onto a brass rod.

"Thanks, I'm just looking." He shrugged his poncho over the briefcase.

"I thought the army supplied you boys with all the housewares you needed."

"I'm shopping for my wife. My fiancée, I mean. We're getting married next month."

"Too bad. They're either too young or too old—or too married."

He retreated to the more populated part of the room. There, face burning with rage and frustration, he pretended to interest himself in corduroys. Every time he looked up he could see the girl's brunette head showing above the curtain display. He wondered how long he had before the old man came back from the men's room.

At length he heard a scraping noise, and when he looked up the girl's head was gone. A moment later she came past the table carrying the stepladder.

The stout woman had unfolded one of the larger bath towels and was holding it up in front of her as he came around the end of the aisle. Her back was to him. He glanced all around and up, in case there were more stepladders. Then he broke into a lope, drawing out the bayonet.

Just as he got close enough to smell the decayed flowers of her perfume, his foot scraped the floor. She started to turn. He caught her larynx in the crook of his left elbow, choking off her cry. He swooped his right around and up. She sagged in his embrace. As she slid down, spraddle-legged, he caught the strap of her bulky handbag looped around her right wrist with the hand holding the bayonet. Then he stepped back, letting her sprawl the rest of the way onto her back. The dark pool spread swiftly across the buffed linoleum. He opened the bag and closed his hands around a thick cardboardy bundle held together with a rubber band.

"Jesus God!"

He whirled. The man standing at the end of the aisle, thick-shouldered, with short-clipped hair and a soft roll around his middle, wore the blue twill shirt and trousers of a Hudson's security guard. His eyes and gaping mouth were huge in a face gone watery white. Then the mouth clamped shut and his right hand swooped down toward the checked butt of the revolver in his belt holster.

He lunged, closing the distance between them in two long strides and slicing the bayonet's long double-edged blade around in a backhand sweep. The blue twill shirt opened straight across the guard's soft middle, and as the glistening coils spilled out he forgot about the gun and reached with both hands to hold himself in.

That ended the threat. As the guard's knees buckled he swept past and around the end of the display of curtains, where he fell back into a normal pace for a busy department store, closing his poncho over his bloody weapon and the bounty he'd snatched from the woman's bag. He was almost to the escalator when he realized he didn't have his briefcase. He'd dropped it during the first attack.

Just then the old man passed him, leaning on his bamboo cane. He decided not to go back. Not because of the old man, who would certainly be no more trouble than the guard, but because there were too many people too near. It was just luck that the guard had been too deep in shock to cry out before his strength left him. A soldier never sneered at chance, but neither did he ask too much of it.

He walked up the escalator, just like any shopper for whom the mechanism was too slow. He listened for the first cry, the clanging of the alarms signaling for all the doors to be secured. Then he was out on the sidewalk.

The uptown car was on time. Once again he had a token ready and he took a seat at the rear. The rest of the passengers crowded up front. He took off his poncho, folded the bayonet inside to avoid staining his uniform, and sat back to count the number of ration stamps he'd removed from circulation.

He was holding a fistful of recipes clipped from newspapers.

chapter twenty-four

Tino thought Mr. Orr's driver, Barney, was a giant pain in the ass.

Every time the bodyguard shifted his weight while leaning against the gleaming maroon surface of Mr. Orr's DeSoto, the driver looked down with a scowl to see if he had managed to scratch the paint with his butt. Two years ago the little Irish fuck had been rolling Chevies on the GM test track for forty a week and now he was acting like a full partner. But Tino was in a good mood, enjoying the feel of the sun on his back and the sound of the river gurgling past the shore of Belle Isle, and he made conversation instead of a fight.

"Think he's carrying?"

"Who? Mr. Orr?"

"Shit, no. He ain't had a piece in his hand in twelve years. I mean the twerp by the car."

Barney looked at the man in the uncomfortable-looking black suit standing by the black Cadillac with government plates, parked a hundred yards farther down the gravel apron of the freshly blacktopped road that circled the island. The car was a blackout model, with all the chromework painted over. The man's complete attention remained on the two figures standing inside the railing by the Scott Fountain.

Barney looked away. "Sure he's carrying. Would you keep your coat on in this heat if you weren't?"

"I think I'll go talk to him."

"About what?"

"Things. We're in the same line of work."

The man by the Cadillac didn't move his head as Tino approached, but he was sure his eyes did behind the dark lenses of his tortoiseshell glasses. His coat was open.

"Hiya," Tino said.

"Good afternoon."

"You Secret Service?"

"Yes."

"No kidding? You protect the president?" Tino showed off his dental work. Joe Louis had knocked out all his front teeth in 1936, cinching his retirement from the ring.

"I don't work White House."

"Seen him up close, though, I bet."

"Lots of times."

"He walk at all? I see him standing with them canes when he's giving a speech."

"I can't talk about that."

"Top secret, huh? That's why they call it Secret Service."

"Something like that."

"See any action?"

The man was silent for a moment. Then he touched the nosepiece of his opaque glasses. "Took some guns off four male subjects parked by the Reflecting Pool in '39. Said they were shooting ducks. Turned out they were Bund."

"Wow."

"I got a commendation."

"Bonus?"

"No. Treasury doesn't do that."

"Pisser. What kind of piece you carry?"

"Army .45."

"Hey, me too. Ever fire it?"

"Just on the range."

Tino pointed up at the fountain, at a pigeon cleaning its

feathers on top of one of the marble lions' heads. "Can you pick off that bird from here?"

"Sure."

He pointed toward the Italianate arches of the Belle Isle Casino, where a woman held the leash while her wirehair terrier lifted its leg against a low hedge. "Hit that dog?"

"I like dogs."

"You could hit it, though."

"Sure."

"Me too." After another little silence Tino said, "How do you put in for a job with the Secret Service?"

"To begin with, you can't have a criminal record."

"What makes you think I got a record?"

For answer the Secret Service man pointed at Frankie Orr, leaning on the iron railing next to Frank Murphy, Justice of the Supreme Court and former attorney general of the United States.

"How much money you make?" Tino asked then.

"I pay my bills."

"That's the only difference between you and me, bo. My boss pays mine." He turned around and went back to stand next to Barney. "High-hat government fuck."

"Watch the paint," Barney said.

Frank Murphy had a forehead that was outgrowing his scanty hair and thick black-Irish brows thatching the soft dark eyes of a shanty tenor. They masked a machinelike brain and a will of granite. Before vacating the office of attorney general to accept his seat on the Supreme Court, he had been a Detroit Recorder's Court judge, mayor of Detroit following the recall of Charles "Wide Open" Bowles, governor of Michigan, and high commissioner of the Philippines, where he had served for two years as governor-general. He had fought in the trenches of France at the same time Frankie was doing his stretch in the New York State Reformatory at Elmira for putting out the eye of a Rothstein tough named Jake the Kike with a nail in a board during a scrap in the Garment District. In Frankie's mind this made them fellow veterans.

"I should get back here more often," Murphy was saying. The baroque white-marble fountain gushed behind them as they leaned on the iron railing overlooking the pyramid of steps. From their base the grass spread like green felt, beyond which sparkled the river, and beyond that rose the buildings of Windsor and Hiram Walker's distillery, an old Orr associate. "Summer's a sorry time in Washington. It won't let you forget it was built in the middle of a swamp." Murphy's Corktown brogue was evident only when he spoke of Detroit. It would have raised eyebrows among the preening Ivy Leaguers of the Brain Trust.

"Bitch in winter, though," Frankie said. "Michigan."

"That's your ancestry speaking. You lack sod in your blood."

Frankie made no reply to that, not knowing what it meant. He was the only one of the pair dressed for the weather, in one of his trademark dove gray snapbrims, a Dobbs Airweight with ventilator holes above the band, blue summer worsted, solid blue tie on a gray silk shirt with a monogram, and woven Italian leather loafers, hundred bucks a pop since the embargo. The justice was turned out like an Irish civil servant: rumpled black suit, cheap white cotton shirt, lace-up brogans with thick rubber soles. But then Frankie thought it would be a shame to hide swell clothes under a black robe.

"Friend of mine owns a cabin up on Walloon Lake," he said. "Hemingway had the place next door. Why don't I send the key around? You could fish for three months, forget all about Washington till September."

"I can't picture you with a friend who fishes."

"Okay, the joint's mine. I was going to turn it into a road-house, but then the war came along and I couldn't get the material. It ain't in my name."

"A rose by any other. Only you're no rose."

"Roses are for saps. I always send orchids. What about it, Your Honor?"

"Thank you. I prefer to buy my fish in a market. The price is much less dear."

"Not with rationing. Well, suit yourself." Irony was lost on Frankie. "Where you staying, the Book-Cadillac? They give you the presidential? What am I talking about, sure they did. I know a penthouse suite makes it look like a dump. The manager owes me a favor. He'll keep your name off the register. Reporters in this town are a pain in the ass."

"Where would that be, the Griswold House?"

Frankie's face went plank flat. "They tore down the Griswold," he said.

Murphy, watching him out of the corner of his eye, chuckled. "I never really bought that story, about you cutting a man's throat in the Griswold dining room. I thought you spread it yourself to scare the other wops into line. But you know something, Oro?" He pronounced the name with sinister foreignness. "You're a rotten poker player. There's a Friday night foursome at the Columbia Arms would peel you down to your guinea ass: Harry Hopkins, Buckminster Fuller, John O'Hara, and Francis L. Murphy. A button man in silk undies is still just a button man."

"I never was brought up on that charge." His tone was dead dull.

"It don't signify, boyo. I'm not in the fight now. I got Pendergast out of Kansas City where he'd been dug in like a crab for thirty years and put him in Leavenworth. I nailed that Red

Earl Browder and pulled Marty Manton by his ears off the federal bench for graft and threw him behind bars. I'd have got you, too, if Pierce Butler didn't croak just when he did and leave an opening on the Court. The devil was looking out for you that day."

"You too. You'd have gone down the shitter trying to get me."

"Well, we'll never know now, will we?"

Frankie slid back behind his bluff mask. "Let's not fight, Your Honor. Who delivered the vote for you in Detroit when you went for governor?"

"That's because you were afraid I'd run again for mayor if I lost. You knew I couldn't touch you from Lansing."

Frankie was impressed. He hadn't thought the mick bastard was smart enough to figure out his philosophy: If you can't buy 'em, kill 'em. If you can't kill 'em, promote 'em. The Orr triple play. In another minute Murphy would be calling to have Justice Butler's body exhumed. He'd almost have been proud to claim credit for that one; but as Murphy had said, that time the devil was looking out for him. He'd take his support from wherever it came. It was the secret of his survival. *Omerta,* vendetta, the Code of the Underworld—call it what you will—had filled the graveyards and penitentiaries with honorable men, and Frankie was still standing. It was amazing what you could accomplish once you put aside honor.

He changed his tack. "I been following your career. I'm a fan. I read where you're a champion of individual liberty. That means you're for the little guy."

"You were reading about Huey Long, not me. I happen to think the big guy has just as many rights as everyone else."

"That include protection from a crazy cop?"

"Don't shit a shitter. I was a Recorder's Court judge for seven years. I know how things work down here."

"This is a special case. I got a Racket Squad lieutenant threatening to beat me to death in a hotel room if I don't bail him out on a case he can't handle."

"What's the case?"

"This Kilroy thing. I don't know if you heard about it in Washington."

"The wire services picked it up. If Kilroy's selling to you, I'm with the lieutenant."

"That's just it—I checked all my people. Nobody's bought a single ration stamp since before this nut started. My decision. They're too easily traced, not like hard merchandise at all. I'd cooperate if I could, but I got enough on my plate with this phony government prostitution beef. Cops and crooks been busting my balls for twenty years. That maniac Jack Dance threatened to pull the plug on my boy Patsy when he was in an incubator. I can look out for myself. I can't if all my enterprises are shut down."

"So put your people on Kilroy. You might win points."

"They're on him now. No dice. This bird's an independent. He don't even live in the same world, but try telling that to this bug Zagreb."

"Max Zagreb?"

"Yeah. You know him?"

"Only by reputation." Murphy pushed himself away from the railing. He was wearing a little smile. "My advice? Suspend operations. Put all your people on the street and keep them there until they come up with something. A bone. Anything."

"I can't do that. I got overhead."

"Bullshit. The money's nothing to what you stand to lose if Zagreb thinks you're fucking with him. You want overhead? Try six tons of concrete out at Willow Run."

"Put it that way, I don't see no difference between Zagreb and Kilroy."

"Sure there is. Kilroy doesn't have a license to hunt. Mother of God. You don't see it, do you?"

"I guess I'm stupid."

"Not stupid. Not you. Just stuck on yourself. It's not just the murders. Hell, it's not the murders at all; if Kilroy takes a life every day for the rest of the year, the body count won't match five minutes in the Pacific Theater alone. Ration theft is wartime priority. Last month, Roosevelt put an end to the rubber strike in Akron by threatening to try the leaders for treason and hang them. If I'd done that up in Flint when the UAW pitched a full-scale riot in the Chevy plant, the Supreme Court would have had me skinned and stuffed and sent around the country on a flatbed truck as a warning to other governors. But that was 1937. Have you got so self-important you think your government cares if a black marketeer gets himself beaten to death in a hotel room for refusing to cooperate with the authorities in a matter of national security?"

"I got rights like everybody else."

"Is that why you set up this meeting? To tell me you have rights?"

"You're the only person in Washington I know anymore. They shuffle in and out of there like an automat."

Murphy held up a hand. The Secret Service man standing by the Cadillac started that way on the trot. "I don't believe it. What did you think, I'd come down on Zagreb with all the weight of my high office to protect your pinballs and slot machines? Just what in our past history made you think I'd offer to do that?"

"I saved your life."

"What?"

"When you got in as mayor and started pushing over Joey Machine's breweries, he petitioned the Unione Siciliana to hang a tag on you. I was president. I told him you don't kill politicians, the heat ain't worth it. He damned and helled me and called me a yellow pimp, but he wasn't in a position to buck the Unione. Later, when you came back from the Philippines and threw your hat in for governor, he petitioned us again. I said relax, the governor has no authority in Detroit. By then he was raking so much out of the policy racket in Niggertown he thought he was bigger than everybody, the Unione included. He said you was one dead mick whether we said yes or no. That was in October 1935. Remember?"

"That was the month Machine got shot to pieces with two of his men on a restaurant staircase. Tommy-gun job. Pretty messy for post-Repeal. I thought you were cleaning up the operation."

"You knew Joey. He had to go out the way he lived. Point is you owe me."

"You should've tried to collect then."

Frankie watched Murphy descending the steps to where the Secret Service man was waiting. The bald spot on the back of the justice's head had already begun to burn in the sun. "That's all you got to say about me and Zagreb?" Frankie called out. "Bend over and grab my ankles?"

"It only hurts for a minute."

chapter twenty-five

Canal breathed on the filmy window and shook out his handkerchief to rub at it. The linen stuck. He wondered how many cartons of cigarettes it took to turn a pane of glass into flypaper.

"I'll miss this shithole," he said. "It's the first place I felt at home since my old man and old lady moved us out of the boxcar."

Zagreb said, "We wouldn't be leaving it if you and Burke didn't go around telling every punk in the city about the California."

Burke was sitting on the exposed springs of the bedstead with his hands on his knees. "Frankie already knew all about it. You should of seen him when we mentioned it. He shit his pants."

"He'll just have his tailor run up another pair. Anyway too many people know about the place. I'm surprised the press wasn't camping out in front when we pulled up. I saw a Pathé truck parked outside Hudson's."

McReary was leaning back against the door. With his shoulder covering part of the sign that was permanently fixed there, the legend advised guests to SPIT ON THE FLOOR. The condition of the narrow cherrywood planks suggested that its point had been taken. "I never heard of anything like it. This asshole must have balls as big as B-17s." His sister worked at Studebaker.

"How sure are we this asshole is our asshole?" Canal asked.

"We go through this every time." Zagreb repositioned one

of the chairs, then changed his mind and went on pacing. He hadn't sat anywhere but in the car longer than five minutes since the call came in. "You want one of these fuckers to fuck with, or a fucking platoon? Let me know when you've made up your fucking mind. I'll be in a fucking submarine."

Canal winked at McReary. "We got to get Zag laid. He's got fucking on the brain."

Zagreb kicked over the chair. The clatter made everyone jump. Immediately he held up both palms. "Forget it. I'm sorry. Forget it."

"We're all in the same boat," McReary said.

"Don't say that, okay? Say anything but that. You sound like that prick Brandon." The lieutenant plucked a Chesterfield out of his pack. The Ronson wouldn't fire, and he threw it and the cigarette out the window.

Canal and Burke exchanged glances. Burke cleared his throat and asked if there was anything from the lab.

"Not yet. I gave them the number here. This is the last time we'll be using the room, and it's the only place we can talk without some son of a bitch in a blue bag listening in. I'd just as soon sell the story to Hearst myself and cut out the middleman."

"It isn't just the uniform boys," Burke said. "Brandon didn't make inspector by pretending to be Garbo."

McReary said, "Carton of cigs says even if we make the collar he'll grab it."

"I don't care who gets the collar. I want this cocksucker in a cage." Zagreb looked at Burke. "You look too comfortable. Call the lab."

Burke got up from the bed and went out.

Canal tried to raise the window another few inches. When it wouldn't budge he put his detecting skills to work and discovered that two nails had been pounded into the frame to prevent second-story men from opening it far enough to climb inside. No air was stirring through the six-inch gap. "Somebody in the store had to have seen something," he said.

Zagreb said, "The husband's no help. He had a seizure right in front of the prowl-car cops. They took him away in the same ambulance with the security guard. I don't think he saw anything anyway. Guard was DOA at Receiving, never recovered consciousness. Some of the employees were going off shift at the time of the attack. I borrowed a couple of uniforms from the First and Ninth to run them down. Both of them are waiting for their call-up. They've got nothing to gain from running to Brandon or the press. They'll be up to their ass in the enemy in eight weeks."

"Welcome to the club." Canal surrendered to the heat and peeled off his coat. He looked even bigger in his white shirt, sweat through along the strap of his shoulder rig.

Burke came back after five minutes. The hallway where the telephone was was even hotter than the room and he was sweating like an overworked draft horse.

"Two sets of prints on the briefcase," he reported. "One's the floorwalker's; he picked it up. Other set matches a print on the steel scabbard we found inside the case. There's traces of blood inside the scabbard and the case. They're testing it for type now."

"They say they're sending the prints to Washington?" Zagreb asked.

Burke nodded. Seeing that Canal had stripped down, he took his coat and hung it on the back of a chair. It was the hottest June in a decade.

"Put your coats back on. We're getting copies of those prints and calling every recruiting center in the city."

"I thought I'd let them draft me," Burke said.

"This guy wears a uniform. He isn't selling the ration stamps he steals; he's taking them out of circulation, like a good American. Good Americans volunteer for military service."

Canal shrugged into his wilted coat. "Then why ain't he killing Japs or Krauts instead of Detroiters?"

"Because Uncle Sam doesn't put cuckoos in uniform, that's why."

McReary, amused, looked glum. "Since when?"

Zagreb ignored him. "This guy was rejected for military service, probably on a psycho, and he didn't do cartwheels over it. He hit the beaches in his own hometown. But his prints are on record. They print you at the same time they're sticking their finger up your ass and telling you to piss in a cup. That's to make sure they don't induct known criminals."

"We don't know none of this for sure," Canal said. "All we know is some kind of uniform's missing from the inventory the Jew cleaner kept, and maybe the Polack woman in Hamtramck was buying a magazine subscription. You put those two things together and came up with Willie Gillis with a knife."

"A bayonet. That scabbard's standard army issue. Kilroy's got military on the brain. If you got a better theory we'll run it out."

The telephone rang in the hall. McReary, standing closest to the door, went out.

Canal said, "Well, I ain't got one. But they don't hang on to them prints. They send them on to Washington, where they go into about a million files."

"We can narrow that to thousands by sorting out the rejects."

Burke said, "Maybe hundreds. There can't be *that* many cuckoos in the metro area."

Canal snorted.

"Some nuts fool doctors." Zagreb speared a cigarette between his lips and patted his pockets for his lighter, forgetting. Burke struck a match. "Thanks. We'll put the psychos on top of the list, but we have to include ulcers and flat feet."

"Be easier if we had a description," Canal said.

"A name would be nice, too, and a social security number if he's a Roosevelt man. Or we could sit around Thirteen Hundred drinking gin rickies and wait for him to turn himself in. Since we don't have any of those things, let's use some of those extra rations Uncle Sam lets us have for shoes."

McReary returned and shut the door. "That was Bertriel on the horn, from the Ninth. He's with a Cathleen Dooley in Redford; she lives with her mother. Part-time clerk at Hudson's. He thinks she might have got a look at Kilroy. A good look."

"Thank Christ." Canal reached for his coat. "I traded all my shoe rations to my brother-in-law for liquor."

chapter twenty-six

They parked the black Oldsmobile behind a Michigan Ice Company wagon drawn up to the curb. The wagon's inventory was dripping through the tailgate into a puddle on the asphalt. When they braked, a sharp earthy stench announced to the occupants in front and back that they'd rolled into a pile of fresh horseshit.

Burke, who cleaned and maintained the car, swore and smacked the steering knob with the heel of his hand. "Why don't they drive trucks? Even the dairy companies are selling their nags for glue."

"Why make the investment?" Canal asked. "Everybody's getting Frigidaires come peacetime."

"Not me. Katy can go on dumping out the pan. That's five minutes she's not busting my balls 'cause I'm not commissioner."

"You tell her it's because you signed your last sergeant's exam with an X?"

Zagreb stepped down onto the sidewalk. "You boys stay here and duke it out. Baldy and I are going in with Rembrandt." He tipped his head toward the lanky plainclothesman unfolding his articulated legs from the backseat. He was carrying a flat tin of charcoals and a sketch pad the size of a billboard.

Canal said, "Burke and me ain't good enough for Redford?"

"You guessed it, Starv," McReary said. "I can't figure out why everybody calls you a dumb Polack."

"Me neither. My grandfather wiped Polack off his saber every Sunday."

Zagreb slammed the door and leaned on the sill. "This is a girl who still lives with her mother. I don't want to scare her off by coming in with a pair of gorillas."

"Go ahead. Me and Canal'll sit here and pick fleas off our backs." Burke popped the glove compartment and took out a flat pint of Bushmill's. Suddenly he grinned at the back of the ice wagon. "Hey, we can have this panther piss on the rocks."

The three men who had gotten out started up the stoop of the little brick house. The sketch artist asked Zagreb if his men always did their drinking right out on the street.

"Just since we confiscated six cases from a market operation on Watson." He grinned. "You want to join the Racket Squad, Officer?"

The man shook his head gravely. "I'm M.R.A."

"I thought the Supreme Court threw that out," McReary said.

Zagreb was still grinning. "Not NRA. *M*.R.A. Moral Rearmament. You know, keep Mae West off the screen."

"That's the Catholic Church," said the artist. "We're more serious. We started the national defense movement in 1939. People make fun of us, but if we got started ten years sooner, we wouldn't have this mess in Europe."

McReary said, "Don't forget Japan."

"The Japs were a lost cause from the start. Did you know there's no word for morality in any of the Oriental languages?"

"Did you know Lana Turner spelled backwards is Anal Renrut?"

"Okay, cut it out. Time to serve and protect." The lieutenant knocked on the door.

It was opened almost immediately by a stocky young man in a Detroit police uniform. Zagreb introduced him as Officer Bertriel, who filled them in from the contents of his pocket notebook and led them into the living room. The lieutenant shook hands with Mrs. Dooley, a tiny woman in her early fifties with finger-waved hair washed in a silver-blue rinse, seated in an armchair in a gray dress closed at the throat with a small emerald clasp. Cathleen, her daughter, was sitting on the end of the davenport. She was larger than her mother and dark-haired, wearing a white blouse and gray calf-length skirt, strap sandals on her bare feet, and leg makeup to simulate nylons. She nodded at each of the three newcomers, but kept her hands folded in her lap. She looked pale.

The living room was almost antiseptically clean. Seating himself, Zagreb suspected the plastic slipcovers had just been removed from the upholstered furniture. A fifteen-year-old radio stood in a corner on spindled legs under a beaded scarf and a bowl of wax fruit. On the wall above the armchairs hung a large plaster crucifix across from one of those trick pictures of Christ whose eyes were open or closed depending on the angle one looked at it. McReary, the son of Protestant parents who hadn't seen the inside of a church since he was ten, got up from his armchair and sat on the end of the davenport opposite Cathleen Dooley so he couldn't see it. It *was* sort of spooky. A jumble of family pictures in silver frames crowded the mantel of the imitation fireplace, and a low Chippendale-style tea table displayed copies of *Collier's, Life,* and *The Michigan Catholic.*

"I told the policeman I don't think that young man killed anyone," Cathleen Dooley said. "He was a soldier."

"Not a sailor," Zagreb prompted.

"No. They wear white caps and those cute bell-bottoms. He had on a cap with a shiny visor and a cape."

"Cape?"

"One of those waterproof things, rubber or something. It

was raining, or it had been. The street was wet when I went outside."

"Was he carrying a briefcase?"

"No."

"No he wasn't or no you didn't see one?"

She frowned, concentrating. She wore bright red lipstick, and it exaggerated both the expression and her pale coloring. "I suppose he might have had something under his cape. But he was too good-looking to kill anyone. Killers are small and ugly, like Peter Lorre."

"We'll get to that. What color was his uniform?"

"Brown."

"Brown like army?"

"I think so. I don't know."

"Officer? Enlisted man? Did you see any gold?"

"I don't know."

"The slicker would've covered his insignia." McReary sounded smitten. He admired large-boned women with slim ankles.

"Tall or short?"

"Oh, tall."

"Very tall?"

"Very. Not like a giant, I don't mean that. Just nice and tall."

"How tall are you, Cathleen?" Zagreb asked.

She hesitated. "Five-six."

"Tell the truth, dear." Mrs. Dooley looked at the lieutenant. "She's five-eight. Her father was six feet five. He laid the bricks for this house without help. I keep telling her she should be proud of her height. It's no picnic going through life having to ask strangers to take things down from shelves."

Zagreb kept his attention on the girl. "How much taller was he than you?"

"I don't know."

Shit. "If he didn't do it, that will come out. We just want to talk to him. He might have seen something."

"I wasn't being stubborn. I couldn't tell how much taller he was because I was looking down at him. I was on a stepladder. I was putting up a curtain display."

"Then how do you know he was tall?"

"He looked tall. He was very slim and everything was in— proportion." Her cheeks showed color for the first time. She looked down at her hands. "He said he was getting married next month."

Zagreb was glad he'd left Burke and Canal in the car. Canal would have broken something by now.

"Cathleen, this is Officer Gleason. He's a police artist. You can help him draw a picture of the man you saw."

"Really? Just like on *Gangbusters*?"

"Just like that, only less noisy. But you have to give him a description. Don't just say he was good-looking. Some women probably think Peter Lorre's good-looking."

"*Blind* women," McReary said.

"Shut up. I mean quiet. Cathleen?"

The lanky artist pulled up an ottoman and sat down, bracing the open pad against his raised knees. He placed a squat piece of charcoal against the paper.

"He looked like a movie star."

"Cathleen!"

She looked at Zagreb. Her lips made a defiant red line, like a Kilroy cut. "I mean a *specific* movie star. I just can't think of his name." She turned. "Ma, you remember. *Billy the Kid.* We saw it last summer."

"I can't help you, child. All the actors look alike to me since Valentino died. I cried for a week."

"Robert Taylor."

They all looked at Officer Bertriel standing next to the blinking Christ.

"I like Westerns," he said.

Cathleen Dooley went up to her room and came back with an armload of copies of *Photoplay* and *Screen World*. She and Zagreb and McReary and Bertriel went through them while Mrs. Dooley went to the kitchen to put on a pot of coffee. It was McReary who came up with a picture of Robert Taylor in uniform, smoking a cigarette on the set of *Waterloo Bridge*. Cathleen shrieked when she saw it.

"That's him!" Then her forehead wrinkled. "You don't suppose it really was him?"

McReary, whose miswired scowl said he was pleased with himself for finding the shot, said he'd be sure and get her an autograph at the booking.

The page was torn out and Gleason, the artist, clipped it to the top of his pad with a borrowed hairpin. Cathleen, swept up into the hunt, stood behind him. Together they put a visored cap on Taylor's sleek head, lightened the hair at his temples, and increased the space between his eyes. After Gleason had erased and drawn the chin along slightly weaker lines she pronounced it a fair likeness.

Back in the car, Zagreb passed the sheet over the seat for Burke and Canal to admire.

"Wait a minute." Canal sat up straight. "I seen this guy somewhere."

"See *Bataan*?" Zagreb asked.

"Holy shit."

Burke grinned. "This mean we get a trip to Hollywood?"

McReary said, "Forget it. Those gunboats of yours won't fit inside King Kong's footprints at Grauman's."

They dropped Gleason off at 1300. Zagreb told Burke to drive on.

"Where to?"

"Go up Jefferson. Maybe we can catch a breeze off the river."

"Ain't we going to get copies made?" Burke asked.

Zagreb said, "Let's talk about that."

"What's to talk about? We got the asshole's picture."

"Put yourself in the asshole's place."

McReary said, "That's a stretch."

"Shut the fuck up. That horse isn't around now. You can stop trying to impress her."

"You're talking about the woman I love."

"You're Kilroy," Zagreb told Burke. "You get back home tonight from a good day's slashing, pick up your milk and the *News*, open the paper, and there's your kisser on the front page. What do you do?"

"You mean after I shit a brick?" Burke waited for the light to change at Jefferson. "Go underground."

"Anybody would, and ordinarily that'd be good enough for me. That was before this fucker took his act to fucking Hudson's downtown. That's like sticking it up our ass and breaking it off. I want him walking around where we can get at him. I want a name and address to go with his picture. I want to pull him out of his house and throw him down on the sidewalk on his face and stand on his neck and yank his wrists behind him and hook the cuffs on and make 'em bite. That won't happen if we put him in tonight's early edition."

"Sounds personal."

"You're goddamn right it's personal. First time I've felt like this since December '41."

Canal uncovered his teeth, but it only made him look wolfish. "You felt that way, how come you ain't out busting Japs?"

"Roberta and I were together then. I thought I was needed at home." Zagreb watched the scenery roll past. "Nobody needs me now."

They were passing the sprawling Stroh's brewery, chimneys pouring charcoal smoke into the sky to rival the coke ovens at Rouge. Canal cranked his window down the rest of the way to smell the river, or maybe the hops. "You're counting plenty on those fingerprints being on file. Even then it'll take time. Meanwhile all we got is his briefcase and bayonet scabbard. He's still got the part that cuts."

"We'll hoof his picture around the recruiting centers like I said. Then if the FBI craps out too we'll go public."

McReary groaned. "Drop me off at Woolworth's. I'm out of Dr. Scholl's."

Burke said, "If he slices up another old lady and it gets out we had his picture and didn't circulate it, Witherspoon will see us off on the next troop ship to the Aleutians. Be jitterbugging with polar bears come Christmas."

They drove along with this vision past the Belle Isle bridge, already shuddering under the weight of cars. In a rationed economy the island offered the only escape from the deadhammer heat of the city.

Canal broke the silence. "Trouble is we ain't got the manpower. Department's got more holes in it than the Maginot Line. Three days ain't what it was before Pearl."

"I've got an idea where we can find recruits," Zagreb said.

chapter twenty-seven

Gidgy kept his car spotless from habit, but when he got the call from Frankie Orr's receptionist—English white woman, could talk with a cock in her mouth and make it sound like caviar—he drove it out of the garage on Hastings where he paid an exorbitant fee to the Greek who owned the place to keep it safe from thieves, vandals, and pigeon shit and washed it again in the vacant truck bay of a place he owned a piece of on the East Side. He used a clean bucket and bubble bath, then two coats of Johnson's Wax, eradicating smudges from the whitewalls with white shoe polish.

The car was a 1939 Auburn, bottle green with black fenders and running boards, side-mounted spare, and exhaust pipes exposed like plates of ribs on both sides of the hood. He'd taken over the title from a bookie on Fourteenth who didn't have any use for it on the bottom of Lake Erie with a Chevrolet short block tied around his neck. Gidgy had replaced the garish custom leopardskin upholstery with full-grain black leather, chromed the pipes, and tied a little suede pouch to the gearshift containing the wing bones of an African eagle, his family legacy, smuggled across the Atlantic in a slave ship in the rectum of his great-great-grandfather, the second most powerful witch doctor in his village. The *most* powerful witch doctor had spiked his broth with toadstools and sold him to white traders while he was insensible.

That was the legend among the Gitchfields, in any case. Gidgy suspected the old man was a dock laborer who had gotten drunk and fallen into the hold, and that the bones belonged to a chicken that had perished no earlier than 1900, and no farther east than a kitchen in Baltimore. But when your family tree was kindling you snatched at twigs. The pouch had gone with him every place he'd lived since he was fifteen.

He took Mack to Cadieux, wanting to let the twelve cylinders speak their piece but not daring to. It wasn't the gasoline; he had twelve forty-gallon drums sitting in a private garage on Michigan. He didn't want to call attention to a colored man driving a nice car through neighborhoods so white they hurt his eyes. He didn't admire the houses as they got bigger nor the lawns as they turned a bluer shade of green. That would be like a Jew from the Warsaw Ghetto admiring Goering's garden.

He hadn't wandered far from Paradise Valley in years, and never for more than a few hours. Gidgy felt no special kinship with others of his race—if you believed that old story about his great-great-grandfather, treachery knew no color, and the policy war of 1931 had pitted black against black, with the wops coming in at the end to mop up—but he was sensitive to hostility from outside. He could feel the change for the worse since the hillbillies came up to work the plants. With them, however, he knew where he stood. Grosse Pointe was a confusing mix of New Deal do-gooders and rednecks in shirt boards, and he lacked a program to sort them out. In Detroit his enemies were loud and obvious. Up here he couldn't tell which marble hall might end in a back room with a white sheet and a hood hanging in it.

The scenery hadn't changed much since his last visit. Depressions didn't peel the paint off mansions or cave in their front porches; they just moved one set of residents out and another in, without affecting the outside. The big-big places, forty-some rooms looking out on Lake St. Clair, were in the same hands they had always been in, stained green with old auto money. Those sons and daughters of machinists only entered the stock market after the crash, picking up blocks of shares in their own companies for pennies on the dollar and then sitting on them, waiting for the economy to turn around. Now they were living off fat defense contracts. When the war ended and people started buying cars again the world would gain several dozen billionaires.

One thing was missing from the colonials and Queen Annes, not that he'd have noticed if he hadn't heard the story: the ornamental scrollwork. When the defense drives came along and the country asked the Midwest's wealthiest citizens what they would donate, they had magnanimously given up their wrought-iron railings. They had replaced them with topiary and decorative walls of brick and stone, straightened their ties and smoothed their skirts, and sat back on their wallets, secure in the knowledge that they had Done Their Part. Somewhere in the ocean, some fuzzy-faced kid might even now be lying in his berth in a submarine, feeling the shudder of enemy depth charges and thanking Grosse Pointe for the square inch of iron fleur-de-lis that stood between him and a watery grave.

A careful driver, Gidgy kept both hands on the wheel at all times. This increased the discomfort caused by the heavy Colt M-1911 .45 semiautomatic lodged in the chamois leather lefty holster under his right arm, like a goitrous growth. In case the pistol failed him he had a .32 Smith & Wesson revolver in the left saddle pocket of his gabardine jacket. He never went armed in his neighborhood. He figured if someone was willing to come after him in the record shop or in the furnished room around the corner where he lived like a monk—just him and a phonograph and thirty-six suits made to his order at Clayton's—his card had come up and nothing he did would change that. But he had nightmares about breaking down here in the whitest four square miles south of Vancouver, where a fidgety rich homeowner could sweep him off his doorstep with a charge of double-O buck and there was no one to come forward and say he hadn't intended to rob the place. Robert Leroy Parker Gitchfield, who prided himself on never having stolen a dime off anyone he hadn't killed for a better reason, which was spoils, not stealing, lived less in fear of death than of being labeled a common thief when he wasn't around to tell his side.

Finally he swung between a pair of granite pillars and up the long limestone drive to Francis Xavier Oro's house. This was two horizontal planes of concrete separated by a row of opaque glass, commissioned from Frank Lloyd Wright by the auto pioneer whose widow had sold it to Frankie. Gidgy, who had heard the story from Frankie himself, shook his head at the sight of it there among all those Swiss chalets and English Tudors. If *he* knew that was wrong, why didn't people with money know it? It depressed him, an intelligent man if not an educated one, to think that brains had no place in the formula for success. He felt he was doomed for life to shoulder the burden of thinking for cretins who could afford to hire it done.

Climbing the shaded flagstone steps to the painted-steel door he knew he was being watched. A decade at the top had refined Frankie too thoroughly for the gaucherie of armed guards at the gate, but he would have men stationed around the grounds and behind upper-story windows. The battle tactics he himself had introduced to Detroit had superseded the unwritten edict against going after rivals in their homes or endangering their families: the life of his own newborn son had been threatened in the maternity ward, and Big Nabob, the boss of the old Black Bottom and Gidgy's early mentor, had been shot to pieces along with his blonde mistress in the bedroom of his garish apartment on Frankie's order, touching off the numbers war. Gidgy himself felt no nostalgia for the passing of the old ways. In his experience, rules of conduct were drawn up for people to obey who didn't need them.

The doorbell made no sound at all on his side of the thick steel slab, a bulletproof improvement on Wright's fiberglass. It was opened by Tino, who accepted the .45 and .32, laid them on a table suspiciously convenient to the door, and patted down the visitor thoroughly but without rancor; Tino liked Gidgy, who in return for Frankie's ear during an old dispute had gotten him into a whorehouse on Harper that dealt exclusively in light-skinned colored girls from the islands. Beatrice Blackwood, an alumnus, had smoothed the way with the madam, who ordinarily set her sights higher than low-grade muscle, the bodyguard's employer notwithstanding. Tino must have had a good time that night, because even friendly drop-ins to the Orr estate had been known to head straight from there to their chiropractors.

Gidgy followed the big man down the long hallway that bisected the house, then left into the west wing. He'd heard Frankie had had the place redesigned to create two separate households, one for his wife, the other for himself, with his kid spending alternate nights with his mother and father. Catholics. He himself had married six times and divorced four. A divorce hadn't been necessary the last time because technically he was still married to his fifth wife; just because the bitch never signed and sent back the papers didn't mean she should stand in the way of his happiness. Wife No. 6 hadn't seen it that way and left him with an empty safe-deposit box at Detroit Manufacturers Bank and a barlow knife between his fourth and fifth ribs.

Poor Frankie. All that work and money, and now he was forced to live in quarters larger than all of Paradise Valley.

The room where they ended up was some kind of den. The

ceiling was lowered by way of amber glass panels to less than seven and a half feet—causing Tino to duck his head instinctively as he held the door for Gidgy—and lighted indirectly after the fashion of the rest of the house from behind soffits. The muted effect went with the fixtures: steel gray wall-to-wall carpet, walls of palest blue, almost white, a radiophonograph in a bleached wood cabinet that reminded the visitor of a coffin. A solo violin was playing softly on the turntable; Gidgy's knowledge of music outside his specialty was spotty, but he thought it was either Fritz Kreisler or Yehudi Menuhin. He took the S-shaped object of bent plywood in the corner for modern art until he saw a stack of buff-colored envelopes on it and realized it was intended for a desk.

Mounted on one wall was a deluxe map of the world printed in bright colors on cork. It looked at first like a war map. Then Frankie, who was standing in front of it, reached up and drew down a canvas screen attached to a ceiling roller to cover it, and he suspected it represented something else.

"Gitch, how are you? How's the store?" He shook Gidgy's hand.

"Just fine, Mr. Oro. Jimmy Dorsey was in last week, bought out all my Leadbelly."

"That's fine." He wasn't listening. "You know my son Pasquale? I'm showing him around, you'll be working for him someday."

He hadn't noticed the boy, sitting at the far end of the room in a chair shaped like a potato chip. Gidgy hadn't seen him in a couple of years, he must've been what, nine, ten then. He didn't appear to have grown any. A pair of crutches with foam-rubber pads leaned against the wall beside his chair. Gidgy said hello and got a grave nod in return. There was no family resemblance that he could see.

Frankie leaned back against the bentwood desk with ankles

crossed and arms folded. He was making an effort to be casual, Gidgy thought, in white flannels and an eggshell-colored cardigan over a blue silk shirt. A foulard scarf, honest to Christ, tucked down inside his collar just like David Niven. He always thought you had to have gone to Oxford to get away with that. At least finish high school.

But you didn't laugh at Frankie. Not even in your head.

"I got a shipment of tires coming up from Akron next week. Think you can unload a couple hundred from Niggertown?" Frankie always used the word without offense. Gidgy, who like him came from a neighborhood where wop, kike, mick, and split were almost terms of affection, accepted it in the same spirit.

"I thinks so, Mr. Oro. I got somebody at Willow Run. Them boys clocks up the miles on the commute."

"Good. Got room in the garage?"

"It's pretty full of gasoline right now. I can sell short, make room for maybe fifty. Guy I know has a secondhand furniture store on Oakland, four thousand square feet and lots of it empty, everybody's hanging on to their old stuff till after the war. I could buy in for twenty-five hundred."

"Don't ever sell short. Nobody ever got to be Henry Ford by taking a loss." Frankie went to the radio-phonograph and opened the door to the record-storage compartment. It contained a gray steel safe. He worked the dial, removed a brick of bills, peeled some off, and returned the rest to the safe. He closed up and handed the bills to Gidgy. "That's two thousand. Get a bargain."

Gidgy put the bills in his inside breast pocket. Then he waited. Frankie hadn't called him all the way up here to talk about tires.

"What are your plans for after the war, Gitch?"

Shit. Maybe the man was just lonely, no one to talk to but his runty crippled kid, who hadn't opened his mouth since Gidgy got there. "Drugs."

Frankie nodded, approving. "Weed? Horse? Pills are a bitch. Too easily traced."

"Horse mostly. Market's solid, never goes below a certain line. I figure it to go up when the boys get back."

"In Niggertown?"

"Everywhere. Them army medics spray morphine around like Flit. Gonna be plenty of vets walking around with Purple Hearts and monkeys on their backs. Too many for the V.A. to bring down."

"That's one of the reasons I like working with you, Gitch. You don't think like a nigger." As he spoke, Frankie went back to the canvas screen, pulled it down, and let go. As it snapped up into the roller, the map of the world was exposed. A megaphone-shaped pattern of pins extended eastward from Michigan across Europe.

"I got confidence in our boys. We're going to win this war, but we're going to have to pound the Old World flat to do it. After the Krauts surrender and the rebuilding starts, the shortage of construction materials will make Prohibition look like fly shit on the ledger. I own pine forests in the Upper Peninsula, two brick factories in Toledo, a steel mill in Sandusky."

"Sounds almost legit."

"That's the front. They'll be up to their asses in amputees, they'll need morphine and penicillin. The Red Cross won't be able to score enough through regular channels. Then there's the luxuries, liquor and cigarettes and chocolate bars. Forget whores, the war widows will be underselling us there for the next fifteen years. We'll make it up in eggs and milk."

"You got cows and chickens?"

"I got the people who got the cows and chickens. I also got connections." He pulled the screen down again and turned toward the desk, lifting an eight-by-ten envelope off the stack. "Here. Have your people show these around. Call me if they click."

The envelope was stenciled DETROIT POLICE DEPT. OFFICIAL BUSINESS. Gidgy unwound the string and pulled out a glossy sheet of cardboardy stock, a photocopy of an artist's drawing of a man's head wearing a cap of some kind, police or military. "Who is it?"

"That's what the cops want to know. I'm helping out on an investigation. The lieutenant's a friend. Just find out if anybody's seen him and let me know."

There were other sheets in the envelope, all identical. He counted fifteen. "That's it?"

"That's it. You got my home number?"

"You want me to call you *here*?"

"Only if it's outside office hours." Frankie glanced at his Curvex. "I'll call you when the tires are in."

A black Packard Eight was parked behind the Auburn, where a man in blue serge held open the door while his passenger struggled to separate his four hundred pounds from the backseat. Fat Tony Reno, who kept the sports book downriver, wasn't getting any skinnier. A rusty Plymouth coupe belched its way up the drive. The Ballista brothers, cheap fuckers loansharking in Pontiac.

Come for their envelopes.

Letting out the clutch, Gidgy shook his head over a changing world. No more wrought iron in Grosse Pointe. Southern rednecks tracking chicken shit into Paradise Valley. And Frankie Orr, dreaming of world conquest with his nuts firmly in the grasp of a lowly city lieutenant. The New Deal was full of jokers.

part four

Lights Out

Elizabeth let Dwight into the living room at Sojourner Truth, told him she was late getting ready and to make himself at home, and flew back to the bathroom. He glimpsed yellow robe and her head wrapped in a towel like Carmen Miranda's headdress only no fruit, and never got the chance to say hello. Alone with the big Zenith, he switched it on and tuned in the ball game. Pitching in relief for Trout, Hal Newhouse was smoking the whole Cleveland side in the sixth.

Earl came in whistling from the bedroom, tucking in the tail of a half-and-half shirt, inexpensive cotton except for a silk collar and cuffs. "What's the word, brother of mine? Say, who died?" He pulled Dwight's charcoal gray tie out of his coat.

"I splashed barbecue sauce on the other one."

"You can't wear that to the track. People think you came to bury a horse." Earl undid the tie, slapping aside Dwight's hands as he tried to stop him. He jerked it from around his neck, draped it over his own shoulder, and untied his own, gold turtles on a ruby field. Dwight protested, then gave in and put it on. Earl helped him make the ends even. Then he went back into the bedroom and came out tying a green one with red sailboats.

"How many ties you got?"

"Gate, I got better things to do with my time than count my ties. Where *is* that woman? We'll miss the daily double."

"How you feeling?"

"With my fingers." He held them up and wiggled them. Then he went into the little yellow kitchen, took down a bottle of Four Roses from a cabinet, and splashed some of its contents into a water tumbler. "How about a bracer? Them bleachers get hard."

"No, thanks. And you know what I mean. You tell Elizabeth where you was the other night?"

"She didn't ask. I thought maybe you told her."

"You know better than that. You a junkie, Earl?" He lowered his voice on the last part.

"Do I look like one?"

"You could. I don't know what one looks like. I thought you was going to start staying away from guys like that Gidgy."

"Didn't say that. You got cash? Track's no fun you don't put something down." He fished a roll of bills out of his pants pocket and unwound the rubber band.

"Where'd you get that? Gidgy said you took your last cut in cocaine."

"This an advance. I'm lining up customers for some tires. I can get you a set."

"I got mine recapped just last month."

"Recaps are no good, you see 'em all along the highway from here to Willow Run. These are on the house, little brother. Thanks for not saying nothing to Lizzie."

"I'll roll on the caps a while longer. One Littlejohn with a court date's plenty."

Earl's face went blank as a slab. He snapped the band back on the roll and returned it to his pocket. "Do me a favor, Dwight? Don't bleed all over my rug from them holes in your hands."

"It ain't that. One of us has to look out for Elizabeth if the other one goes to jail."

"I know, babe." He laid a hand on Dwight's shoulder. "I ain't such a much as a big brother. Ma was telling me all the time, look out for Dwight. I tried, you know what I'm saying? Then

I'd forget. Too much Pa in me, I guess. You always was the hope of the family."

"That's horseshit, Earl. If it weren't for you, we'd still be in Eufala unloading cotton for a dollar a day."

"I always was the idea man, but you're the one that sticks. That's why I want you to take them tires. I see things, you know what I'm saying? I see things, and I know if anything happens, Lizzie'll get took good care of. Who's going to do that if I'm in the joint and one of them recaps blows and my little brother winds up smeared all down the apron?"

"I guess I'm taking the tires," Dwight said.

Earl showed his gold tooth. He squeezed Dwight's shoulder and let go. "Whitewalls, what do you say?"

"No. I'd have to repaint the jalop to live up to 'em."

Elizabeth came out, wearing a summer cotton dress with shoulder pads and white pin dots on deep blue, her white platform sandals emphasizing the muscles in her calves from pushing carpet sweepers and standing on tiptoe to dust the tops of cabinets. She had coral polish on her toenails and a white carnation over her right ear that made her look a little like Billie Holiday.

"I'm feeling lucky this fine Saturday," she said, pulling on a pair of white cotton gloves. "I'm thinking of putting two dollars down on a horse with a name that hits me right. Who's running?"

Earl put on his zoot-suit coat, pulled a rolled-up *Racing Form* from a side pocket, and smacked it against his palm. "Number Three in the second's called Steady Dee."

Her sudden smile was like a flashbulb going off in Dwight's face. "Earl, be a good husband and fetch me my purse."

Steady Dee came in at five to one.

It was the daily double. Earl had ten down in addition to

Elizabeth's two. When he explained to her that they had just made one hundred and twenty dollars, she screamed and threw her arms around him and they almost tumbled off the bleacher seat. Dwight, who had kept his money in his pocket—he was superstitious about betting on himself—basked in their ecstasy and the sun on his back. It was a warm clear day at the state fairgrounds, not as humid as it had been, and the crowd had broken out its brightest prints and whitest flannels. There were more straw boaters than he'd seen in one place since before the war. Except for Pearl Harbor he'd never considered himself especially patriotic, but when "The Star Spangled Banner" played over the public-address system and the crowd rose in a body with hand on heart, he felt a lump as if he'd swallowed a cotton boll. The drink and hot-dog vendors, exempt from rations on the retail end, had to keep going back to empty their apron pockets to make room for more cash.

Earl split the one hundred and twenty down the middle, spread the sixty on two horses in the third, and cleared twenty when Fear Itself placed and Betty's Gams won. Elizabeth hugged them both. Dwight smelled her warm moist skin mingled with the citrus perfume.

When Earl came back from the booth, he announced he'd split again, betting thirty on Happy Daze to show. Happy didn't. Dwight stayed out of the argument when Earl proposed doubling down in the fifth race. He did over Elizabeth's protests, and won again when a filly named Once in a While came in by half a length at two to one. By then he'd bought and consumed six Pfeiffer's, and this time Dwight took a hand, or rather two arms, and restrained him physically from placing the entire day's winnings on the nose of Peace in Our Time. Peace finished with the pack. They left before the seventh, one hundred and seventy dollars to the good.

In Dwight's car, Earl handed the money over to his wife with a flourish. She tucked it into her bra, but not before separating his original ten and giving it back. "Ain't we going to celebrate?" she asked.

Nearing Kern's Department Store, Earl told Dwight to pull over.

"This a nightclub now?" Dwight asked.

"Just do like your big brother says."

Dwight found a spot and spun the Model A into it. Earl had his door open before he set the brake. He said he'd be just a minute and loped through the nearest revolving door.

Elizabeth, who had ridden in the middle with her feet on the hump over the driveshaft, slid over to the passenger's side. "Now what's that boy up to?" She peered out the window as if she could see through the wall of the building.

"Whatever it is, it won't make a lick of sense to nobody but Earl."

She watched the people whirling in and out through the doors. "I don't even know if I thanked you for bringing him home."

"You did, but you didn't have to. He's my brother."

"Sometimes I forget he's the older one. Was you two always like that?"

"Sometimes I think so. When I was little it was different. I was a runt, bigger kids picked on me all the time. Earl was there and whaled the tar out of 'em. Sometimes they was too big, they whaled the tar out of him. It didn't matter none how big they was, though. He waded right in."

"Now it's you does the wading."

He moved his shoulders. "It was Earl's idea to come up and work in the plants. I never would of took the chance on my own."

"Glad you did?" She was looking at him now.

"Most of the time." He rubbed a hand over his face; he'd worked the swing shift Friday night and had gotten only three hours' sleep. "Hell, all of the time. Or I should be. Sometimes you forget things wasn't so great back home."

She rearranged herself on the seat, placing her back against the door and gathering her legs beneath her. "Earl's got his heart set on getting rich. What you got *your* heart set on, Dwight?"

He looked through the windshield. He hadn't taken his hands off the wheel. "I'm trying to put money aside. I don't want to work with my hands my whole life. They got schools up here will take coloreds."

"I had a cousin went to college. He's a pharmacist in New Jersey."

"Well, first I got to finish high school."

"That's a good plan, Dwight."

"It's a plan."

The door behind Elizabeth opened suddenly. She grabbed the back of the seat to keep from spilling out and scrambled back up onto the hump in the floor. Earl, one foot on the running board, planted a green paper Kern's sack on the seat and took out a clamshell box.

"What'd you do?" Elizabeth's tone was accusing.

"Just take the box. I feel like a street peddler here."

She took it and tipped back the lid. A watch with a tiny square face and a gold expansion band lay inside the blue velour lining. The legend on the face read UNIVERSAL GENÈVE.

"It's a Chronograph," Earl said. "I'm getting tired of you axing me what time it is all day long. Here." He took back the box, slid the watch off the form, and threaded it onto her slim wrist. "How's it feel? They can take out some links or put some in."

"You got this for ten dollars?"

248

"I didn't go to the track with just the ten. Anyway, I got a account. You like it?"

"It's beautiful. Earl, we can't afford it."

"Sure we can. Axe Steady Dee. Shit! I almost forgot." He reached into the sack and took out a sapphire blue tie bisected by a vertical spear embroidered in silver thread. "I wants my tie back, by the way." He tossed it in Dwight's lap.

Dwight picked it up, felt it, looked at the tab sewn to the back. "This is silk. I didn't know you could *get* silk."

"You can get anything if you got the cash. Henry Ford don't wear no rayon."

"I'd be scared to wear it. What if I get barbecue sauce on it?"

"Then you take it to the cleaners. They got to make a living just like you and me. It's good for the economy. Put it on."

"You can't run around spending money like this, Earl. How often you have a day at the track like today?"

Earl reached across Elizabeth and put a hand on Dwight's knee. His expression was as close to solemn as it ever came. "I can't think of nobody who'd put up with a jackass like me for a brother like you do. Not for a silk tie or a Brooks Brothers suit and a pair of Thom McAns. I done told you I'm nobody's idea of a big brother. Just let me do this. It's all I can swing."

Dwight smiled and undid the tie he was wearing. The gold tooth in Earl's grin caught the sun.

The rearview mirror was inadequate. Elizabeth took charge, evening out the ends and seating the knot so that there was no untidy dimple below it. She smoothed the shank along the placket of his shirt and smiled. "You look like Joe Louis on the town."

"Speaking of doing the town," Earl said. "What time is it by that Chronograph?"

She made a business of turning her wrist so that the jewels in the bezel glinted. "Five of six."

"I knowed it was suppertime. My belly's growling like a old lion. Let's hit Carl's and then do some clubbing."

"The Forest?" Dwight felt uneasy about facing Beatrice. Despite what Gidgy had said, he was afraid he might have given her grief over telling Dwight about him.

"I'm tired of the Forest. We're hitting the Trocadero."

Elizabeth took in her breath. "I'm not dressed for it!"

"Sure you are. Show 'em the watch. If that don't get us in I'll blind the doorman with this here." He dove into the sack, brought out a square box, and slipped a heavy silver ring onto his right pinky finger. It was set with a swirly blue stone. "It's a tigereye," Earl said, rocking his hand right and left to catch the light. "I was looking for a fire opal, but they wanted too much. Anyways I like this better. What do you think?"

Dwight said, "It looks like a blue marble."

"What do you know? You was going to wear a black tie to the track."

"It was gray."

"How about it, sugar? Is it the flash, or is it the flash?"

"It's the flash," she said.

He said, "Ha!" crumpled the sack, tossed it to the floor, climbed onto the seat, and jerked the door shut. "Well, fire it up, little brother. Push that little button there on the side, Lizzie; that starts the stopwatch. Let's see how many records we can bust between here and the restaurant."

Dwight readjusted the rearview mirror and stomped on the starter.

chapter twenty-nine

Xavier Cugat and his orchestra had opened up a third front on the stage of the Club Trocadero.

In the background, the musicians in their scarlet coats laid down a barrage with marimbas and trumpets while their black-tailed general worked the floor, beating his palms and stamping his patent leathers. Between them a handsome conga player pounded artillery out of a torpedo-shaped drum, his hair in his eyes. The singer, a Latin goddess of war in shimmering white with an explosion of red rose in her hair, chick-chick-a-boomed the chorus of "Cuban Pete" into a microphone that resembled nothing so much as a grenade. The dance floor was a whitecapped Nördsee of couples doing a frantic rhumba. The entire building shook like the hull of a destroyer under enemy fire.

A suspicious-looking doorman collected the six-dollar cover charge from Earl and turned them over to a greeter in tails and a dark study, who conducted them to a tiny table near the short corridor to the rest rooms. Dwight, seeing Earl's face go flat, feared a confrontation from which they could not possibly emerge victorious. His brother's sudden grin as he stepped in to hold Elizabeth's chair, which the greeter was obviously not going to do, filled him with relief. It occurred to him then, briefly, how much of his life had been lived according to Earl's mercurial temperament.

Earl, fully ensconced as host, ordered Old Taylor and soda for himself and Dwight and a cherry Coke for Elizabeth. Their waiter glanced speculatively at Dwight, but did not ask for proof of age. He wasn't asked often, although sometimes in the past his brother had been when he himself had not. He wondered at just what point he had begun to look like the older of the two Littlejohns.

The music was too loud for conversation. When their drinks came they lifted their glasses, making up their own toasts in their heads, and drank. It amused Dwight that Elizabeth could not resist eating her cherry first. Most women, the ones he had observed anyhow, saved theirs for last if they ate them at all. In some things, he decided, she would always be a girl of fifteen.

The nightclub was filling rapidly. Dotted with ferns and dwarf palms in clay pots, its ceiling an aviary of papier-mâché parrots and its adobe-textured walls covered with bullfight posters and lattices strung with flowering vines, it looked as if it had been dug up by the roots in downtown Rio de Janeiro, or what someone who had never been closer to Rio than a Cesar Romero movie at the Capitol thought it might look like, and replanted square in the middle of the Rust Belt. At any moment Dwight expected a fat *generalissimo* to waddle in on the arm of a blond American starlet.

Earl leaned over and yelled in Dwight's ear, "Makes you want to run down to Mexico, don't it?"

"South America," Dwight said.

Grinning, his brother nodded and sat back. He hadn't heard a syllable.

A cigarette girl drifted by, wearing fruit on her head and a dress that showed she hadn't any stretch marks. Earl caught her attention, laid a dollar bill on her tray, took a box of Parliaments, and refused change. She beamed her thanks and cruised on. Earl offered the box to Elizabeth. She took one. He lit it and one for himself off a table lighter shaped like a pineapple. Dwight wondered when his brother had switched from Luckies. They saw each other almost every day and he was conscious that they were losing touch.

He was conscious, too, never had his mind off it for long, that he hadn't held up his end of the bargain with Lieutenant Zagreb. He'd had every intention, after bringing Earl home from the record store on Erskine, of reporting to the lieutenant that Gidgy was his brother's link with the black market; he'd even thumbed a nickel into the slot of a pay telephone a block from Sojourner Truth and dialed two digits from the card Zagreb had given him. Then he'd hung up. There was something about Gidgy's eyes, or rather the absence of them in that long solemn face behind the smoked glasses, that told him he had more to fear from him than he did from the police.

It had taken him the better part of forty-eight hours, on four hours' sleep, to convince himself he wasn't a coward, that he wasn't afraid for himself. There was Beatrice, who had directed him to Gidgy in the first place, and who would certainly be caught up in repercussions if the Racket Squad raided Abyssinia Records and Sheet Music. There was Earl. And in all cases there was Elizabeth.

He'd been thinking a lot about her since Beatrice had asked him who he wanted to find Earl for, himself or his sister-in-law. Shit, who was he kidding, he'd been thinking about her a long time. It took a near stranger to tell him why.

He watched her now, smoking her cigarette like a grown-up lady, moving her shoulders to the clickety beat from the bandstand, leaning over to hear something Earl was saying, then tipping back her head and laughing, showing a horseshoe of perfect teeth and the long smooth line of her throat. She caught him looking and winked, then turned her head to look at the band. The wink warmed him as if he were standing up to his neck in the Gulf off Mobile.

Beatrice Blackwood was a smart woman.

The rousing tune ended on a sting of brass. The crowd clapped and hooted, and Cugat went immediately into "My Shawl," a romantic ballad with the drums and Bolivian scratchers shunted into the background. Earl stood, a little unsteadily, burlesqued a bow from the waist, and gripped the back of Elizabeth's chair. She shot a concerned glance at Dwight, who smiled back and lifted his glass in a gesture of blessing. She rose and accompanied Earl to the dance floor.

The waiter came by. Dwight ordered another round, asking for the bartender to go a little more heavily on the soda and lighter on the whiskey, and paid for it. The waiter withdrew without a word or even a nod. Dwight reminded himself that that would have passed for hospitality unprecedented in Eufala. He was thinking too much of Alabama lately. He'd spent most of his nineteen years wishing he were anyplace else.

The drinks arrived just as Earl and Elizabeth returned, Earl apologizing for his two left feet, Elizabeth telling him to stop, he was just fine. Dwight noticed a faint limp as she headed down the corridor to the ladies' room.

"Next slow one's yours, little brother." Earl plunked himself down and drank. "I should of waited for a jitterbug."

"You'd wait a long time with Cugat."

He made a face over his glass. "Starting to water down the booze. Your idea?"

"It's early yet."

"Dwight, you're gonna make somebody a great wife."

The band threw itself into "South of the Border," sealing off conversation; which Dwight thought was just as well.

Elizabeth returned, smiled thanks at Dwight for her fresh Coke, and ate her cherry. They listened to the music, and then she and Dwight danced to "Cielito Lindo." She'd freshened her scent in the ladies' room. He knew she couldn't afford any but the most common kind, yet he'd never smelled anything quite like it on any other woman. He decided she had a natural musk that changed it and made it exclusively hers.

"What you going to study?"

He started. "What?"

When she smiled with her lips closed she looked just like Lena Horne. "You said you was putting money aside to go to school. What kind of classes?"

"Mechanics."

"I thought you didn't want to work with your hands."

"Not forever. I want to own my own garage, pay other people to work with their hands for me. But that don't figure to happen right away. Even Henry Ford didn't start out in a white shirt."

"No. He just started out white."

He looked at her.

"I don't mean to shoot you down," she said. "It's just all anyone in this town ever talks about is Henry Ford, Henry Ford, Henry Ford, like he's God. All he done was build himself up from flat ground. When you're colored, you start in a hole."

He thought about that. "At least I ain't digging it any deeper since I come up here. That's a step in the right direction."

"I love you, Dwight." She laid her head on his shoulder. "You're the best brother."

When they got back to the table, Earl had ordered another round. His glass was already half-empty.

"Let's go to the Casanova," he said. "This spick music's giving me the Tijuana trots." His speech was slurring.

Dwight said, "I'm hitting the head. Then I think we better go home."

"Whassamatter, you don't wanna miss *Lum and Abner*?"

Dwight went down the corridor. His bladder was close to bursting.

There was a short wait for a urinal. When one opened up he

stepped toward it. The man standing next to it turned away, zipped up, and put a hand against Dwight's chest. "That one's busted, boy."

He looked up into the man's beefy, flushed face. He wore his hair long and greasy to his collar and he had an old triangular scar on his left cheek that might have been made by someone's ring. He smelled as if he'd been soaking in a tubful of beer.

Dwight said, "It ain't busted. I just seen somebody using it."

"You like looking at white men's peckers?"

Dwight backed away from the man's hand and walked around him. When a hand grabbed his shoulder and started to turn him he turned into it and swung his right fist up from the floor. He felt the jolt all the way to his shoulder when he connected with flesh and bone. Something struck him from behind then, a sharp blow to a kidney, and his bladder let go. When he turned that direction, a black light burst in his head. He tried to stay on his feet, but someone pushed him and someone else tripped him and he felt himself going down, with things striking him from all sides. He tried to get up, but a blow to the back of his neck flattened him. He was being kicked now. He curled himself into a tight ball. The harsh lemony disinfectant on the floor and the stench of his own urine burned his nostrils. His ears roared. Kicking and kicking, grunts behind the kicking. Something gave way with a snap and more kicking. The door swung open, drifted shut slowly against a percussive wave of frantic Latin music from the stage, clacking castinets and brumping brass, maracas rattling like shattered bones. He was wading in black water, he kept losing the bottom and ducking under. The burning in his nostrils increased, as if they were filling with water, but he knew it was blood. For a while he tried to stay above the surface. Then he gave up and let himself go. No one could hit you when you were underwater.

He awoke in the ambulance, the siren screaming in his ears, but the shock of the pain and the rhythm of movement made him dip back under. The pain woke him again when they were rolling him up a ramp, and again when he was being washed. He was aware of being bumped through a pair of swinging doors, of a sharp wave sweeping the length of his body as he was lifted from gurney to bed, details that afterward he wasn't sure he hadn't dreamt. He came to full consciousness aching all over and hearing Earl's voice, close but muffled behind a gauze curtain hung from rings on the portable rail surrounding the bed: "I don't see why we can't take him home, if nothing's busted."

"Listen to the doctor, hon." This was Elizabeth.

"He has two cracked ribs and a concussion." This was a new voice: male, white, tired. "Closed head injuries are tricky. I've seen men sustain beatings far less severe, go to bed with nothing more than a slight headache, sometimes not even that, and in the morning they're dead. We need to hold him overnight."

"Sure you ain't just trying to up the ante? Ford don't cover this."

"Earl! I'm sorry, Doctor. He's drunk."

"This is Detroit General. We don't have to fill beds on a Saturday night. Your brother's the eleventh brawl victim brought in here since I came on at eight. I'm told that's some kind of a record since they repealed Prohibition. All but two of them were colored."

"What's going on?" Elizabeth asked.

"I don't know. The other night I heard Edward R. Murrow saying the London Home Guard has Airedales that whimper when they hear enemy bombers approaching—gives them an extra second or two to activate the air-raid sirens. After a few months in the emergency room you get to be like one of those dogs. All the time I was getting ready for my shift I had a feeling this was going to be a long weekend."

chapter thirty

Max Zagreb was feeling more like the youngest lieutenant in the Detroit Police Department than he had for some time.

The sea of uniforms that greeted him when he entered the briefing room represented the largest assembly of street patrolmen gathered at 1300 since war was declared. The median age was forty-five. The youngest reserve on hand was almost forty, and there was at least one sixty-year-old in attendance who had been called out of retirement to free a desk cop to fill a vacancy left on foot patrol by an officer currently serving with Halsey. The sheer number of gray heads made Zagreb feel positively adolescent. It both amused and alarmed him to think that there were men present who had walked the beat in the domed helmets and handlebar moustaches of the Edwardian era.

"Looks like a D.A.R. meeting," McReary said.

Burke said, "You'll get there soon enough, Jackie Cooper."

Zagreb told them to shut up. He drummed his fingers on the cardboard file he held.

The four detectives stood at the bottom of the basement stairwell, waiting for Obolensky, the turnout sergeant, to finish his opening remarks to the officers fidgeting on their creaky folding chairs. The subterranean room smelled strongly of mildew and chicory coffee, heavily adulterated with the harsh root because of rationing. It was 6:10 A.M. Sunday, June 20; ten minutes earlier, a hand grenade dropped in the vicinity of the huge medieval-looking electric coffee urn on the yellow pine table at the back of the room would have wiped out the department's uniform division. A blue fog of cigarette smoke clung to the exposed pipes and bundles of electric wire between the ceiling joists.

Obolensky confined himself in his parade-ground yell to the dates and major details of the murders committed by Kilroy between the final week of May 1943, when it was believed Ernest Sullivan was slain and his body pushed into the river, and last Tuesday, when Florence Kitchen, sixty-four, of Dearborn, and Edgar Goss, forty-nine, a security guard employed ten years at J. L. Hudson's, were killed in the department store in the presence of approximately forty shoppers and employees. Then he introduced Zagreb, who came forward and spread open his file folder atop the podium.

"Kilroy has been identified," he said. "Teletype received from the FBI yesterday afternoon matched prints found on the briefcase and bayonet scabbard he left behind at Hudson's to Ladislaus Ziska, born 4-20-1918 in Ypsilanti. Don't bother trying to spell the name, it's on the sheet Sergeant Canal is handing out." The big plainclothesman was making his way down one side of the room with a stack of mimeographed pages. "Father Wenceslaus Ziska, Bohemian, naturalized citizen, served in the AEF during the First World War, present whereabouts unknown. Divorce decree issued *in absentia* by Washtenaw County on grounds of desertion 12-7-31. Mother deceased 8-30-39 of trauma to the trachea caused by strangulation, possibly at the hands of a fellow patient, although her son was questioned by the Ypsilanti police and released for lack of evidence. Case remains open.

"On 12-8-41, Ziska attempted to join the army, but was rejected for mental instability. At that time he was living in a furnished room on Mount Elliott. He left it a month later without leaving a forwarding address." Zagreb had apologized to the young woman who was living there now, a ball-bearing inspector at the Hudson naval gun factory in Centerline, for knocking her down when she opened the door to clear the field of fire in case Ziska tried to go out a window. "He has a 1937 Nash sedan registered in his name at the old address. Medium gray, Michigan license John Thomas six eight two nine."

All this was on the sheet, but Zagreb was pleased to see most of the officers recording the information in pocket notebooks. Mimeos got lost all the time, while piles of shabby spiral pads, scribbled all over with doodles on the covers, were always turning up among their personal effects when they died or were killed in the line of duty. They never threw them away. He was one brass hat who placed a knowledge of shorthand ahead of marksmanship in his evaluation of the rank and file.

"From age eleven to fourteen, Ziska was raised in a succession of foster homes, in only one of which his residency exceeded six months. In 1932 he was convicted of arson after his sixth and final foster home burned to the ground, injuring both his legal guardians, Rudolf and Esther Muenster. Mrs. Muenster died of complications following a sixteenth skin graft one year and one day after the fire; twenty-four hours earlier and a charge of murder would have been brought against Ziska. Upon his release from the Monroe County juvenile facility in 1936, he petitioned for the return of a U.S. Army bayonet, serial number nine three seven six one four Edward, dated 1916, which he claimed had belonged to his father. His petition was granted. We believe this is the weapon used by Ziska in five murders." He turned the page.

"Ladislaus Ziska is twenty-five years old, brown hair and eyes, five-ten-and-a-half, a hundred and sixty, no scars or other distinguishing marks. One female eyewitness in Hudson's has remarked upon his resemblance to the actor Robert Taylor."

This brought the first laugh of the morning. "No photos are available, since the juvenile authorities don't take mug shots. We have a police sketch of the suspect based on the eyewitness's description, copies of which Sergeant Obolensky will hand out at the end of this briefing." He held it up.

"Psychiatric report filed at the time of Ziska's rejection for military service reads as follows: 'paranoid schizophrenia with persecutory patterns and delusions of grandeur.' In layman's terms, a nut." More laughter. "Not a joke, gentlemen. It means he doesn't scare. Up until Hudson's his victims were all elderly and frail, not the type to put up much of a fight. They now include an armed professional security guard in his forties and healthy. The very fact that he would extend his activities to a busy downtown department store in broad daylight indicates he has no fear of being captured or killed. Ziska likes to dress up as a soldier. Soldiers are trained to be prepared to die for their oath. Just like police officers."

He was no longer reading from his prepared statement. He paused to let the last comment sink in, then pronounced the three words that no lieutenant of the Detroit Police Department had used since the demise of the Purple Gang:

"Shoot to kill."

The press conference was set up in the ornate mosaic lobby of the City Hall, and briefly attended by Commissioner Witherspoon, who stayed long enough to have his picture taken with the officials involved, then breezed on out before the first question was hurled. Inspector Brandon, still glistening from a visit to his barber, put on glasses to read off many of the same remarks Zagreb had delivered at 1300, then introduced the lieutenant with a little push from behind. Only the temporary podium kept Zagreb from falling among the agitated reporters. His first impression was of a herd of drop-front Speed-Graphic cameras wearing hats.

"Lieutenant, any chance this guy's really a serviceman?"

"No, we checked with all the branches. There's no record he applied with any of them after the army rejected him."

"Think he's working for the enemy?"

"We're operating on the assumption he's a loner."

"Where's he selling the stamps?"

"Ration stamps are traceable. So far no stamps issued to any of Ziska's stamps victims have shown up in circulation."

"Isn't Ziska a Kraut name? Sure he isn't fifth column?"

"It's Czechoslovakian."

"What's his motive?"

"It's just a theory. We think he's a superpatriot, or considers himself to be one. He thinks he's helping the war effort by targeting hoarders."

"Any chance he's right?"

"No, those are tactics more worthy of the enemy. Ziska's no hero."

"How many cops you got on this case?"

"Commissioner Witherspoon has committed the entire department to bring Ladislaus Ziska to justice."

"How will that affect what's going on in Paradise Valley?"

Zagreb shielded his eyes. The jinking flashbulbs had blue bubbles swirling between him and the reporters. "Who said that?"

"Ray Girardin, *Times*."

The voice belonged to a man standing on the edge of the crowd. His suit was less rumpled than the general lot although no more expensive. He had a tired face, all loose skin, as if the skull beneath had begun to recoil from the things its owner had witnessed. Only his eyes remained prominent: large, luminous, not quite as protuberant as Sergeant Canal's, but hardly less unnerving.

"Hello, Ray. Where've you been keeping yourself?"

"Here in City Hall. Mr. Hearst thinks I'm too dignified to go on chasing kidnappers and bank robbers the way I did in the old days."

"What's this about Paradise Valley?"

"Well, not just the Valley. We've got unconfirmed reports of clashes between whites and Negroes throughout the city since early yesterday evening. Shouldn't the department be keeping some officers in reserve in case of a full-scale disturbance?"

"Clashes are nothing new. We've got a lot of people up from the Jim Crow South working side by side with colored employees in the plants. We've been handling the brawls pretty well so far."

"Two weeks ago the KKK launched a full-scale strike at the Packard plant because three Negroes were promoted. The army had to be brought in to investigate. It doesn't sound like the police handled that one at all."

"The police aren't going anywhere, Ray. We'll be right here in town if the Civil War breaks out all over again. Meanwhile we've got a psycho killer to put behind bars."

"Version I heard was you gave orders to shoot to kill."

"You said that, I didn't."

Zagreb took a question from Rolf Owen of the *News*. Out of the corner of his eye he saw Girardin flip shut his pocket notebook and walk away.

The police sketch of Kilroy, with captions identifying him as Ladislaus Ziska, ran on the front pages of special editions of the city's three major dailies and those tabloids that had survived the Depression and the wartime paper shortage. Within an hour the switchboard at 1300 was jammed with calls reporting Ziska had been sighted, as close as Greektown and as far away as Ann Arbor. Officers were dispatched to interview those callers who had not immediately been tabbed as crackpots. Zagreb and the Racket Squad heard about every call and stayed put in the squad room.

"I still say we should of went back and hung Frankie out his office window by his ankles." Canal tossed a quarter into the Town Club crate next to the coffee urn, a smaller cousin of the giant in the basement, made change from the nickels and dimes already there, and poured himself a fresh cup; fresh being a benevolent description of the stuff that issued from the spout. The container hadn't been dumped out and recharged since early that morning.

"It wouldn't help," Zagreb said. "Vice and Burglary both picked up characters with the Kilroy sketch stuffed in their pockets. He got them out on the streets okay."

"I meant just for fun."

McReary's telephone jangled. He rewrapped his tongue sandwich from the Grecian Gardens in wax paper, dumped it in his wastebasket, took his feet off his typewriter leaf, and answered it.

Burke said, "What brand is Girardin drinking these days? Think he believes that riot crap?"

"*Times* is holding on by its teeth. An old-fashioned berserk murderer isn't enough to boost circulation anymore." The lieutenant fired up a Chesterfield. He'd found his Zippo in the lining of his raincoat.

"He was on police beat too long. He wants to be commissioner."

Canal gulped scalding coffee. Zagreb, who had been waiting ten minutes for his to cool, decided the sergeant's mouth and throat were lined with asbestos. "I expected to feel swell when we had a name for Kilroy. I'm thinking we lost him for good the minute we found it out."

"That's what I like about you, Starvo. Always see the dark cloud around the silver lining."

Canal made a farting noise in Burke's direction.

McReary cupped a hand over his mouthpiece. "Zag, you might want to take this."

"Who is it?"

"Ziska's landlady."

chapter thirty-one

Comfortable?" Elizabeth asked.

"I'm fine," Dwight said.

He was sore all over, and his cramped position on the passenger's side of the Model A didn't help. His body was laced with painkillers, but his swollen face burned and the lump of bandage on the side of his head where they'd shaved it to stitch up a scalp laceration caused by the steel toe of a work boot made him feel lopsided. The tape around his abdomen was so tight he couldn't fill his lungs, which he guessed was the idea; the two fractured ribs were pinching him enough as it was. His arms and legs were a rainbow of bruises. When he thought about it, the insides of his knees and elbows were the only parts of him that didn't hurt. Babies in the womb had the right idea. It was only when you came out of the curl that you got in trouble.

Earl climbed in on the other side of Elizabeth and punched the starter. "You're staying with us a couple. You ain't in no shape to do for yourself."

Dwight said nothing. Who was arguing? As they pulled away from the curb he watched with detachment the nurse rolling the empty wheelchair back through the doors of Detroit General Hospital. Receiving, most folks called it, on account of it was all the time receiving patients in a shot and battered condition. Place boasted more doctors and nurses with wound trauma experience than any other hospital outside the theaters of war.

"Who pulled me out?" Dwight asked then.

"You mean out of the toilet? Who you think? Who's in charge of making sure you don't get your head beat off?"

He looked at Earl, seeing for the first time that his brother's right eye was swollen almost shut. It bunched up like balloons when he grinned back.

Elizabeth said, "Well, the bouncer pretty much had the job finished when you got there. Otherwise I'd be driving you both home. If I knew how to drive."

"Thanks, Earl."

"Shit, little brother. It's my job." He turned out of the driveway onto Grand. "Only I wisht you talked the cops out of hanging on to that Hupmobile stick."

Night had fallen, a particularly dark one with almost all the illumination in the city provided by streetlamps and automobile headlights; blackout curtains were a requirement everywhere, and although air-raid drills were less frequent than they had been at the panicky start of the war, the heavy material was still in place in most windows. He'd never seen so many in use at one time. Without visible lights the downtown skyscrapers made black oblongs against a slightly lighter sky. The houses looked evacuated. He hadn't noticed that before, and wondered if the morphine in his bloodstream had distorted his outlook. It made him feel uneasy, as if he had entered a city preparing for siege.

Earl and Elizabeth's block was even more desolate. Theirs was the only car on the street, and the tickety sound of the motor echoed off the blank fronts of the houses on both sides.

"Sure is quiet," Elizabeth said.

"Good." Earl turned into their driveway. "Some kind of fight happening on Belle Isle. They was talking about it in the lobby when I was waiting for you and Dwight. They said a bunch of whites attacked a colored woman on the bridge, throwed her baby into the river."

"My God, Earl!"

"It's just crazy talk."

Elizabeth made up the studio couch. Dwight had insisted on it and won his point, because it was big enough to sleep only one comfortably, and anyway he wasn't about to put them out of their bedroom. His jaw was too sore to chew. It was too hot for soup, so she mixed a pitcher of eggnog and he drank two glasses through a straw, the hospital broth he'd had for lunch having had no staying power. The pills he took after supper made him drowsy. Earl lent him his pajamas and helped him into them and Elizabeth tucked him in. He went to sleep saying something about what a good mother she'd make. He didn't know where he got that, maybe from Mammy Yokum. His and Earl's mother had never been known to do anything of the sort.

He had a wet dream. It must have been the morphine or the pills, he didn't get them as a rule, and when he awoke hearing unfamiliar voices, he was mortified and looked down at himself quickly to see if the stain showed. But the blanket covered him. It took him another minute to place one of the voices as it came to the forefront. It was Gabriel Heatter's. Someone was listening to the network news.

". . . including actor Leslie Howard, were aboard the plane when it was reported missing and are believed dead. On the home front, Edward J. Jeffries, Jr., Mayor of Detroit, has deployed two hundred police to quell widespread rioting between Negroes and whites in his city, and may request Michigan Governor Harry Kelly to dispatch units of the state police and national guard. To forestall further violence, all the saloons in the city have been ordered closed and owners of pawnshops and hardware stores instructed to remove all firearms, ammunition, and knives from their shelves and display windows and lock them up in the wake of rumors of atrocities committed by whites against Negroes and vice versa on Belle Isle, a popular recreation spot in the Detroit River. Colored clergymen and civic leaders have denounced the rumors as erroneous. We have reports of motorists, colored and white, pulled from their cars and beaten.

"In Washington today, President Roosevelt met with . . ."

There was a squeal of static, a trill of dance music, laughter from a studio audience, a piece of the Barbasol jingle. Dwight twisted his head, sending a bolt of pure pain from his neck to the top of his skull. Elizabeth, wrapped in her yellow robe, was standing in a crouch in front of the radio with her hand on the tuning knob. The glow from the dial drenched her taut face in a jack-o'-lantern shade of orange.

"What's going on?" Dwight asked.

"I don't know. I can't find a station that knows nothing. Most of them are signing off. It's almost midnight. That's good, isn't it? They'd stay on the air if anything was wrong."

He recognized the signs of early hysteria. "Where's Earl?"

"I don't know that either. He was fidgety, he said maybe he could find out what was going on. I asked him not to go out. He said he'd be okay on foot, he can run where he can't take the car. That was an hour ago. I tried to call. It rang and rang and nobody ever answered."

"Tried to call where?"

"The Forest Club." She went on twisting the knob. "The stations don't know nothing. One says they're all over Paradise Valley. The other says they're downtown."

"Who?"

"White people, Dwight. Who you think? White people."

chapter thirty-two

Burke cruised past the address and parked the big Oldsmobile against the curb across from it. He killed the engine, but no one got out right away. Against the setting sun the house was as individual as a milk cap: two narrow stories of white frame built during the last war from available materials, pegged into a hill with the basement at ground level. It had red-and-white awnings and a shallow porch with potted plants on the railing and a rocking chair that didn't look as if it had been sat in since the Armistice. A 1939 Buick with a dull coat of dark blue chalky-looking paint was parked nose-first in a separate garage with the doors open.

"Looks like a place where somebody's mother lives," McReary said.

"So did Ma Barker's." Zagreb looked at his Wittnauer: Nine hours had elapsed since the press conference. Time enough for any would-be Jack the Ripper to have fled halfway across Canada. "What's the name, O'Reilly something?"

McReary got out his notebook. "Aura Lee Winsted, G.A.R. Her late husband served with the Twentieth Michigan, invalided out at Cold Harbor. She's still collecting benefits."

"We better hurry," Canal said. "She must be a hundred."

"Don't bet on it. A lot of sweet young things latched themselves on to shaky veterans in their last years. Be getting pension checks till 1990." Zagreb inspected the load in his .38, then put it back under his arm. "Baldy, you're with me. You others keep an eye out for Robert Taylor."

Canal said, "I got piles on my piles. Let Baldy stick with Burke."

"I don't need you scaring any widows."

"She's heard a thousand war stories. What's to scare?"

"Okay, but keep your mouth shut."

"That's when he's scariest," McReary said.

Zagreb and the sergeant climbed the flight of concrete steps leading from the driveway to the front porch. The screen door was hooked. Zagreb rapped on the wooden frame. The woman who came out to peer at their IDs and unhook it stood barely five feet in low heels and weighed ninety pounds. She wore a tailored blue cotton suit with padded shoulders, pinched in at a waist that Canal could have encircled with his big hands. Her hair, worn in a Prince Valiant cut with bangs straight across, was died a corn shade of yellow, a sharp contrast to the leathery tan of her face, which when she smiled broke into stacks of wrinkles. She wore orange lipstick and rouge and white-framed eyeglasses with an Oriental slant. She shook hands with both detectives—hers were encased in white cotton gloves—and led them into a living room done all in shades of white and cream and yellow. A white shag throw turned a camelback sofa into a polar bear and a buttermilk-colored Fada radio shaped like a bullet stood on the shallow fireplace mantel. If Mr. Winsted had left behind any souvenirs of his Civil War service, none was on display in the living room.

Her offer of lemonade declined, the three sat. The lieutenant asked about Ziska.

"That's not his name," she said. "I don't think he's the man you're looking for, but he looks like the picture in the paper and he drives a gray car, I think it's a Nash, but I don't know much about kinds of cars. He's on invalid leave from the Army

Air Corps. He was wounded in combat. Now he sells war bonds."

"Not magazine subscriptions?" Zagreb asked.

She pursed her orange lips, remembering. Then she shook her head. "No. He said war bonds. He's been living here almost three months. A very nice young man."

"Did he say where he was wounded?"

"The leg. The left one, I think. He limps sometimes."

"What battle?" Canal asked.

Zagreb shot him a sharp look.

"He didn't say. I don't think he likes to talk about it. My Orville was the same way. He talked about his friends in the Twentieth, his sergeant, the things they did in town, but never Cold Harbor. Everything but that."

"What name did he use?" Zagreb asked.

Wrinkles stacked her forehead. "Orville?"

"Your boarder."

"Oh. William Bonney."

On the landing outside the apartment, Zagreb asked Mrs. Winsted how long Bonney had been out.

"All day." She sorted through a ring of keys attached to a Red Crown tab. "He doesn't keep regular hours. He goes where the War Department sends him. Toledo sometimes."

It was a three-room flat, no kitchen. "This was Orville's study, where he kept his war mementoes. I donated them to Greenfield Village. We slept separately the last ten years; he had nightmares. I turned the closet into a bathroom after he passed on. These days a person just can't get along on widow's benefits."

There was a table, a mohair sofa going threadbare on the arms, a three-drawer sideboard supporting a Philco tabletop radio, a *National Geographic* map of the European Theater on the wall with flag pins stuck in it. Canal went into the bedroom, came out right away shaking his head, and opened the door to the bathroom.

"Look out!" Zagreb jerked his .38.

His heart thudded in his ears, a Krupa drum crescendo. Then it tailed off. What had looked like a man jumping out of the bathroom was just an empty uniform hanging on the back of the door. The chocolate brown tunic draped a wooden hanger with khaki trousers folded neatly over the bottom bar and a dress cap with a shiny black visor on the hook above.

Canal, who had unholstered his own revolver, swiveled his eyes Zagreb's way, reddened, and returned the gun to his armpit. Savagely he reached up and unhooked the hanger.

Mrs. Winsted was watching from the open door to the landing. "He must not be working today after all. He always wears it when he sells bonds."

"Zag."

Canal had exposed a black waterproof poncho hanging behind the uniform.

Zagreb said, "Yeah."

Canal searched the uniform pockets while the lieutenant went through the shirts and underwear in the sideboard. The corner of a small square of stiff paper stuck up out of the crack between the bottom and back of the top drawer. He pulled it out. It was a gasoline ration stamp.

"That doesn't really mean anything, does it?" asked Mrs. Winsted. "Everyone has stamps."

"It may mean something that he has just one."

"He probably carries them with him. It's a good habit to get into. I'm always going off and forgetting mine and having to come back."

"Nothing in the pockets," Canal said.

"Check the bathroom."

The landlady had come into the apartment and stood looking around. "He's the neatest tenant I've ever had. Must be the military training. Orville was the same way until the last couple of years." She looked at the gateleg table. "That's where I put his meals when he's been too busy to stop anywhere. I never charge him for them. I consider it part of my contribution to the war effort."

Canal swung shut the medicine cabinet. "Clean. Toothbrush and paste and shaving stuff. No prescriptions."

"How often does the trash man come around?" Zagreb asked Mrs. Winsted.

"Just once a week now. Wednesday. It used to be twice, but they're all in the service now."

"Where do you put your trash?"

"There's a bin out back."

"Could we take a look?"

"Certainly." She touched the bare table. "I wonder what he's done with the oilcloth."

He drove back from Warren in a state of cold fury.

His supervisor at the messenger service had given him only five packages to deliver that morning, but the destinations were literally all over the map: one in Hamtramck, two in Birmingham, a fourth in Royal Oak, and the last in Warren, where he had been forced to simmer in a waiting room for two and a half hours because the package was a level 4, meaning it was to be placed in the hands of the addressee only, and the addressee was stuck in a meeting. He couldn't even go away and come back later because the man's secretary had no idea how long he'd be hung up and said he had to catch a train for Chicago as soon as he came out. There was the whole day shot. He was going to have to find a job that gave him as much freedom without running him ragged because there weren't enough employees to go around.

To make matters worse, he'd blown a tube or something in his car radio. The dial glowed when he switched it on, but all he got when he twisted the tuning knob was various kinds of static. It wouldn't have meant so much if he hadn't been tied up all day. For all he knew the war had burst wide open. He had an uneasy feeling he was missing something important.

On Woodward, waiting for the light to change at Grand, he spotted a *Detroit News* box under a streetlamp and strained to see if he could make out the headline on the issue on display. His own face stared back at him from the front page.

He set the brake and got out, leaving the Nash in the traffic lane with the door open, thumbed a nickel into the slot, and snatched out a copy. As he turned away, a man in a wilted-looking Palm Beach suit and cocoa straw hat was looking at him on the sidewalk. He stared back until the man lowered his head and resumed walking.

The driver of the car behind his was blowing his horn when he slid back under the wheel. The light had changed. He drove through the intersection, then swung over into a parking space in the next block, leaning over to skim the story on the front page in the pool of light from the streetlamp. Then he threw the paper into the backseat and wheeled back out into traffic. He broke the wartime speed limit in the first quarter mile.

Zagreb and Canal followed Mrs. Winsted downstairs, through a kitchen with a gas refrigerator and range, and out the screen door in back. She turned on the floodlight over the driveway. From behind the steamshovel–shaped trash bin they could see the Oldsmobile parked on the street, its interior in shadow. Zagreb hoped McReary wasn't talking Burke's ear off. Baldy was a stakeout disaster.

He tipped back the lid. The stench of rotted vegetables came out in a gust. He took off his coat, exposing his shoulder harness, draped it over the iron railing of the back steps, and leaned in to sort through the stained paper sacks and empty cardboard boxes inside.

"I could use a hand here," he said.

Canal said, "Shit," under his breath—the landlady was standing on the back stoop, watching—and peeled out of his coat.

Zagreb pushed aside a bundle of newspaper, but it rolled back down against his arm. When he picked it up to shove it out of the way, its weight surprised him. He grasped it in both hands and tore it open. It was stuffed tight with ration tickets.

"What?" The sergeant couldn't see.

"Kilroy was here."

Tires scrunched to a halt on the asphalt driveway. Zagreb looked at the blunt hood of a gray Nash. From old habit his glance flicked down to the license plate—JT-6829—then up to the face behind the windshield, automatically superimposing upon it the artist's sketch. For a microsecond, a splinter in the eye of Time that Zagreb would relive for the rest of his life, their gazes locked.

Then everything was movement. Gears crashed, Zagreb pulled his hands out of the bin and reached under his arm, the car went into reverse, the black Oldsmobile started up and swung away from the opposite curb into a U-turn, Burke trying to block the driveway. Canal, whose reflexes were fast for a man half his size, went into target-range stance in front of the garage, perpendicular to the street with his right arm extended and his revolver at the end. It barked twice. The windshield on the driver's side collapsed.

But the car kept moving, picking up speed as it bumped over the curb. Its bulbous left-front fender struck the sleeker one of the Oldsmobile, shattering a headlight. Another crash of gears and then the Nash shot forward, two wheels jumping the sidewalk.

Now Zagreb and Canal were in the street, broken glass crunching underfoot, their shooting arms raised in perfect parallel, guns double-banging like carpenter's hammers slightly out of synch. A bullet struck the sloping trunk with a clank. Another clipped the side-view mirror on the driver's side.

Canal clawed open the back door of the Oldsmobile and piled in. Zagreb put a foot inside, pounding the roof with the hand holding his gun. "Go! Go! Go!"

Burke cramped the wheel and pressed down the pedal, turning the U into an O. Zagreb bounced down onto the seat, drawing in his other leg just as the car's momentum swung the door shut. As they straightened out, picking up speed, Burke flipped on the siren. McReary unhooked the handset from the dash to call for backup.

"What the fuck he come back for?" Canal was panting. "He must've seen the papers, heard the radio. Why didn't he just keep going?"

"He came back for something," Zagreb said.

"What, his razor?"

"No. His uniform."

chapter thirty-three

Dwight put on the clothes he'd worn home from the hospital, the ones he'd had on when he was beaten in the men's room at the Club Trocadero. Earl and Elizabeth had spent the night in the waiting room and had not thought to go home and bring back a change. Just sitting on the toilet lid, raising one leg to put on his pants, sent waves of pain throughout his body, but he'd refused Elizabeth's help and didn't want to take any medication because he needed to stay alert. When he pried himself to a standing position and looked at his reflection in the mirror above the sink, he thought he looked as much like Joe Louis as he had Saturday night, only now it was after the Schmeling fight.

There was blood on his shirt. On a sudden inspiration he picked up his suit coat, groped in the pocket on the right side, and brought out the necktie Earl had bought him to celebrate his big day at the track. When he put it on and dragged down the knot, it covered the worst of the stains. It was what the well-dressed search parties were wearing this season.

When he came out of the bathroom, Elizabeth was dressed, in a one-piece frock and the platform shoes she had worn to the fairgrounds. "I'm going with you. You ain't in shape to drive."

"You don't know how. Anyway, somebody has to stay here in case Earl comes back or calls."

"Look at your poor face." Her voice broke.

It hurt his split lip to grin, but he managed it. "You ought to see the other guy's fist."

"Dwight, I'm scared."

"You know Earl. He's probably pitching pennies."

"I'm scared for you."

He didn't know what to say to that, so he said he'd be back soon.

He was relieved to see the street was quiet, even though it was an unnatural quiet that under ordinary circumstances would have disturbed him. Quiet came before and after trouble. Trouble was noisy.

The A started sluggishly; all that condensed humidity on the manifold and wires. It was a warm night, but his blood was running slow from drugs and aftershock, and the damp in the upholstery made him shiver. He turned on the heater.

After a few blocks the quietness began to get eerie. Even the curfew, spottily enforced as it was, hadn't been this successful at keeping people off the streets. There was always someplace to go late at night in a city like Detroit, blind pigs and twenty-four-hour coffeehouses. Sojourner Truth seemed to be holding its breath.

He welcomed his first glimpse of a pair of headlights as he moved farther east. He stopped to let a streetcar pass, its row of lighted windows and silhouetted passengers a cheerful vote for normality.

The car had become uncomfortably warm. He turned off the heater and cranked down his window. He smelled cooling asphalt, the scorched odor that clung to bricks and concrete overheated during the day. A sharp stench of fresh horseshit, left by an ice wagon or a mounted police patrol, crept into his nostrils, not an entirely unpleasant smell under the circumstances. There was life in the city, reassuringly mundane.

As he neared Jefferson, a darting light caught his eye from the left side of the street. Someone was trotting his way on foot, waving a flashlight. He downshifted and applied the brake, but he kept his grip on the hand throttle. Other circles of light approached the car behind the first.

Someone leaned his weight on the running board, depressing the springs on that side. A flashlight flared in his face, blinding him. Then it was switched off.

"Sorry about that, colored brother. I had to see was you black first." Something metal snicked in the void: the safety catch of an automatic.

As Dwight's vision readjusted itself, he saw a broad male face framed in the open window, thick-mantled along Masai lines, with a wide flat nose and a downturned cicatrix of a mouth, as if it had been carved into the face with a knife.

"Who are you?" Dwight asked.

"Volunteer with the Reverend Horace White of the Plymouth Congregational Church. We done been deputized to restore order."

"Deputized by who?"

"Well, that's still being worked out. Cops don't want us going heeled."

"You got a gun."

He waved it, a shiny piece that looked like a trick cigarette lighter. It twinkled under the corner lamp. "Just this little old .25. You wisht you had one too, you heard what I heard. Maybe you does. Where you headed?"

"The Forest Club."

"How come?"

"I'm looking for my brother."

"Your brother bust you up like that?"

"No. He got me away from the ones that did."

"Well, you turn around and go back home. Your brother be along directly, if he ain't dead or in jail."

"What's going on?"

"Coloreds say a colored woman and child got murdered on

the Belle Isle bridge. Whites say a gang of coloreds raped a white woman there and kilt her. Either way there's folks running around with rocks and sticks."

"And guns."

The man smiled for the first time, showing more teeth than Dwight had ever seen in one mouth. "I could swing or throw, I be in the nigger leagues."

"I got to find my brother."

The smile shut off like a light. "Just don't come back and say you wasn't warned."

The man pushed himself off the running board and walked back the way he'd come. There was a conference of swirling flashlight beams, then they split up and went off in different directions.

He took side streets from there. Something told him there would be more interruptions if he used the main thoroughfares. Then, three blocks from the Forest, he saw more lights and a row of sawhorses painted with red-and-yellow diagonal stripes erected across the street. A police barricade. He killed his lights, drifted over to the curb, and set his brakes. From there on he'd be better off on foot.

"Hey! *Hey!*"

The cry, coming from behind as he backtracked to the previous block, spurred him to a faster walk; he was in shadow and thought he could vanish if he pretended he hadn't heard. Then a whistle shrilled.

"Stop! Police!"

He stopped. He knew better than to turn. Footsteps came up swiftly from behind him, then stopped.

"Put your hands on top of your head and turn around."

He did so. A flashlight beam, several times stronger than the one he had already faced, struck him full in the eyes. He squinted and waited for it to be turned off. It remained on.

"Why the hell didn't you stop?" The voice was full of gravel.

"I stopped."

"I meant the first time I yelled. You deaf?"

"I didn't think you meant me."

"You see any other niggers around? You see *anyone* else around? What the hell happened to your face? You been mixing it up?"

"I got attacked in a men's room."

"Try to blow somebody didn't want blowed?"

"No, sir. I just wanted to use the urinal."

"Where was this toilet?"

"The Trocadero."

"Well, la-de-fuckin'-da. When?"

"Last night."

"Them bruises look pretty fresh."

"I got stitches under this bandage." He waggled the elbow on that side of his head.

"What's your name, boy?"

"Dwight Littlejohn."

"What you doing out past curfew?"

"Looking for my brother."

"He lost? How old is he?"

"Twenty-two."

"Don't he know the way home? That's old enough, even for a jig."

Dwight said nothing.

"Let's see some ID."

The flashlight moved down then, to the middle of his body. It was intimidating in appearance: as long as Dwight's forearm and encased in hard black rubber. Everything a cop carried was a potential weapon, from the handcuffs on his belt to his thick rubber soles. This cop was big, all Detroit cops were big, a massive dark silhouette gleaming here and there—his sidearm, the polished oak stick hanging from his belt down past his knees like a monster dick—with purple balloons swirling around him. Another couple of minutes' exposure and that powerful beam might have cooked Dwight's retinas for good.

He had his thumb almost in his hip pocket when he remembered he hadn't taken his wallet.

He played for time. His brain was as slow to get started as the Model A. The damn painkillers had deadened all his best instincts. "What's the trouble, Officer?"

"Nothing a great big shipment to Africa wouldn't fix. Come on, come on. You playing with a hole in your pocket or what?"

Something made a loud clank in the direction of the police barricade at the other end of the block. Patrol car headlights illuminated the area. Dwight saw the flat cap of an officer as he bent down to retrieve his nightstick from the sidewalk. The big cop turned his head that way two inches.

Good as it was going to get.

Dwight spun around and ran, propelling himself forward as much to run out of his own dizziness as to get away. He knew he weaved a little. Later when he'd had a chance to think about it he'd figure it might have saved his life. The cop didn't shout or blow his whistle. Dwight heard something, a flat clap like a book hitting the floor, and kept running, turning a corner he sensed was there but couldn't see, it was that dark and he still had the purple balloons. He heard the noise again, flattened further by the corner of the building that had interjected itself between him and it. Only then did he realize what it was.

He couldn't believe he was being shot at. Why was he being shot at? For running? Jesus Christ, for *running*? If he felt better he'd have been scared.

What strength he had snapped like a string. He slowed to a trot, then a walk. His pulse was hammering in all his cuts and bruises, his cracked ribs pinched his lungs as he gasped for air, sharp pricks as if he were being stabbed repeatedly with an ice pick. He couldn't tell if the pounding he heard was in his ears or if the cop was closing in, taking aim at his back. He wondered, his body screaming the way it was, if he'd even feel the bullet.

Ahead of him the sky glowed green. Then it glowed pink. Then green again. He recognized the neon sign of the bowling alley next to the Forest Club. He found comfort in it. The world couldn't be falling to pieces if they were still bothering to feed juice to the sign.

He made a game of it. If he could make another five steps before he was shot down, made that, if he could make another five, made that, another five still, now he was on the sidewalk in front, now he was reaching for the door, now his hand was on the handle, now he was pulling it open, now he was climbing over the threshold, the steep threshold, the Mount McKinley of thresholds, now he was in. The door sighed shut behind him, and there was no bullet, no gun, no cop. Fat fucker had probably been too lazy even to pursue him around the first corner.

He was in the Forest, but it wasn't the Forest, not like this, not at this hour of a balmy night late in June. Where was the music? Where were the people? The juke was lit up, but it was silent. The rose-colored lights burned softly above the bar, the big mirrored ball, veteran of a hundred dance marathons before the end of the Depression finished all that, dangled from the ceiling striking reflected sparks over the empty littered dance floor. Just for him?

"Back right on out that door or I'll blow you through it."

Not just for him.

"Beatrice?" He shielded his eyes. His pupils were threatening to secede from his body.

"Dwight? Dwight Littlejohn?"

He spotted her then, standing in front of the bar in the low-cut black evening dress she wore most nights, lowering an antique shotgun with two great big curly hammers like iron ears and the barrels sawed off clear back to the wooden stock. She eased the hammers forward, one at a time.

"What happened here?" he asked.

"Nothing. Here."

"I'm looking for Earl."

"He's in back." She swiveled a shoulder in the direction of the door behind the bar. She was still holding the shotgun in both hands across her thighs, like a baton.

It was a small room with a desk and a lamp, an oddly domestic one with a fat china base and bluebirds printed on the paper shade. Cartons of Old Taylor and Ten High were stacked against the back wall. Earl was sitting in the desk chair, an ordinary kitchen job with a steel-tube frame, facing the door. His legs were splayed out in front of him and he had the coat of his zoot suit folded over his arms in his lap. He smiled when Dwight came in, showing his gold tooth. His face shone with sweat and the white of his bruised eye formed a glittering crescent between the puffed lids.

"Why so late, Gate?" he said. "Take the slow freight?"

"Car didn't want to start. You all right?"

"Fine as shine, little brother. You leave Lizzie all alone?"

"The neighborhood's quiet. I didn't know what we might run into. What's going on?"

"Night started out the same as all the rest," Beatrice said. She was leaning against the doorframe, the shotgun dangling at her side, her other hand gripping that arm. "Drinkin' and dancin', dancin' and drinkin'. Then some horselick I never seen before grabbed the mike away from the singer and said a bunch of whites raped a colored woman and strangled her and throwed her and her baby off the Belle Isle bridge.

"You'd of thought somebody yelled fire. Everybody went tearing for the door. Earl tried to stop them."

"Everybody was having such a good time," he said. "I said, why bust up the party?"

Dwight didn't like the played-out-record sound of his brother's voice. Earl never got tired. "What'd they do?"

Beatrice said, "I didn't see it. I just heard about it. Maybe it ain't true. I don't believe that Belle Isle story neither."

"Tell me so I won't believe it," Dwight said.

"Twenty or so boys stopped a streetcar, just stood on the tracks in a bunch so the motorman had to pull the brake. They piled in and pulled out all the white folks riding on it and beat the shit out of them. Men and women."

"Jesus."

"Stopped some cars, too. Busted open the windows with bricks and dragged the drivers and passengers out onto the street and stomped them. I heard glass busting. Not for a while now, though. Maybe they went on home."

"Maybe they didn't," Earl said. "They wasn't tired enough to just stop. Should of went on dancing. Everybody was having such a good time."

"I called the ambulance twenty minutes ago. Probably all tied up in the white neighborhoods."

"An ambulance what for?" Dwight asked.

Earl said, "It don't hurt now. It did some at first. Well, bad. I'm cold, though. How come you went out without no coat, little brother? Catch your death."

"Why don't you put yours on?"

"Can't. I'm using it."

Dwight looked down then, at the coat in Earl's lap and what it was soaked with. The entire front of his shirt below the tab of his racetrack tie was stained almost black. Dwight's knees buckled and he followed them on down and threw his arms around his brother, holding him tight as if he could stop the bleeding with his own body. It had seeped through Earl's coat and he could feel it, clammy-slippery, through his shirt.

"Razors got no place on a dance floor," Beatrice said.

Dwight felt Earl's fingers in the hair at the back of his head. He looked up. The gold tooth was gleaming bright, as if it were drawing the light from Earl's heavy-lidded eyes. "Tell Lizzie it only hurt some at first, Dwight. It don't hurt now."

chapter thirty-four

He swung right onto Jefferson, nicking a red light and drawing an angry horn blast from the driver of a Hudson starting across the intersection. A shoe-heel moon, swollen on the horizon, stamped its image on the river and made a jagged charcoal line of the blacked-out cityscape on the Canadian side, where air-raid sirens rang out more frequently than in the U.S., in sympathy with compatriots in London. The wailing coming from the car that turned behind him might have belonged to yet another drill.

He had no doubt Mrs. Winsted was responsible for the presence of armed detectives outside his apartment. He should have foreseen it. Aura Lee was a Southern name, there was something of the faded belle about her; it was a victory for her to have outlived her Yankee husband and drawn money from the Union for so many years, money that could have been spent on arms and provisions. She was no more loyal to the country of her birth than an Irish saboteur was to Great Britain. He had suspected for some time that she was a hoarder, but had banked his suspicions because the apartment was convenient to his activities and he hadn't wanted to spoil his home base. It was a textbook example of what could go wrong when you placed tactics ahead of strategy.

He took one hand off the wheel to spread open the copy of *Life* on the seat next to him, peeling aside Deanna Durbin's smiling face to run a thumb along the bayonet's smooth vane. It would find its next sheath in Aura Lee Winsted's abdomen.

The sensation would be as satisfying as closing his fingers around the wasted neck of that woman at Ypsi State, the brittle bones popping like hollow reeds.

But first things first.

The proximity to West Jefferson had been one of the points in favor of choosing the apartment. As one of the four best routes out of the city, it led straight as a bayonet through all the downriver communities, bang-bang-bang, like rooms in a railroad flat, and westward to the open gravel roads of farm country, where he had room to maneuver in case of enemy pursuit. The cover of night was a bonus.

Traffic was light at that evening hour. He let out the Nash's engine, changing lanes handily to get around the occasional slow-moving vehicle. The blast of cool air through the gaping hole in the windshield struck him full in the face, bringing all his brain cells to life. He had never felt so alert, not even when he was using the bayonet. He'd heard of this happening under fire. It was under just such conditions that heroism was born.

Ahead and to the right, the River Rouge leviathan hove into view with the explosive force of a convoy of battleships under full steam, stacks belching fire as its coke ovens smelted down thousands of tons of toasters, teakettles, and worn-out Model T's and reshaped them into fleets of jeeps. Almost directly across from the enormous city of plants stood the stockade and barracks of historical Fort Wayne, the military installation built to protect Detroit from a Confederate attack that never took place, now finally serving its patriotic duty as a temporary storage place for light and heavy armored vehicles waiting their turn to be shipped overseas. That entire stretch of highway glittered like the rainbow bridge to Valhalla.

Glittered a little too much.

As he topped the low rise, red flashers dyed the car's inte-

jitterbug

rior the color of blood. A pair of Detroit black-and-white prowl cars were parked nose to nose across the avenue to form a roadblock. He saw the peaked caps of the officers lined up on the other side with shotguns and revolvers leveled across the long hoods and turtleback roofs.

"Step on it." Zagreb was leaning forward across the back of the front seat, .38 in hand. "You got an egg under your shoe?"

Burke said, "I got it against the firewall now. He must have a Spitfire under that hood."

"I see his taillights." McReary had both hands on the dash.

Canal said, "Bullshit. He's got them off by now."

Burke said, "Not at the speed he's going. Even he ain't that nuts."

"Who we talking about?" Canal asked.

Zagreb told them to shut up. "That roadblock should be coming up."

McReary said, "I wouldn't count on it. We caught a squeal on the two-way when you two were busy collecting trash. Some kind of free-for-all on Belle Isle. There might not be any cars available."

"That would just about take the cake. When two drunks batting each other with beer bottles get more love from this department than a maniac with a knife, it's time to join the navy."

"Why all the time the navy?" Canal asked the lieutenant. "What's so fucking great about ships?"

"Easier on my piles. There it is! We got the block."

The red glow half a mile ahead was like a stuttering sunrise.

One of the taillights disappeared.

Burke swung up the side-mounted spotlight by its handle and switched it on. Its beam shot out, striking the gray car broadside. "He's turning."

McReary said, "Into what, the river?"

"Fuck the river," Zagreb said. "That's Fort Wayne."

The iron gate was chained and padlocked. He kept his foot on the accelerator, trying to regain the speed he'd lost when he made the turn. He struck square on. The chain held. He hit the steering wheel with his chin, chipping a tooth. Crunching the pieces, he backed up and hit it again. The hood buckled, a headlight went out. Still the chain held.

The siren was getting closer. He didn't look that way, or the other to see if the officers from the roadblock were headed his direction. He backed all the way to Jefferson, slammed the transmission into low, accelerated steadily, shifted into second, and pushed the pedal to the floor. The other headlight went out upon impact. The gate sprang open, he downshifted to avoid stalling, then sped up again and threw the cane directly into third. The entire frame shuddered, but the engine roared, and the speedometer slid up to fifty.

Straight ahead was the Georgian pile of the barracks, a penitentiary-like building given over to a military museum. He tried to turn, but one of his tires rubbed a bent fender and he had to wrench the wheel hard to the right. He bucked up over a decorative border of whitewashed stones and across grass, inches short of the building's granite front. He'd been trespassing a full thirty seconds before the MP stationed in the guardpost inside the gate woke up, shouldered his M-1 rifle, and fired the first angry shot ever heard on the grounds of Fort Wayne. The bullet whistled high over the roof of the Nash.

The guard's sloth enraged him. What if he were a saboteur?

The MP probably wasn't twenty and could pass for sixteen, a real Willie Best, jug ears, freckles, and all. His white helmet looked too big for him. In his dress khakis and crisp armband he might have been a boy playing soldier. He was back in the guard box cranking up his telephone when Zagreb got out of the car and approached him, stepping around the twisted debris of the gate. He was holding his badge folder out in front of him.

"I'm a lieutenant with the Detroit Racket Squad," he told the guard. "The man who crashed your gate is a suspect in five homicides."

The MP silenced him with a white-gloved palm, finished his report, and hung up. Immediately a whooping siren started up and banks of stadium lights mounted on fifty-foot poles slammed on overhead, flooding the compound with their merciless white glare. Zagreb had to shout.

"Is there another gate?"

"No. He'll have to come back this way if he's coming out at all."

"We'll just go on in and make sure."

"I don't think so. This is a government restricted area."

"That's okay, son. We won't steal anything."

The guard raised his rifle.

Just then Canal, McReary, and Burke came up. They had their revolvers out.

Zagreb said, "Son, you don't want to die for your country without ever getting out of it."

"This is my detail," the young man said. "I could get shot by firing squad anyway."

"If they were going to do that, they'd do it for letting the nut with the Nash get by you. Lower the piece and come with us. When we nail this guy I'll tell your CO you did it. You'll make sergeant."

"I am a sergeant. And I can't leave my post."

"Well, we're in hot pursuit of a fugitive in a multiple-homicide case. That means where he goes, we go. Even if it's the White House. I'd tell you to look it up in the manual, but I don't have time. Lower the piece or I'll shoot you as an accessory."

"I asked for combat. They put me in charge of a parking lot." The rifle came down.

Back in the car, Burke drove carefully over the twisted pieces of iron. "What do you think they'll do to him?"

"Somebody has to hang by his balls, and it won't be his commanding officer. Put on some go." The lieutenant sat back.

They turned onto the grass, following the ruts made by the previous car. After a minute the spotlight picked up a reflection. They slowed down, then stopped. The Nash was parked past the end of the barracks. The door hung open on the driver's side and a cloud of thick steam was hissing from the smashed radiator. Burke killed the headlights, leaving the spotlight trained on the car, and they alighted and fanned out to surround the vehicle.

Canal had brought the flashlight from the glove compartment. He stood back and shone it through the windows. When they were sure no one was inside he stepped closer and directed the beam onto the front seat. Nothing was there but a magazine, open to a spread on bathing beauties.

"Okay, we take it slow from here," Zagreb said. "We got us a wounded bear."

He didn't feel hampered in any way by the loss of his car; quite the reverse. He was always more comfortable on foot. He kept in excellent shape with calisthenics, and his options broadened when he wasn't loaded down with heavy machinery. The towering lights had destroyed his cover, but the compound was swarming with troops from the Quartermaster Corps sprinting toward prearranged stations, and a figure moving with assurance and an apparent knowledge of his destination drew less curiosity than someone skulking in shadow. Ahead of him, on the other side of a chain-link fence, sat rows and rows of armored vehicles, lined up in formation as if prepared to trundle toward an enemy stronghold on West Jefferson. He tucked the bayonet's naked blade up his sleeve and sprinted that way.

The fence was higher than it looked from a distance, twelve feet at least. He didn't hesitate, but started climbing quickly. He balked at the coils of barbed wire on top, then unzipped his two-tone jacket and draped it over the wire. He heard a shout then, but he kept moving, pulling himself up and over, not hastening but not wasting time either. When the first shot rang out he was on the other side of the fence and letting go. The bullet missed.

He hit the ground rolling. The impact emptied his lungs, but he knew if he paused to catch his wind he was lost. He rolled to his feet and ran, taking in air with painful stabbing sobs. The bayonet had torn his sleeve when he landed. He untangled it from the material as he ran. There was more shooting. He zigzagged, just like John Garfield in *Air Force.* Zeroes strafing him, bullets stitching up the earth at his heels.

The harsh white light made stationary monsters of the light and heavy tanks inside the compound, like a herd of mastodons flash-frozen in mid-migration by advancing glaciers. He slid between two of them, drawn instinctively into the shadows. Their molded-steel jackets were cool to the touch, the camouflage paint fresh enough to give off a strong smell of turpentine. He moved deeper into the herd, putting yards and tons of armor plate between himself and his pursuers, seeking the center of the iron womb. The proximity of so much martial machinery made his nipples hard. His erection actually put a hitch in his stride.

At length he poked the bayonet under his belt, slanting the blade backward, and clambered up onto a fender. The day's humidity had condensed into droplets on the smooth metal; the moisture seeped through his clothes, chilling him with the thrill of risk. He was Humphrey Bogart in *Sahara,* the lone survivor of his unit wiped out in North Africa, becoming one with his tank, prepared to sell his life dear.

And now he was atop the turret, with its 37-mm gun up front and fifty-caliber machine gun mounted on a swivel at the back. He ran his hands over the hatch, found the handle. It swung up and over silently on oiled hinges. He put a foot inside, groped with it and found the rungs welded to the side. Swung his other leg inside and climbed down into blackness. The raw steel smell was overpowering.

He touched invisible switches and handles and protuberances about which he knew nothing: the movies he'd seen had been disappointingly silent about such details. In any case the tank was hemmed in by its brothers and he couldn't have gotten it out even if he could start it and figure out how it was propelled. He climbed back up.

The siren continued to whoop, but beneath it he heard shouts and knew they were inside the fence, searching the tanks and the spaces between. With his legs still inside the turret he hunkered behind the rear-mounted machine gun, gripping it by its fisted handle. An electric current bolted through him on contact. The black pall of sky overhanging the artificial illumination went bright, the painful blue of the cloudless canopy of the Pacific. *Bataan,* the final minute of the last reel, Robert Taylor in his tin hat and sweat-soaked fatigues, like Bogart the lone survivor of his unit, a week's worth of black beard smudging his handsome face, itself twisted into a mask of hate, swiveling the big machine gun right and left, slamming round after round into the hordes of Japanese swarming up from the beach, hot brass shells spitting out of the ejector and splinking onto the sand, each one representing another dead enemy.

He found the trigger and squeezed. Nothing. Not even a click. The gun wasn't loaded. He burst into tears. Then he stopped himself with a sharp snuffle of snot, crawled up over the turret, and slithered along the fender on the other side. He reached back and slid out the bayonet. The handle felt more natural than had the grip of the gun. It was the friend of so many campaigns, so many victories against the enemy at home. He couldn't believe he'd despaired. And because he couldn't believe it, he wiped the episode from his memory.

Zagreb, bunched up with his squad and quartermaster's men at the gate in the chain-link fence, had been forced to wait an endless minute for a corporal to show up with a key to the padlock. Canal had wanted to shoot it off, like in the movies, but Burke, ever the squad's ground to common sense, had pointed out that if the bullet didn't bounce off and kill one of them, it would almost certainly jam the lock so it couldn't be opened without a hacksaw.

Then the gate was open and they were inside and spreading out to search among the columns of silent tanks, the detectives with their badge folders hanging out of their breast pockets to avoid getting themselves shot by the army. Zagreb could feel the hair on the back of his neck prickling his shirt collar. He hadn't felt that since he was in uniform, hunting among the boxcars in the Penn Central railroad yard for a Jackson parolee who had raped and murdered a nurse on Cass. He knew how

Frank Buck must have felt tracking a wounded predator into the bush.

He wished they'd turn off the siren. The tanks' metal fittings, cooling from the day's heat, made noises that might have belonged to a man clambering over them, and that constant hooting was no help in determining the difference. His knees and neck ached from squatting to peer between the tracks and hoisting himself up and craning to see above the turrets. He stopped often to change hands on his gun and mop his palm on his trousers. The butt grew slippery again almost immediately.

He stopped and held his breath. Several yards to his right he heard a noise that might have been a man sobbing. The sound broke off suddenly. In the aftermath he couldn't be sure that it hadn't been just the echo of the siren off a curved metal surface, like a propane tank ringing after a cherry bomb was set off. But then it shouldn't have stopped, because the siren was still going. He moved that way.

He was having trouble keeping his bearings. It was like searching a cornfield with ten-foot stalks on all sides, obliterating the horizon. He put a hand against the side of a tank that was smaller than some of the others, no more than fourteen feet long, for rest and to consider his direction. He felt a slight vibration through the metal, as if something was moving across it. He looked up at the turret.

A dark flying figure blocked out the sky. He whirled to bring his gun around just as the full weight of the figure struck him and bore him to the ground. An arm went across his throat, choking off his cry. He struggled, tightened his grip instinctively on the .38, then another arm snaked across his front and something pricked him above his belt and jerked back in a hooking movement. It stopped, worrying at something; it was hung up in the strap of his holster. He braced a knee against the ground and shoved back with all his weight. The grip broke. He scrambled to his feet, stumbled against the fender of the tank, grabbed it for balance, and spun around, holding the revolver.

He'd seen the face before, earlier than the police sketch. He didn't know where. The young man had fallen into a sitting position on the torn earth with his back against the steel wheels of the neighboring tank. He'd struck his head; he shook it, then opened his eyes, looked around, and lunged for the shining steel bayonet that had fallen near his right foot.

"Stop!" Zagreb cocked the hammer.

Ziska froze with one arm extended. His eyes moved from side to side, and the lieutenant realized they weren't alone. Canal and McReary had come around the corner of the tank with their guns out. At the opposite end of the long aisle between the vehicles all in line, Burke approached on the run, his long, revolver-carrying shadow stretching out in front. Shouts getting close, more running feet. The soldiers had heard Zagreb's cry.

The man on the ground relaxed then, shrinking in on himself. His sleeve was torn, exposing the flesh where his arm lay limp and pale between his knees. He was a broken thing.

Zagreb said, "Hey."

Ziska took a moment to respond. He looked up without lifting his chin.

"Pick it up."

The lieutenant was no longer sweating. His skin was cool and he could feel through it the man's emotions, the tension in the other detectives as they watched, the vibration of combat boots approaching. Burke, the fourth horseman, had caught up; he felt his heart thudding from the hard run. Ziska, visibly reassembling himself from his shattered pieces, was a dead ringer for his image in charcoal. He looked exactly as he had when Cathleen Dooley had seen him, just before he slaughtered two people in J. L. Hudson's in the middle of a weekday afternoon in wartime Detroit.

Kilroy reached out tentatively. Then he scooped up the bayonet and braced his other hand on the ground to hurl himself forward.

Four guns barked and kept on barking until they clicked empty.

chapter thirty-five

On a sultry Saturday in July 1943, Lieutenant Max Zagreb decided to devote his day off to doing nothing. That wore thin by afternoon, and he dug himself out from under a pile of pulp magazines—the slicks just reminded him of Ziska and his subscription-salesman cover—and went to see a movie.

The feature at the Fox was *Frankenstein Meets the Wolf Man*, but he was mostly interested in seeing the newsreels. The war had busted wide open beginning on June 22, when B-24 Liberators from the Ford Willow Run plant carpet-bombed the Ruhr industrial valley, flattening German munitions factories from Recklinghausen to Antwerp. Then on July 10, America invaded Sicily, pouring onto the south coast from the Pantelleria jumping-off point and plowing inland behind Patton's Seventh Army. Montgomery's Eighth landed three days later. Caught between the Americans and British, the Italians began to retreat like Mussolini's forehead. The Pathé cameras dwelt on teenage gunners poking bucket-size cartridges into boiler-size breeches, but the real story was that the war was being fought between Henry Ford and Alfried Krupp, wobbly-kneed old men with smelting furnaces for hearts. The capacity crowd applauded each dubbed-in explosion. Zagreb figured they were there for the air-conditioning.

The auditorium was silent through the next segment, a follow-up on the Detroit riots. Some of Governor Kelly's 1,000 National Guardsmen were shown patroling the littered streets with M-1 rifles, backed up by five thousand federal troops in jeeps and armored cars dispatched by President Roosevelt, who on Monday, June 21, declared martial law in the city. Carpets of shattered glass glittered on the sidewalks and pavement, looted suits and dresses abandoned in the getaway rush festooned the sills of empty display windows, a group of patrolmen and civilian volunteers wearing special armbands were shown rocking an overturned Chevy coupe from side to side in an effort to right it. The narrator's stentorian voice intoned the statistics for the two-day toot: thirty-four dead, nine of them colored; six hundred injured; property loss nearly two million dollars; one rumor of rape and murder on Belle Isle, false.

Missing from the newsreel were a number of details that Zagreb himself would never repeat, lest he risk both his job and his draft-exempt status. Four colored men removed from the Woodward Avenue streetcar by eight patrolmen on the promise of safe passage, then turned over to a white mob and beaten to death. A colored boy, unidentified, stomped and pummeled by a gang of white men and boys in T-shirts until his brains leaked out his ears on the front steps of the Federal Building. An eyewitness reported on camera the stoning and beating death of Joseph Horatiis, a white doctor answering a call in the riot area, by Negroes who dragged him from his car. No footage went to the carloads of rednecks armed with rifles and shotguns, quartering the streets for colored game like drunken deer hunters.

It was no wonder, caught (like the Italians) between the rape of Detroit and the liberation of Europe, the fate of a five-time killer (perhaps six; sheriff's deputies in Washtenaw County had identified a body found in a patch of woods near Willow Run as a girl last seen attending a movie with a man whose description closely matched Ziska's), tracked down and shot by police when he refused to surrender, barely made the national wires, and then only one paragraph.

He left the theater before the final confrontation between the Wolf Man and Frankenstein's flattopped monster. It reminded him too much of his marriage. At Michigan, he was held up through two light changes by a procession of cars headed for Jefferson, part of a publicized memorial service on Belle Isle for the victims of the riots. It included rattletrap touring cars filled with armband-wearing members of Reverend White's church and officials of Otis Saunders' Double-V Committee, a Negro community group; Cadillacs and Lincolns containing the Junior League wives of automobile manufacturers; various motorists and passengers unknown, probably friends and family of the slain; Robert Leroy Parker Gitchfield's unmistakable Auburn, Gidgy at the wheel showing more brotherly regard than Zagreb would have expected of the most notorious black marketeer in Paradise Valley—and wasn't that Beatrice Blackwood, the Forest Club's most popular barmaid, riding shotgun?—and a couple in a battered Model A, colored kid with a face that looked like it was still healing from the events of last month, and his pretty light-colored girlfriend, both dressed in black. Zagreb felt vaguely certain he'd met the young man recently.

It bothered him, not that it should have. He came into contact with so many people in the course of an investigation; nobody could expect him to remember them all. They didn't all look alike to him. He prided himself on that.